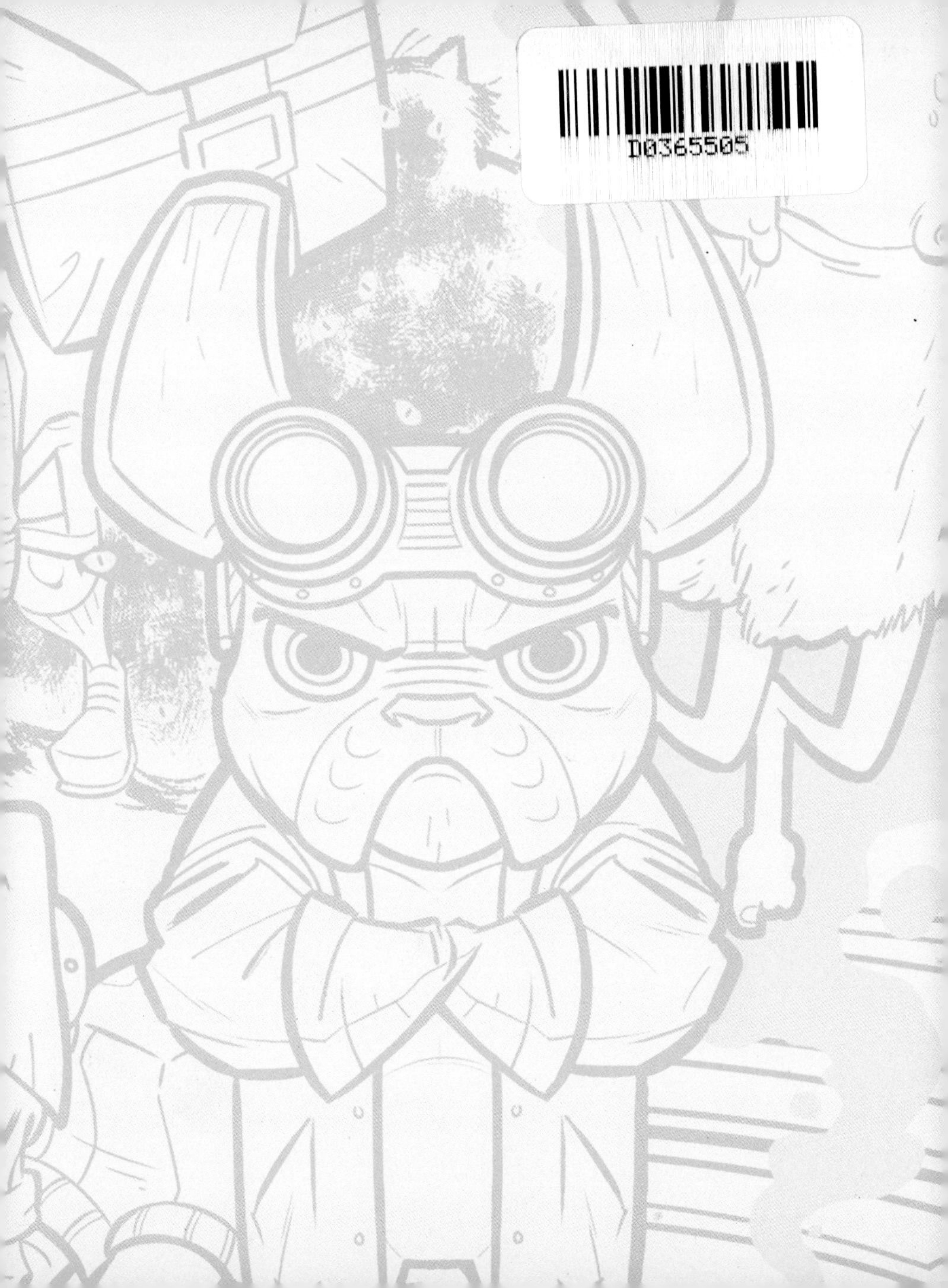

ATOMIC FRENCHIE

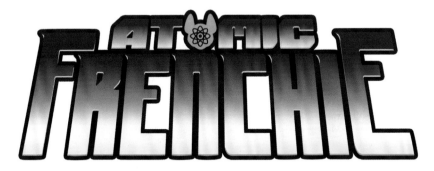

Sit. Stay. Rule.

ATOMIC FRENCHIE

Sit. Stay. Rule.

Thomas E. Sniegoski and Tom McWeeney

INSIGHT
COMICS

San Rafael, California

THE Atomic FRENCHIE

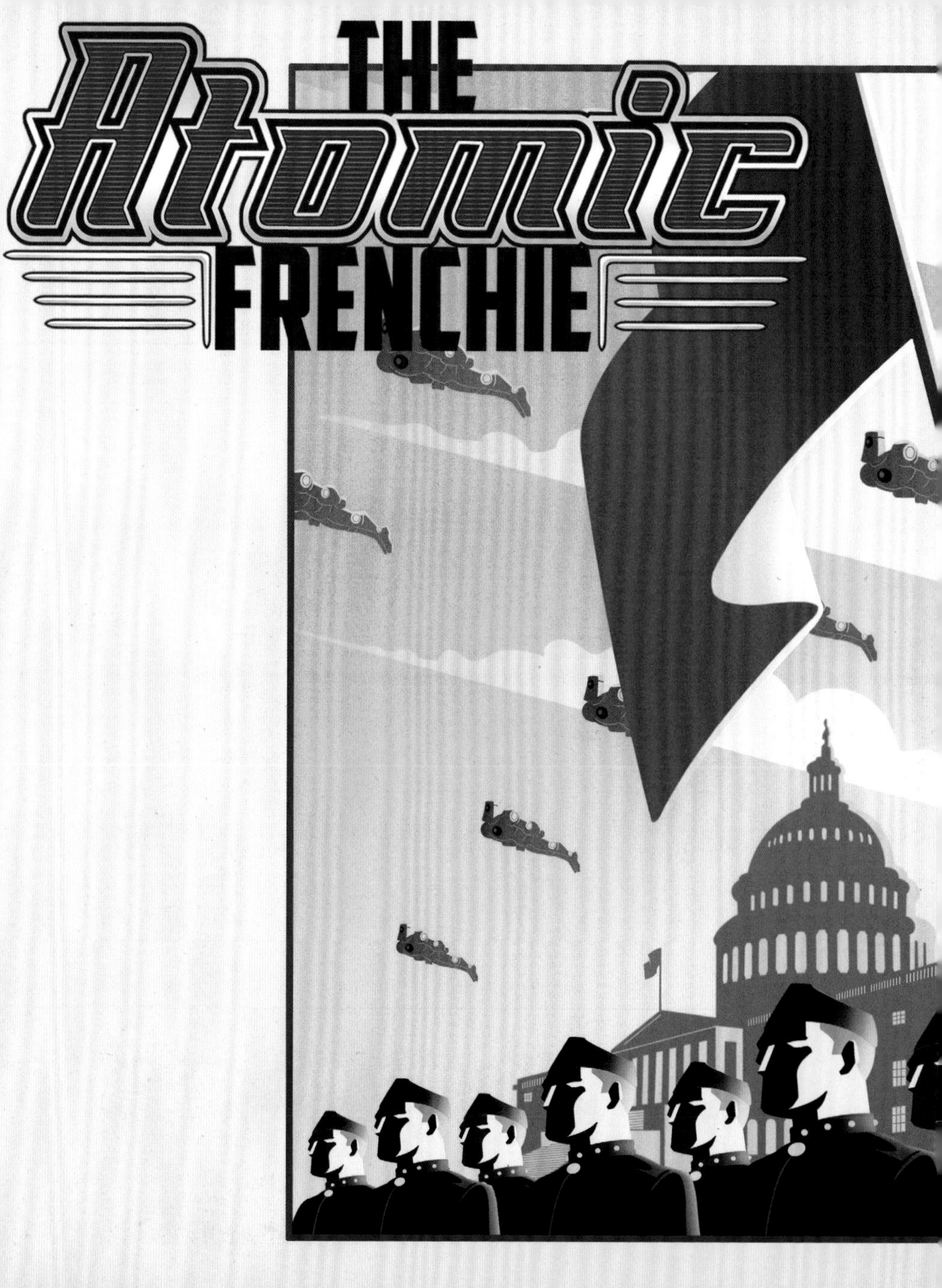

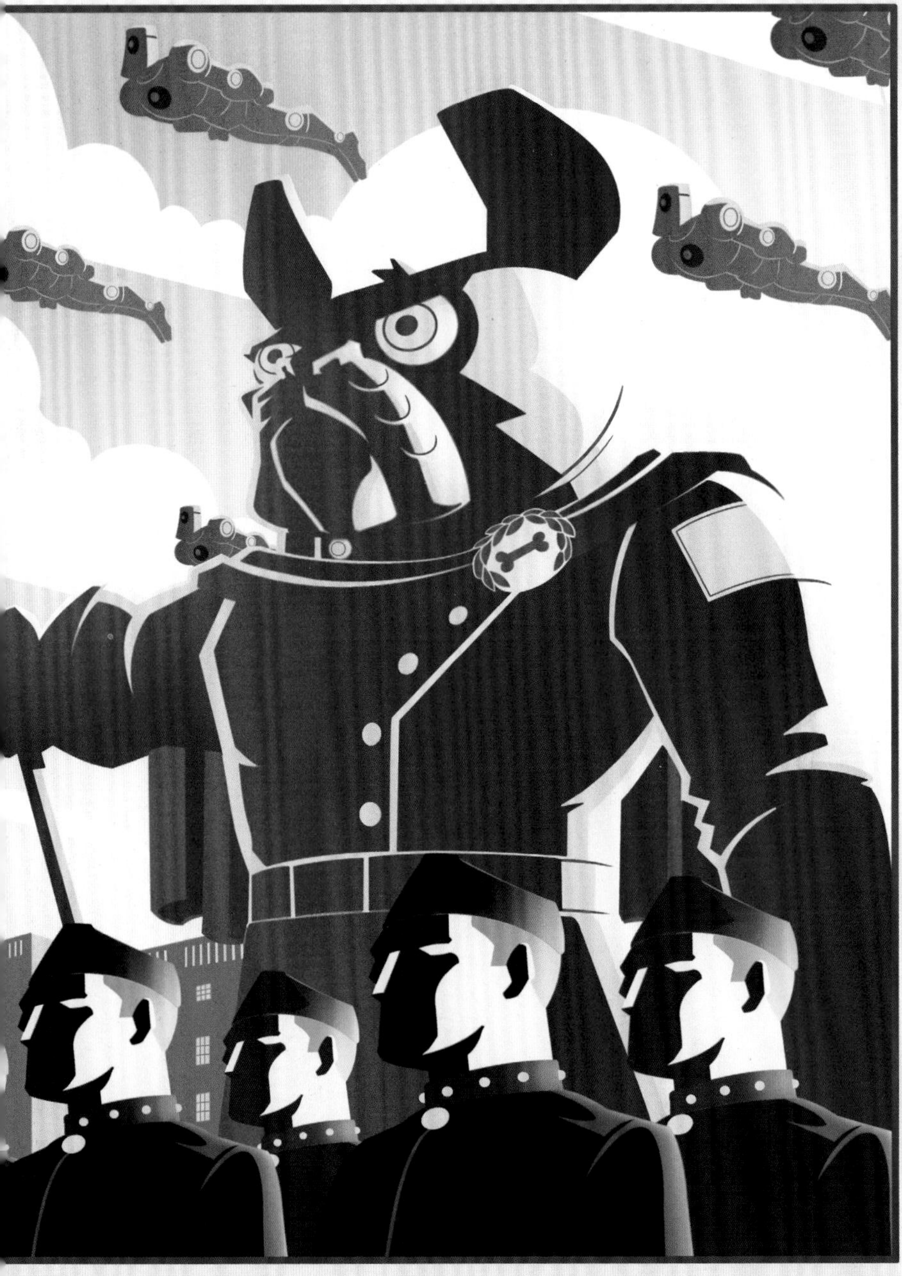

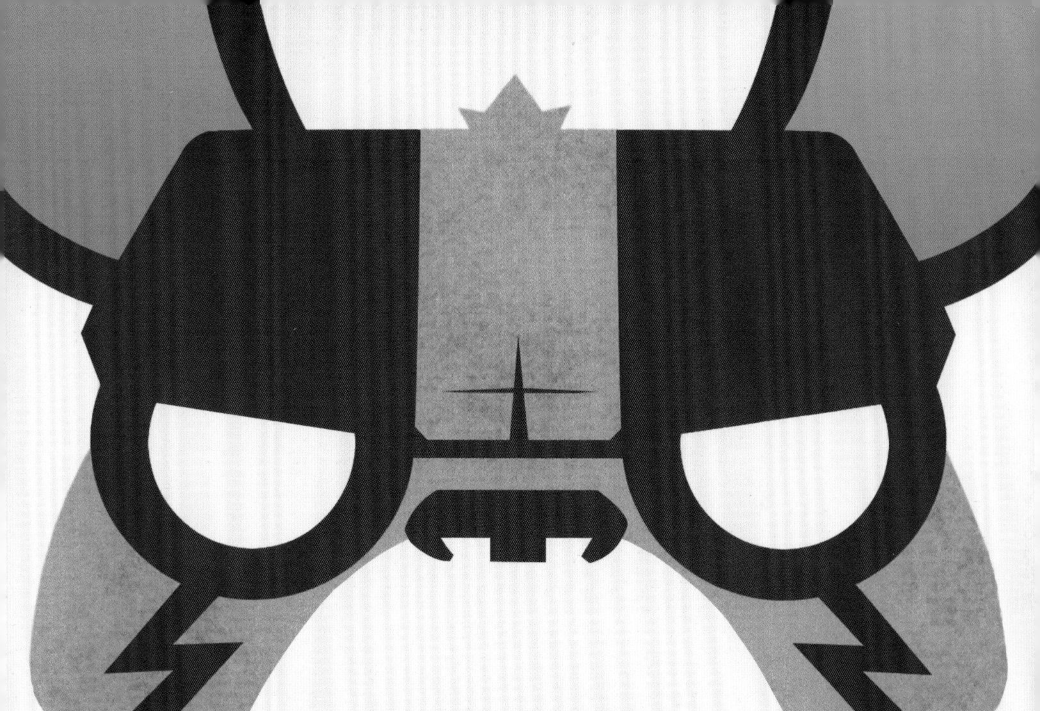

This book is dedicated to Kirby.
I'd like to thank him for allowing Tom M. and me to chronicle his greatness and rise to power.
Long may he reign.
The paw is the law.

—Thomas E. Sniegoski

This book is dedicated to Tom Sniegoski, who invited me into his sandbox and then let me hog all the sand.

—Tom McWeeney

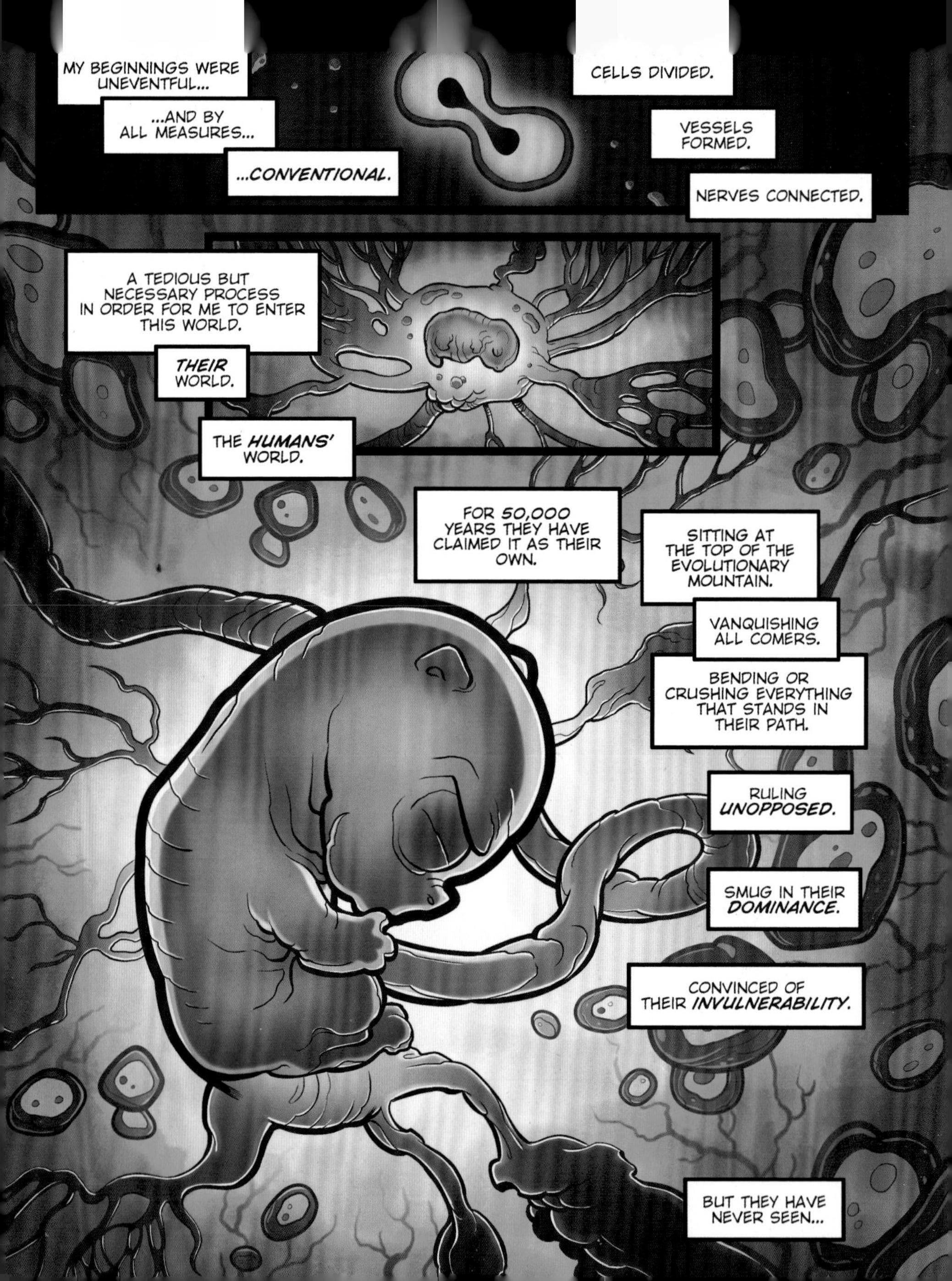
MY BEGINNINGS WERE UNEVENTFUL...
...AND BY ALL MEASURES...
...CONVENTIONAL.
CELLS DIVIDED.
VESSELS FORMED.
NERVES CONNECTED.
A TEDIOUS BUT NECESSARY PROCESS IN ORDER FOR ME TO ENTER THIS WORLD.
THEIR WORLD.
THE HUMANS' WORLD.
FOR 50,000 YEARS THEY HAVE CLAIMED IT AS THEIR OWN.
SITTING AT THE TOP OF THE EVOLUTIONARY MOUNTAIN.
VANQUISHING ALL COMERS.
BENDING OR CRUSHING EVERYTHING THAT STANDS IN THEIR PATH.
RULING UNOPPOSED.
SMUG IN THEIR DOMINANCE.
CONVINCED OF THEIR INVULNERABILITY.
BUT THEY HAVE NEVER SEEN...

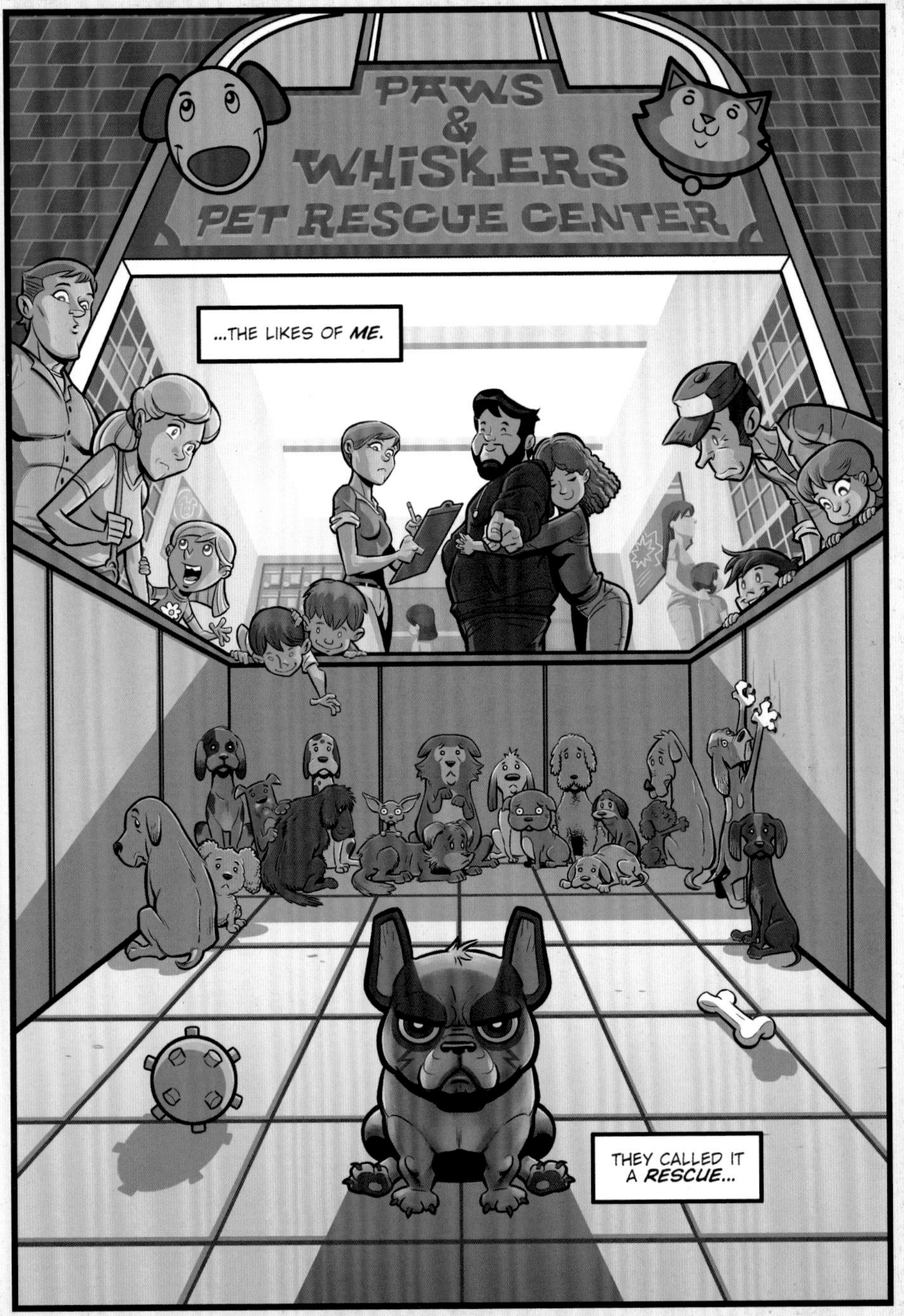
PAWS & WHISKERS PET RESCUE CENTER
...THE LIKES OF ME.
THEY CALLED IT A RESCUE...

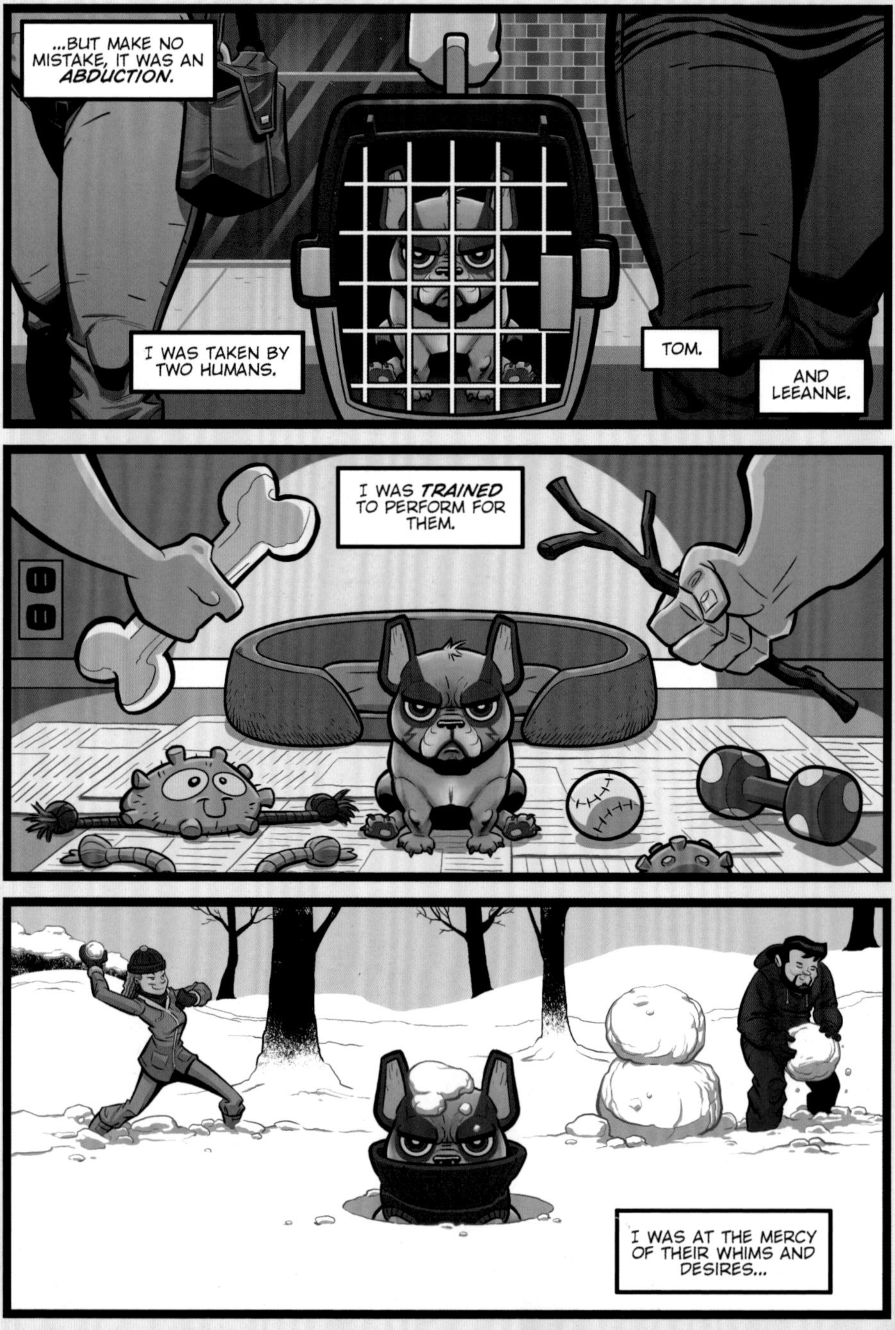
...BUT MAKE NO MISTAKE, IT WAS AN ***ABDUCTION.***
I WAS TAKEN BY TWO HUMANS.
TOM.
AND LEEANNE.
I WAS ***TRAINED*** TO PERFORM FOR THEM.
I WAS AT THE MERCY OF THEIR WHIMS AND DESIRES...

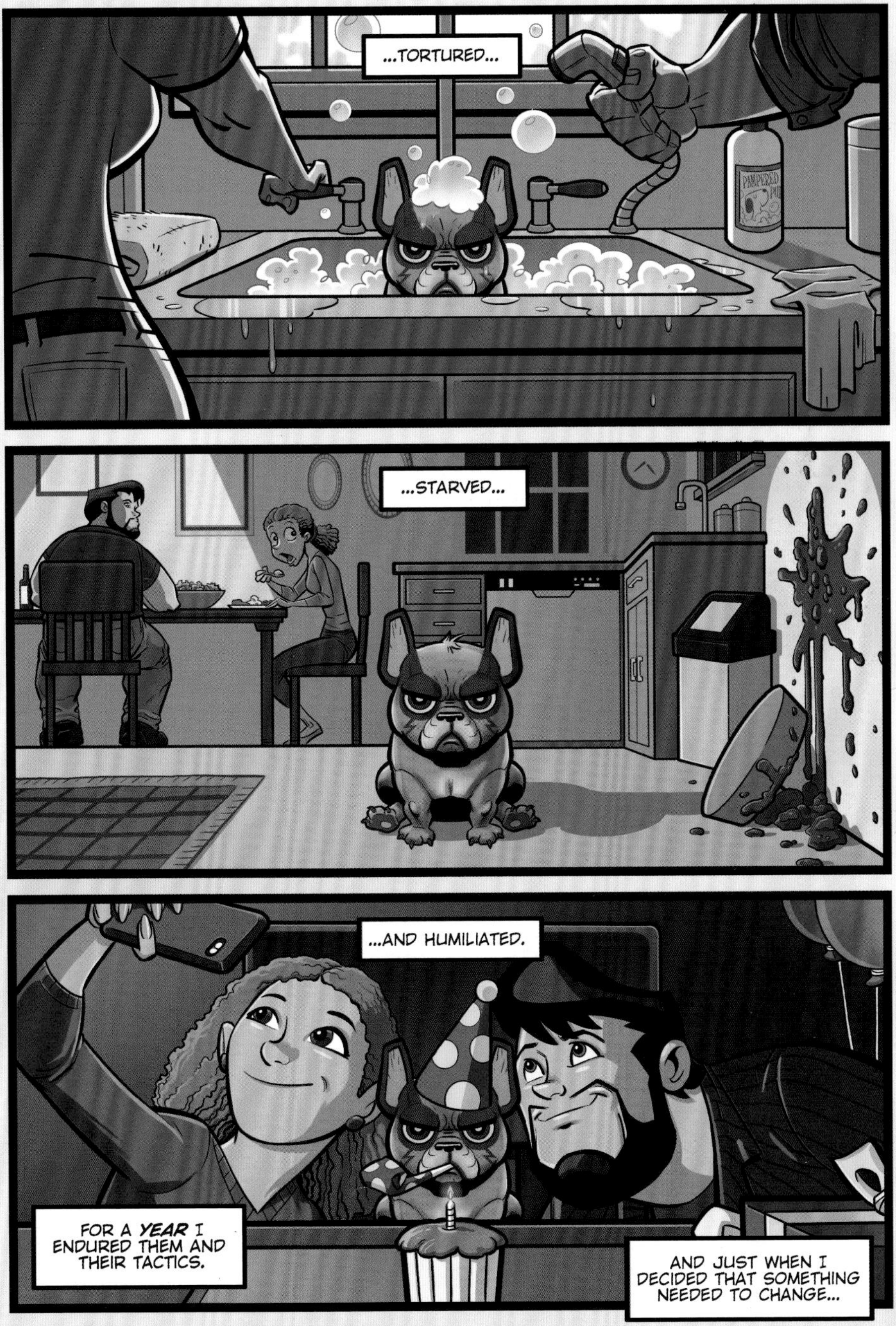
...TORTURED...
...STARVED...
...AND HUMILIATED.
FOR A *YEAR* I ENDURED THEM AND THEIR TACTICS.
AND JUST WHEN I DECIDED THAT SOMETHING NEEDED TO CHANGE...

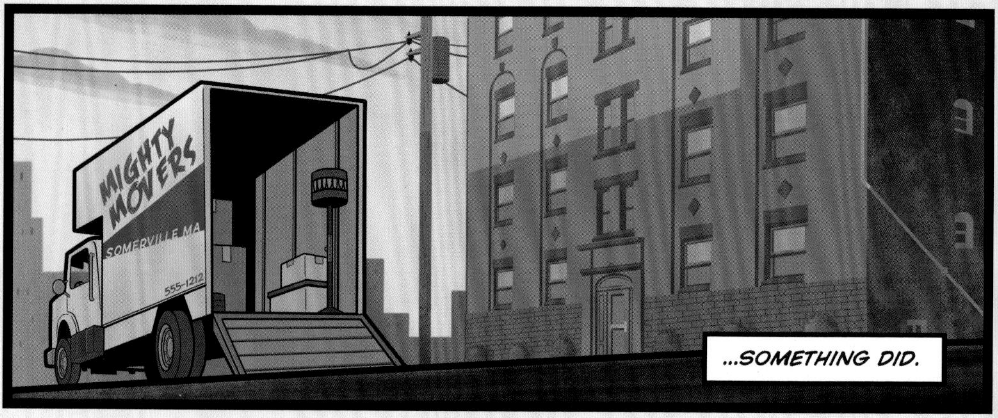
MIGHTY MOVERS
SOMERVILLE MA
555-1212
...SOMETHING DID.

ONE

The modest apartment that Kirby, the French bulldog, shared with two humans and a box turtle was being disassembled.

"What is going on here, OB?" Kirby asked the turtle, who sat quietly in a glass aquarium on a table near the window of a back room.

The turtle stretched his long neck and crawled over the rocks covering the bottom of his tank to peer at the activity around them. "Gee, I don't know," he said after a few moments. "It looks like they're taking stuff away."

"Yes," Kirby agreed. "But to where?"

The Frenchie trotted across the room, claws clicking on the hardwood floor, and jumped onto an ottoman to gaze out the window. On the street below, he saw his humans, Tom and LeeAnne, carrying boxes from the building and loading them into a truck parked on the sidewalk.

Interesting, Kirby thought, watching their every move with his large, unblinking eyes.

"What do you see?" OB called from his tank just as Kirby spotted the old man from across the street shuffling over to speak to his humans.

"Silence, terrapin!" the Frenchie commanded, raising a tiny paw. "I must listen!" He leaned closer to the window, tilting his tall, pointy, bat-like ears toward the conversation below him.

"So, you're leaving the neighborhood?" said the old fool who smelled like pepperoni and medicinal rub.

Leaving?

"Yeah, we're sorry to go, but we've always wanted to have our own house in the suburbs," Tom replied.

House? Suburbs?

"You two will certainly be missed," said he who would soon be dust. "But that dog of yours . . . he is going with you . . . *right*?" The walking corpse laughed nervously as he turned his gaze upward and locked eyes with Kirby in the window.

THE PARK
SIX WEEKS AGO.
WHAT A CUTE DOG!
WHO'S A GOOD BO--
POW!

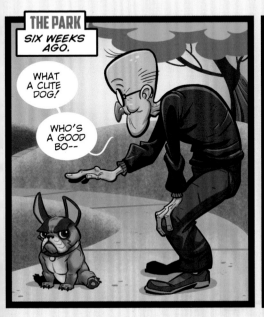

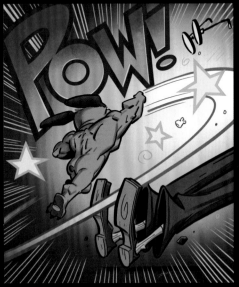

"I've been nothing but nice to him," Kirby muttered indignantly. That ancient bag of withered flesh could have easily met with an "accident" after the many times he'd offended the Frenchie, but Kirby had always been merciful.

"Oh, yes," LeeAnne said quickly. "We're hoping that the suburbs will mellow him some."

"*Hmmmmm*," said the old man, whose bones would shatter like glass if he were to fall just the right way. "Well, best of luck to you both."

Kirby had heard more than enough and turned from the window to consider the facts.

"Well, Kirby?" OB prompted from inside his glass domicile.

"We're leaving this place," the Frenchie said, chewing the words and starting to enjoy their flavor. He jumped down from the ottoman.

"Leaving?" OB squeaked. There was fear in the box turtle's question—fear of the unknown, fear of what it all meant.

But Kirby feared nothing, and this could very well provide him with what had been missing from his boring life . . .

Opportunity.

"We're going to the suburbs," Kirby said, slowly stroking the whiskers on his chin. "Now, doesn't that sound . . . *interesting*."

He began to drool in anticipation.

KIRBY, LATCHED INTO A CAR SEAT...

...COULD ONLY STARE AT THE BACK OF **LEEANNE'S** HEAD...

...AS THE CAR LURCHED AND SWERVED ITS WAY ALONG.

HE SAT...

...AND STARED...

...A SLOW BURNING **BALL OF HATE.**

TWO

Kirby hated riding in the car.

It wasn't that he disliked the wheeled conveyance per se. It was that *he* wasn't in control—and LeeAnne was the worst driver on the planet.

Each time he was forced into the vehicle with her at the wheel, Kirby wondered if he would survive to save the world from its loathsome inhabitants. And the indignity of being belted into the back seat—it was almost more than he could bear.

He often imagined demanding that she allow him to take the wheel. Kirby pictured the shocked expressions on his humans' faces if he were to climb from the back and drop down into the driver's seat.

He would put them both to shame with his incredible driving prowess.

One day that action might be called for, he thought as he turned his attention to the world outside the car's windows. This journey and the potential for new opportunities would distract him from his human's poor driving skills.

The structures of the city gradually diminished, replaced with the green of trees, bushes, and even the occasional empty field.

Where are they taking me? Kirby wondered, tiptoeing on the edge of worry. This far from the city—from civilization—would there even be electricity, or running water?

He took some deep breaths, already concocting a plan to escape the primitive wastelands they seemed to be headed toward. Once back in the city that was his home, he would live in its vast sewer system, forging a great criminal empire in the labyrinthine tunnels beneath the streets.

But he was getting ahead of himself.

First, he would see where they finally ended up.

Then he would decide if drastic measures were in order.

LeeAnne turned into the driveway of the suburban house far too fast, stopping behind the moving truck with a screech of brakes and missing a mover by a hair's breadth.

Tom breathed a sigh of relief and loosened his white-knuckled grip on his seat as she put the car in park.

"We're here!" LeeAnne announced cheerfully, smiling at Tom as she undid her seatbelt and climbed from the car, oblivious to the reactions of her passengers.

"And still in one piece," Tom muttered under his breath as he turned toward Kirby. "Doing okay back there, buddy?" he asked.

Kirby glared, waiting for his stomach to catch up from where it was left at a near head-on collision with a delivery truck three blocks back.

"Let me unsnap you there," Tom continued, leaning into the back seat with a grunt to unbuckle the Frenchie's restraint. "And then you can start getting acquainted with your new home."

New home.

Surprisingly, the words chilled Kirby to the marrow, filling him with great trepidation. What did it all mean exactly? Was this just the next phase in what seemed like an eternity of torment? Or was it truly the beginning of something new?

Tom got out of the car and opened the back door. "Out you go, pal."

Kirby leapt out onto the driveway and stood before the new dwelling. As he assessed the run-down structure, he began to lean heavily toward the continuation of his eternity of torment.

His musings were cut short when Tom tugged on that infernal leash, forcing Kirby to reluctantly follow. Oh, how he longed for the day when he could dispense with such an indignity.

They stopped at the end of the driveway where a smaller but no less rickety structure stood, leaning ever so slightly to the right.

"My own garage," Tom said, the pride and admiration clear in his tone. "I always wanted a garage."

Kirby doubted he would have it for very long, certain that a strong gust of wind was more than capable of knocking it down.

The movers were already carrying boxes and furniture up the back steps and into the house under LeeAnne's direction. He saw OB's tank go by in the arms of a burly man, the little turtle waving excitedly as they passed the Frenchie. It didn't take much to excite OB—a simple piece of banana in his food bowl was akin to winning the Nobel Prize.

If only I could be so easily placated, Kirby mused.

"And this is your yard," Tom was saying to Kirby as he pulled the Frenchie into a patch of crabgrass in serious need of mowing. "Where you'll do all your . . . stuff!"

Hmmmm, yes, Kirby thought with distaste. *Stuff.*

A white picket fence surrounded the yard on three sides. Kirby caught a glimpse of movement on the right side of the yard; the upper half of a melon-shaped head with small, piglike eyes was staring at them over the top of the barricade.

"Oh," Tom said, obviously following Kirby's gaze. "That must be one of our neighbors." He lifted a hand and waved. "Hello!"

THE HEAD QUICKLY DUCKED, THEN *SLOWLY* ROSE AGAIN.

THE *PIGGY EYES* LOCKED WITH KIRBY'S.

"We're just moving in," Tom announced, so very friendly.

"Cute dog," said the creature from the other side of the fence. He made an awful wheezing sound that Kirby quickly determined was a laugh. "Not as cool as mine, but whatever," the mysterious neighbor said dismissively, before going away.

Something sniffed, snuffled, and growled, and Kirby could just about make out a muscular body through the slats of the fence.

He thought it could be a wild boar, or maybe some variety of wildebeest, before deciding that it was indeed just a dog.

How charming.

"Well," Tom said with a smile. "He certainly seemed friendly enough, and he's got a possible friend for you."

Kirby kept his eyes on the fence. He had the impression that the creatures on the other side were going to be a problem—one he would need to address in the not-so-distant future.

But those thoughts were quickly dispelled by something else. At first, Kirby wasn't even sure he'd heard it, but the short hair on the back of his neck bristled, rising up to attention to create a darker strip of fur down the length of his coppery-colored back, and he had the sudden, inexplicable urge to . . .

Howl.

He whipped around, his ultrasensitive Frenchie hearing attempting to pinpoint the source of the sound.

Tom's garage. It was coming from Tom's garage.

Kirby felt himself drawn toward the run-down building, but his progress came to a jarring, choking stop as he reached the end of his leash.

"C'mon, buddy," Tom said, literally dragging the Frenchie back toward the house. "Let's go check out the inside."

Kirby managed one last glimpse of the garage, still hearing the eerie sound emanating from within, as Tom unceremoniously pulled him up the steps and into the house.

THREE

Kirby was not in the least bit pleased.

He had to get outside—to that garage.

"How dare they lock me away," he fumed as he paced back and forth in the sunroom where his humans had barricaded him.

"They don't want you underfoot," OB explained from his aquarium, gazing at the furious Frenchie through the thick glass. "That's all they would need to have you get stepped on!"

Kirby stopped and glared at the turtle. "Is that what you believe?" he asked incredulously. "That this is all for my own good? Imprisonment in this room . . . with you?"

OB shrugged. "At least you've got company."

Kirby snarled, starting to pace again. "If you say so."

He stood before the entryway into the sunroom, his egress blocked by stacks of boxes containing a portion of Tom's vast comic book collection.

Kirby had to get over that wall.

"It isn't that bad," OB continued.

Kirby whirled around. "Come again?"

"This place," the turtle said, stretching his long neck toward the world beyond his tank. "I think this new house is kinda nice and peaceful."

"I despise it," Kirby barked. He walked over to a nearby window and into a patch of warm sunlight. "All this peace and quiet . . . it disturbs my thought process."

"Well, give it a chance," OB said. He always thought on the bright side. "Maybe you'll get used to it, just like you did the old place. Before you know it, it'll feel like home."

"Home," Kirby scoffed. "I'll be dead from boredom long before that." The Frenchie looked away from the view of full, leafy trees, green grass and blooming bushes, and back to the obstacle keeping him from his goal.

"A grappling hook," he said suddenly.

"A what?" OB asked.

"A grappling hook—and a length of rope," Kirby said, his eyes darting about the room. "That's what I need."

"For what?"

"To scale this barricade," Kirby explained, searching for the means of his liberation. "I have to get out of here. I have to get outside."

He remembered the sound from the garage, and the strange effect it had upon him.

"Why?" OB asked.

Kirby almost started to explain—*almost*—but decided against it. Something that mysterious and alluring needed to be investigated by him, and him alone.

"What have I said about questioning me?" Kirby snapped instead. He poked around some of the smaller boxes, searching for something that might be forged into what he required.

"That it isn't good for my continued health," OB answered.

"Precisely."

"Okay then." The dejected OB slowly walked across his tank to take a sip from his water dish. "But the only way you're getting out of here is if Tom and LeeAnne throw you out."

Kirby stopped cold, the little reptile's words stimulating an idea. "Exactly, OB," he said, turning toward the turtle's tank. "How very astute of you."

"What'd I say?" OB asked, the tone of his voice suddenly nervous.

"You have given me the exact means by which I will escape my captivity."

"I have?" OB was clearly clueless about his brief moment of genius.

"You most certainly have." Kirby stepped back into the center of the room. "Now, where to begin," he mused, rubbing his paws together and looking around.

"But I don't get how . . ."

"I just need to be thrown out," Kirby interrupted the turtle. He walked over to a box and pulled it over, spilling its contents.

"Hey! Those are Tom's comics," OB squeaked with fear.

"Can't pull the wool over your eyes, can I?" Kirby said sarcastically.

"You should be really careful with those. I've heard Tom say they're worth a lot of money!"

"Yes," Kirby acknowledged, as he carefully plucked a book from within its protective plastic covering . . .

And tore it in two.

"Eeeeek!" OB screamed. "What are you doing? Are you crazy?"

"Like a fox," Kirby said. He tore the comic book into even smaller pieces and tossed them into the air like confetti. "You really should try this," the Frenchie said as he reached for another of the precious collectibles. "It's quite cathartic."

"Kirby, stop!" OB begged. "Tom is gonna blow his stack!"

The Frenchie froze and thought for a moment, imagining the top of his human's head blowing off and sailing through the air like a furry Frisbee. Then he shrugged. "Exactly," he agreed, and continued to tear up the comic book.

"He's gonna punish you good!" OB warned. "But maybe if you stop now, he won't be so mad!"

Kirby ignored the turtle and looked into the box. "This one looks especially valuable," he said, holding it out toward OB's tank.

"Oh gosh!" the turtle gasped. "That's *Lazer Lasses* #1! It's priceless!"

"Is it?" Kirby said, carefully examining the book before tearing it into shreds. "Then I will be severely punished for sure."

OB squealed in distress as the Frenchie systematically tore his way through an entire box of books. It wasn't until he was halfway through the second box that he paused to assess his work. The hardwood floor was completely covered with shredded, multicolored pieces of comic book pages.

"What do you think?" he asked the turtle.

"I think he's going to kill you!" OB replied.

"That would be a little overzealous—I'm just hoping to be thrown out of the house. Oh, well," Kirby sighed, "we'll just have to wait and see."

He considered tearing up more comics but decided that would be overkill. Although something was still missing—that one final thing to put the cherry on top of the sundae.

He glanced over toward OB's tank.

"Uh-oh," the turtle whispered. "I don't like that look in your eyes!"

"That's it," the French bulldog said. He trotted over to the tank. "The pièce de résistance." He stood on a box and reached into the tank.

"What are you doing?" OB demanded, wedging himself into a corner and pulling his head protectively into his shell.

Without a word, Kirby lifted the turtle's water dish, careful not to spill a drop, and dumped it in the center of the paper-covered floor.

"That should do it," he said, tossing the empty bowl over his shoulder, where it landed on the floor with a clatter.

"I think I'm never coming out of my shell again," OB said, his words muffled.

"I'll take that as a compliment," Kirby replied. He checked his work one last time, making some minor adjustments to the mess of tattered comic books and water.

It was time. Time to draw his humans' attentions to his wonderfully designed carnage. Unfortunately, that also meant that he would have to lower himself to the level of his less intelligent brethren.

He would have to bark.

Kirby closed his eyes, forcing his mind into that place he never cared to visit. A primitive place.

A dog place.

He cleared his throat and let loose the animal hidden deep inside.

"*Woof.*" He listened for a response.

"What the heck was that?" OB asked, poking his beak out from his shell.

Kirby glared. "What do you think? It was a bark."

"Oh," OB said. "Of course it was." He ducked his head into his shell again. "Kind of a sad bark," he muttered.

"I heard that!" Kirby snarled.

"What?" OB whined. "I didn't say anything!"

Kirby glared at the turtle again, then took a deep breath and concentrated on calling forth his primal side.

"*WOOF!*" He looked over to the tank.

"That was a little better, I guess," OB said. "Try it again, but with a little more gusto!"

"Gusto?" Kirby questioned.

The turtle nodded vigorously. "It's always good to do things with gusto."

Kirby rolled his eyes, but gave it a try anyway—anything to get out of this infernal prison.

"*WOOOOOFF!*" came the bark, and he did have to admit—to himself, never to OB—that the turtle might have been right.

The French bulldog craned his blocky head, and cocked a pronounced, bat-like ear to listen.

"Was that Kirby?" he heard LeeAnne's voice from somewhere off in the distance.

"I don't know," was Tom's faint reply.

Several moments of silence followed, and Kirby knew that Tom was listening for him. He cleared his throat once more and unleashed the beast.

"*WOOOOOFFF!*"

And his mighty ears picked up the words he was waiting for.

"You'd better go check on him," LeeAnne said.

Kirby positioned himself amidst the destruction as the sounds of footsteps became louder; he and the remains of Tom's prized collection were the first things the human would see when he reached the barricaded room.

Tom was close, and Kirby tensed in anticipation.

"What's going on, buddy?" he heard Tom ask as he came down the corridor. "Something wrong? You got to go out?"

Oh, yes, Kirby thought, remembering the siren call of the garage. *I've got to go out, indeed.* His eyes were fixed on the space just above the wall of boxes, where he knew the human would appear.

And appear he did.

The man looked as he often did—not too intelligent—with a slack expression and sleepy eyes, and for a brief moment, Kirby thought that his plan might have failed.

But the results were merely delayed.

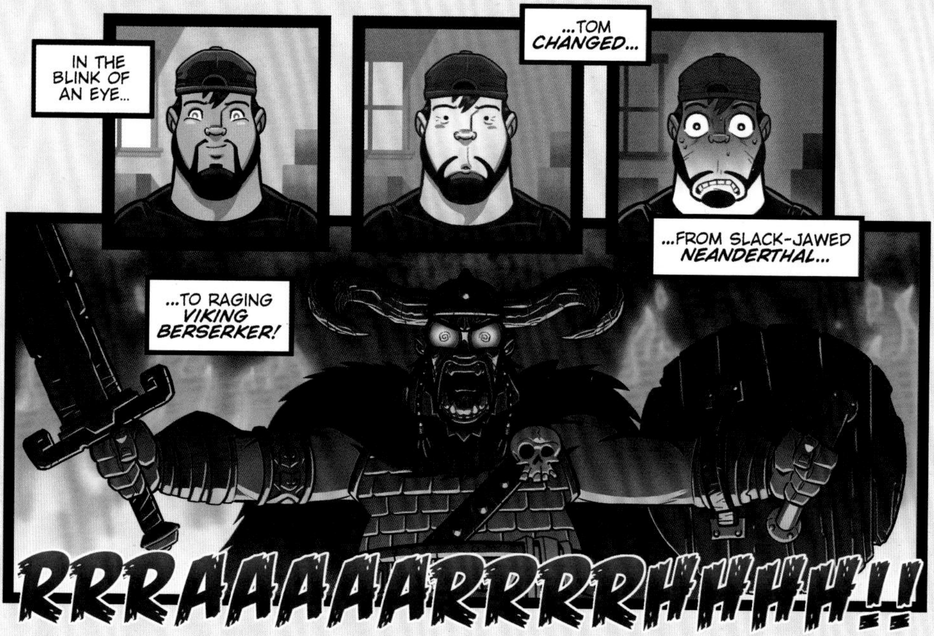
IN THE BLINK OF AN EYE...
...TOM CHANGED...
...FROM SLACK-JAWED NEANDERTHAL...
...TO RAGING VIKING BERSERKER!
RRRAAAAAARRRRHHHHH!!

Kirby would have loved to collect a blood sample from the human, curious if something miraculous had occurred at the genetic level to allow the skin of a human being to turn such a fiery shade of red.

Tom let out a roar followed by a flurry of unintelligible nonsense as he pushed through the stacked boxes to survey all that Kirby had wrought.

The Frenchie locked eyes with his human, waiting for a sign that his plan was about to reach fruition.

Tom's furious gaze fell upon something amidst the destruction and he gasped.

"No," he cried in a choked whisper, leaning forward to pick up a torn and soggy piece of comic book cover with trembling hands. "No, not this," Tom wailed. "Please, not *Lazer Lasses* #1! Anything but that!"

Kirby *woofed* one last time, a gentle prodding, a final reminder that he had been responsible, and punishment—*banishment*—was in order.

Tom turned on the French bulldog. "You!" he roared, the veins in his neck pulsing angrily. "You are a bad dog!"

Yes, Kirby silently agreed. *Yes, I am a bad dog and you must throw me outside.*

As if on cue, the human reached down, grabbed Kirby by the collar, and yanked him into the air.

Yes, that's it, Kirby urged. *That's the spirit!* He caught a quick glimpse of OB inside his tank watching with wide-eyed horror and gave him a thumbs-up as he was hauled from the room. *Success!*

The scolding seemed to go on for an eternity, the humans taking turns as they waggled their fingers in Kirby's face and told him, repeatedly, how disappointed they were.

Yes, yes, get on with it, Kirby thought, not even bothering to make eye contact with the pair as they admonished him.

They took him outside, to the center of the weed-covered lawn, and chained him to a tree. Even this far from the garage, his acutely sensitive Frenchie hearing could pick up the alluring sound.

"Honey, do you think it's safe to leave him out here?" LeeAnne asked her husband.

How cute, Kirby thought. She was actually concerned for his safety, after all he'd done. *Fool.*

"He'll be fine," Tom replied curtly, then took his wife's elbow to escort her back to the house. "He has to learn that there are repercussions for bad behavior."

"If you say so," LeeAnne said, uncertainty in her tone. "You be a good boy," she called over her shoulder to Kirby. "We'll let you back inside as soon as we get stuff put away."

Yes, yes, yes, be off with you, Kirby thought, eager to be alone so he could begin his investigation of the garage.

Finally his humans were in the house and out of sight. The sound from the garage drew him like a beckoning hand and Kirby moved toward it—only to be jolted back to the harshness of reality when he reached the end of the chain.

With a heavy sigh he sat down upon the weed-covered ground and reached up to feel about his fleshy jowls, searching for something hidden away for just such an emergency.

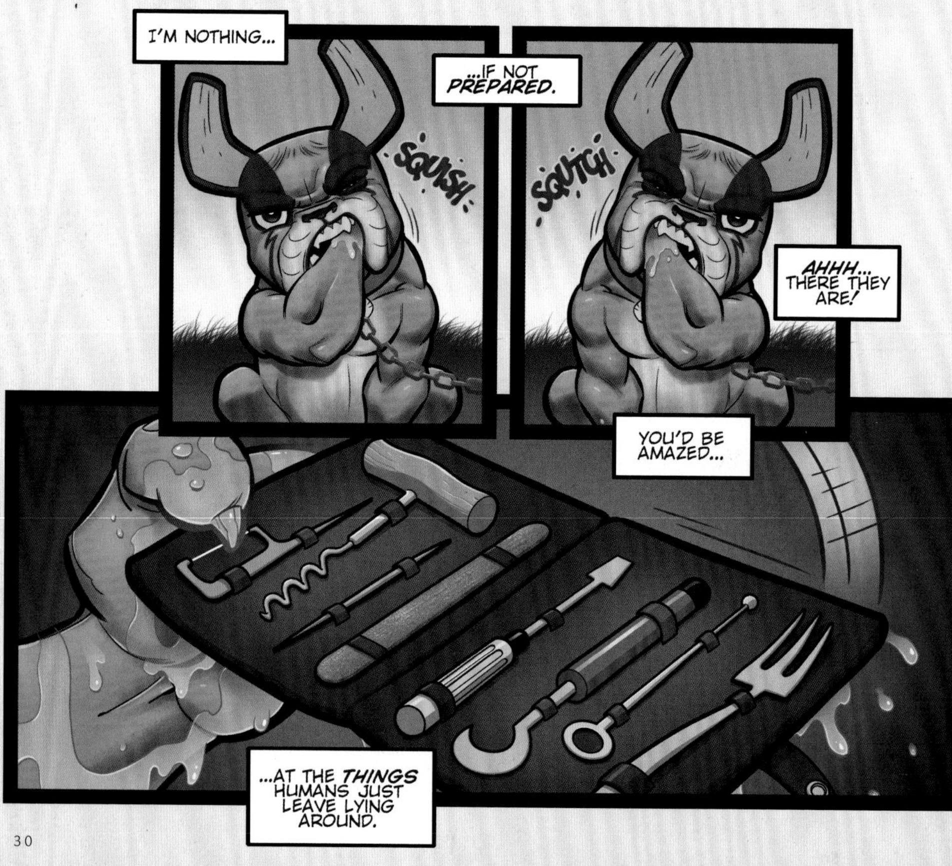
I'M NOTHING...
...IF NOT PREPARED.
SQUISH
SQUTCH
AHHH... THERE THEY ARE!
YOU'D BE AMAZED...
...AT THE THINGS HUMANS JUST LEAVE LYING AROUND.

With practiced precision, he used the tools to unlock the heavy chain from his collar and then returned the tools to his jowls.

Free of his restraints, he cautiously moved toward the garage, circling around the back of the rickety structure so as not to be seen from the house.

The garage's side door was open, and Kirby stopped to listen.

It wasn't just one sound—there were multiple sounds coming together to form a cacophony of noise that called to him. The fact that his humans could not hear it was just further evidence of the inferiority of the human species.

Kirby slipped inside the cool darkness, the scents of dust, rotting wood, and the passage of time tickling his keen sense of smell. His eyes darted about, searching, but found nothing that could be making the sounds.

But still he heard them, close by and yet . . .

If he was any other rational being, he would have begun to doubt his own senses—but he was Kirby.

And in Kirby's world, there was no room for doubt.

He moved farther into the garage, ears twitching. The sounds grew more distinct, but their source continued to remain a mystery.

Kirby hated mysteries with a furious, Frenchie passion.

The garage was filled to near bursting with *stuff* that had obviously been left behind by the home's previous owners. Old, water-stained boxes were stacked along one wall, their corners nibbled by rodents. At the far end, shelves bolted to the wall displayed old jars and coffee cans of various sizes, and to the right of them hung a pegged wallboard where rusted and dust-covered tools still hung. To the right of that, larger wooden crates were pushed up against the garage wall, loaded to overflowing with what looked like scrap metal.

Kirby stood still, eyes taking in every detail of his surroundings, and suddenly it hit him like a rolled newspaper.

The sounds had stopped!

Kirby craned his neck, straining his acute hearing just to be sure, and yes—the strange noises had indeed ceased.

But why?

He spun around, looking to see if anything was different, recalling whether he had done something to affect . . .

He caught movement from the corner of his eye and quickly turned, his gaze falling upon the area of shelving and wallboard.

Seeing nothing out of the ordinary, Kirby slowly stepped forward, eyes darting about the space to find a hint of what he'd glimpsed. It could have been nothing more than a lowly rodent, but something told him that was not the case.

Something was drawing him closer.

To the tools.

Kirby slid a wooden crate over and climbed atop it to carefully study the display of old tools. A hammer hanging from one of the hooks in the pegboard captured his attention. It seemed to be crooked, revealing a clear spot on the board upon which it hung.

"Hello," Kirby muttered, as he reached up and touched a claw to the rusty and dusty old tool.

Wrapping a paw around it, he noticed that it did not come away freely and gave it the gentlest of tugs.

It was not too often that anything surprised the Frenchie, but this certainly did—a sudden whirring sound, a grinding of gears and the turning of cogs.

The Frenchie leapt from the box on full alert, his batlike ears pert, the hackles on his neck and down his back raised to attention as the crates of scrap metal slid apart to reveal an opening.

Fluorescent lights flickered to life, illuminating a staircase that went down, down, down into the bowels of the earth.

Slowly, Kirby stepped forward, stopping just at the entrance of the passage to peer down the steps into the unknown. He was tempted to continue on, but a part of him urged caution.

Instead, he paced before the opening, rubbing the whiskers on his chin and considering the problem before him. Clearly something of great value had to be hidden beyond the passage, and it was mostly likely protected by the most advanced security system imaginable. He thought of wall-mounted lasers with heat and movement sensors zeroing in on their target, slicing them into nicely cauterized ribbon, or strategically placed land mines beneath the floor detonating on contact, obliterating the perpetrator to so much red paste.

That's what *he* would've done. *Hmmmmm.*

Perhaps he would need some assistance.

OB stood tentatively beside Kirby as the two stared into the darkness at the bottom of the steeply descending stairs.

The Frenchie had returned to the house, silently opened the window to the sunroom, and retrieved the box turtle from his tank, telling him that he had need of his aid.

"Where . . . where do you think it goes?" the little turtle asked.

"I don't know, but I intend to find out," Kirby said, slowly turning his gaze from the stairway to the turtle. "With your assistance, of course."

"I don't know, Kirby," OB said, stretching his long neck to gaze down into the opening. "I'm not sure I want to go down there!"

"Of course, OB," Kirby said, sidling up closer to the turtle.

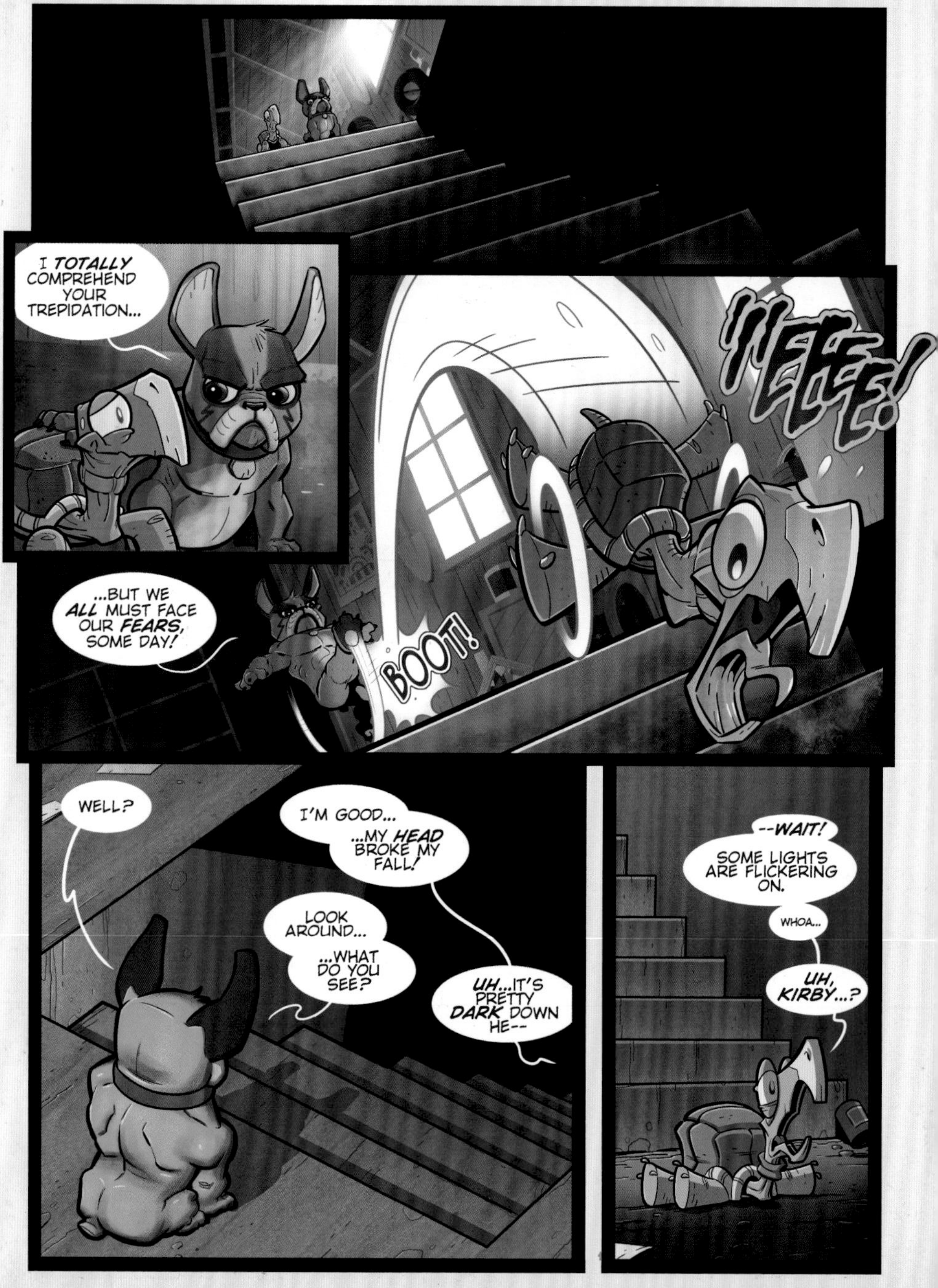

I TOTALLY COMPREHEND YOUR TREPIDATION...
...BUT WE ALL MUST FACE OUR FEARS, SOME DAY!
BOOT!
WELL?
I'M GOOD... ...MY HEAD BROKE MY FALL!
LOOK AROUND... ...WHAT DO YOU SEE?
UH...IT'S PRETTY DARK DOWN HE--
--WAIT! SOME LIGHTS ARE FLICKERING ON.
WHOA...
UH, KIRBY...?

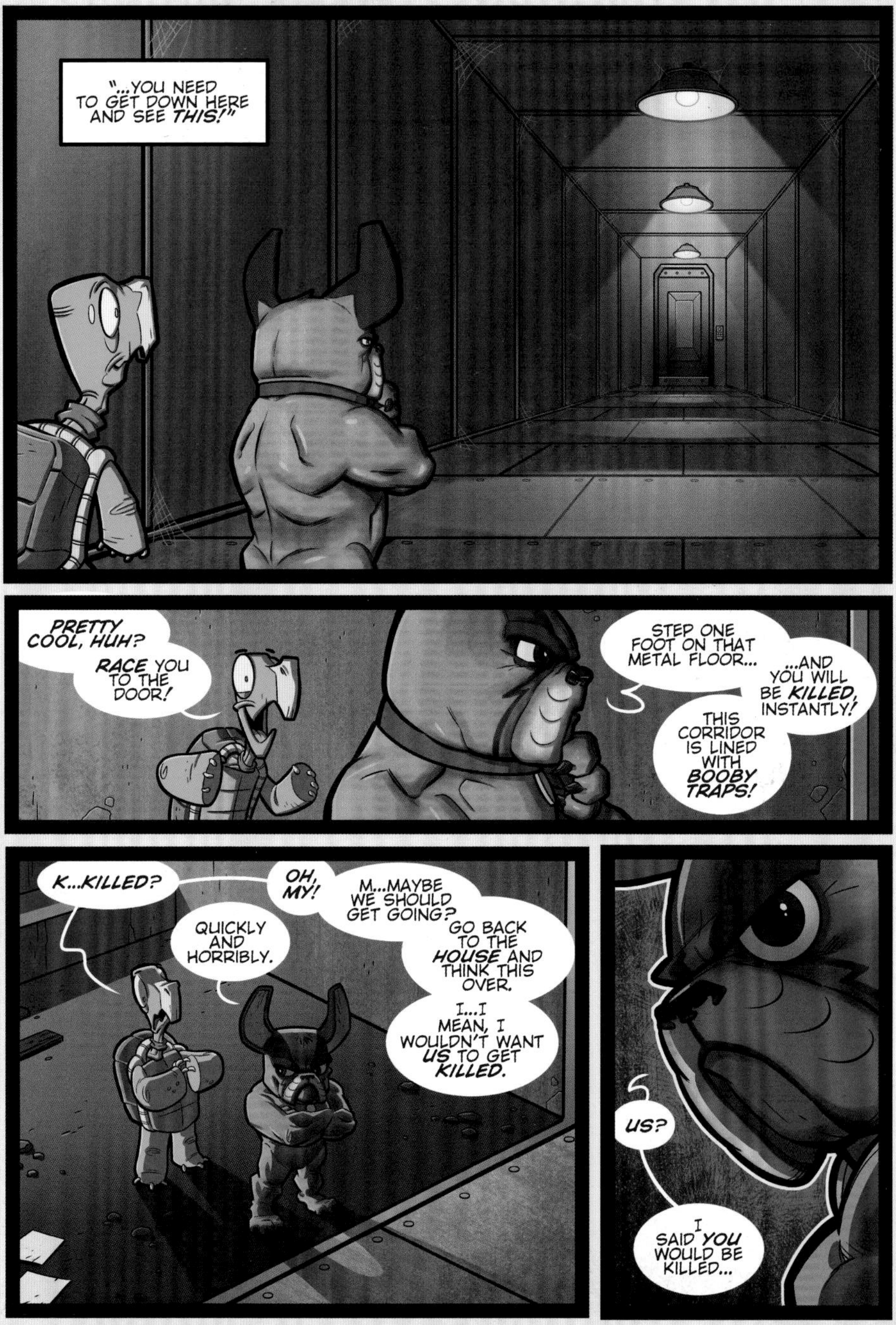
"...YOU NEED TO GET DOWN HERE AND SEE *THIS!*"
PRETTY COOL, HUH?
RACE YOU TO THE DOOR!
STEP ONE FOOT ON THAT METAL FLOOR...
...AND YOU WILL BE *KILLED*, INSTANTLY!
THIS CORRIDOR IS LINED WITH *BOOBY TRAPS!*
K...KILLED?
QUICKLY AND HORRIBLY.
OH, MY!
M...MAYBE WE SHOULD GET GOING? GO BACK TO THE *HOUSE* AND THINK THIS OVER.
I...I MEAN, I WOULDN'T WANT *US* TO GET *KILLED.*
US?
I SAID *YOU* WOULD BE KILLED...

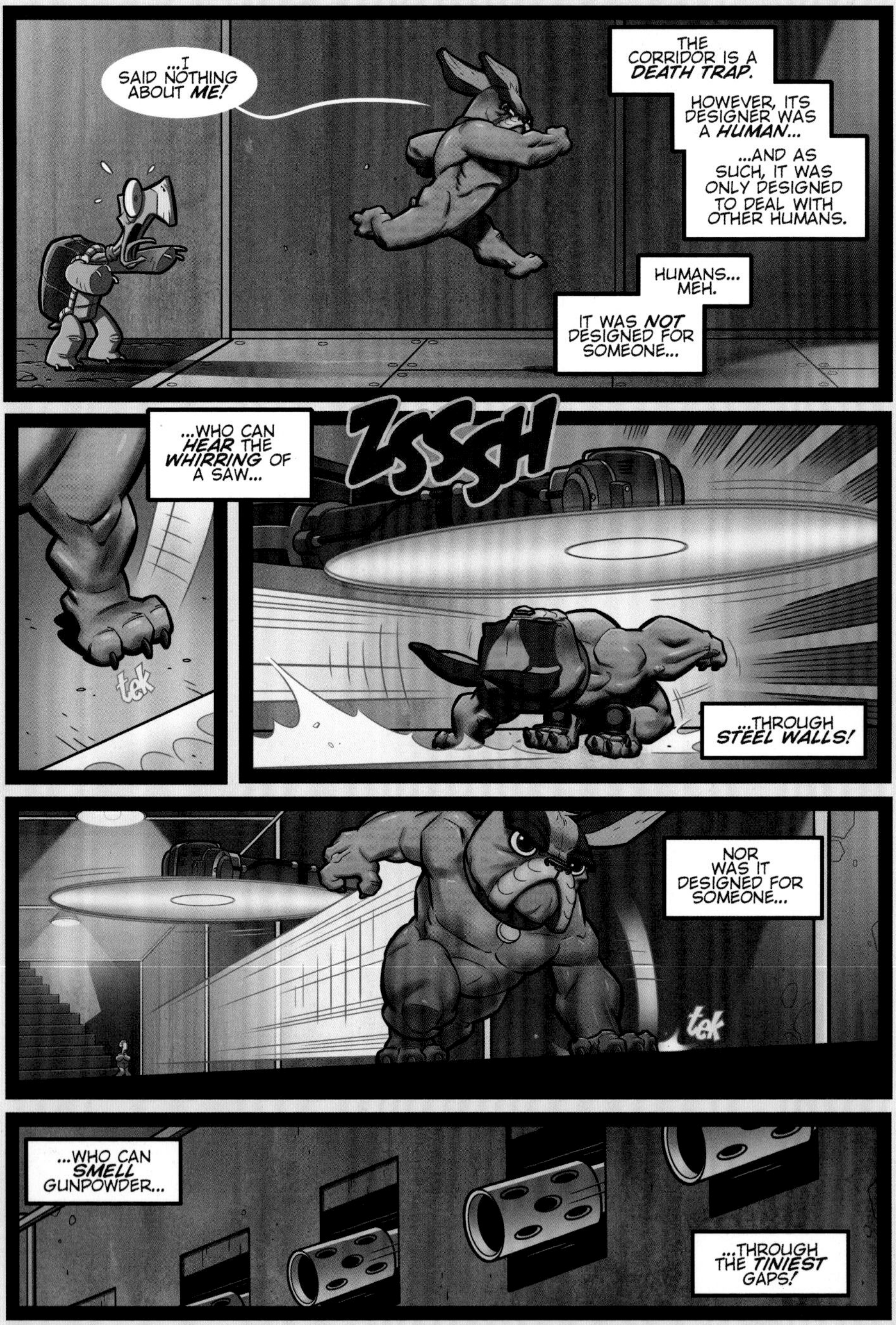
...I SAID NOTHING ABOUT ME!
THE CORRIDOR IS A DEATH TRAP.
HOWEVER, ITS DESIGNER WAS A HUMAN...
...AND AS SUCH, IT WAS ONLY DESIGNED TO DEAL WITH OTHER HUMANS.
HUMANS... MEH.
IT WAS NOT DESIGNED FOR SOMEONE...
...WHO CAN HEAR THE WHIRRING OF A SAW...
ZSSSH
tek
...THROUGH STEEL WALLS!
NOR WAS IT DESIGNED FOR SOMEONE...
tek
...WHO CAN SMELL GUNPOWDER...
...THROUGH THE TINIEST GAPS!

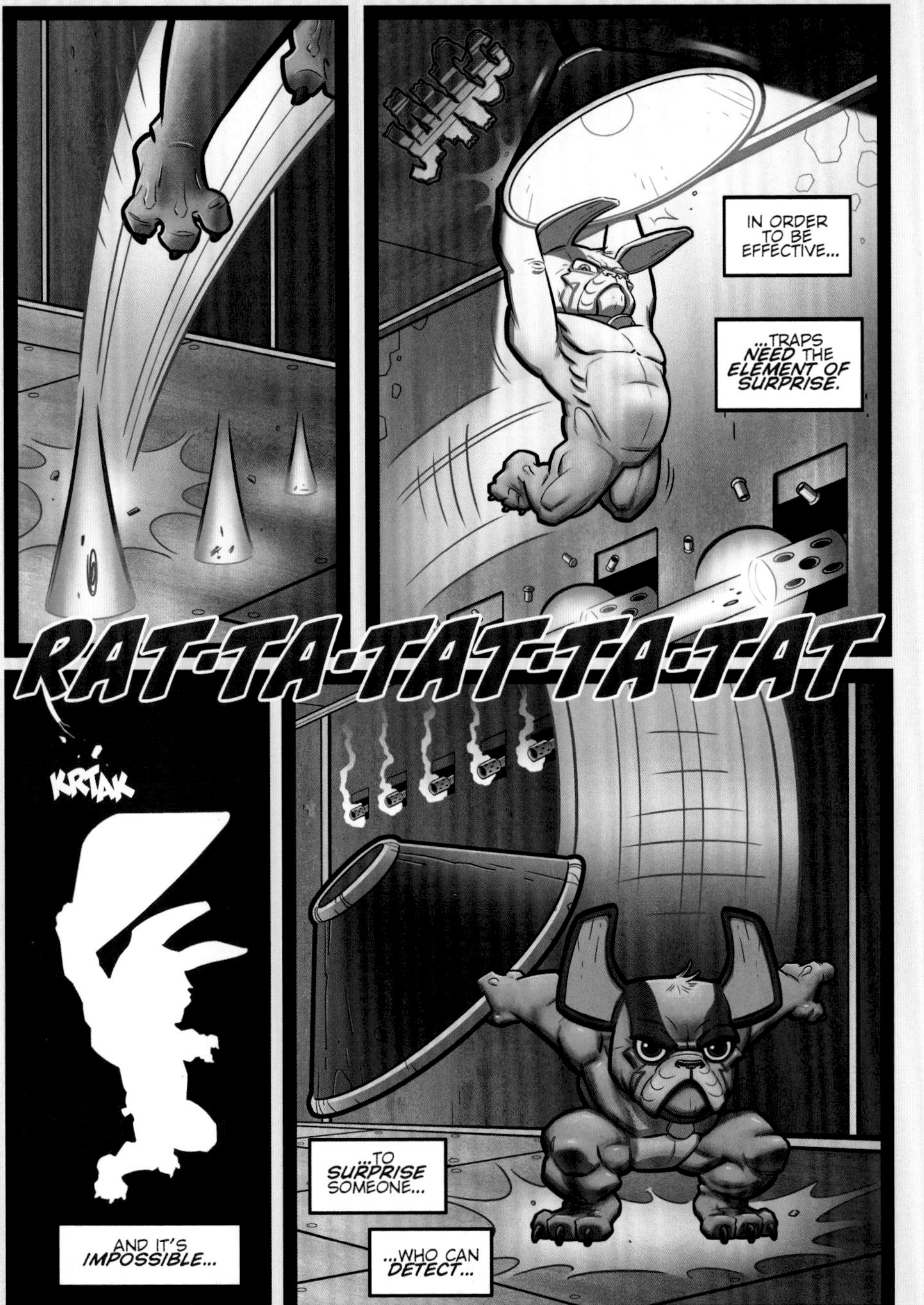
WHIG
IN ORDER TO BE EFFECTIVE...
...TRAPS NEED THE ELEMENT OF SURPRISE.
RAT-TA-TAT-TA-TAT
KRTAK
AND IT'S IMPOSSIBLE...
...TO SURPRISE SOMEONE...
...WHO CAN DETECT...

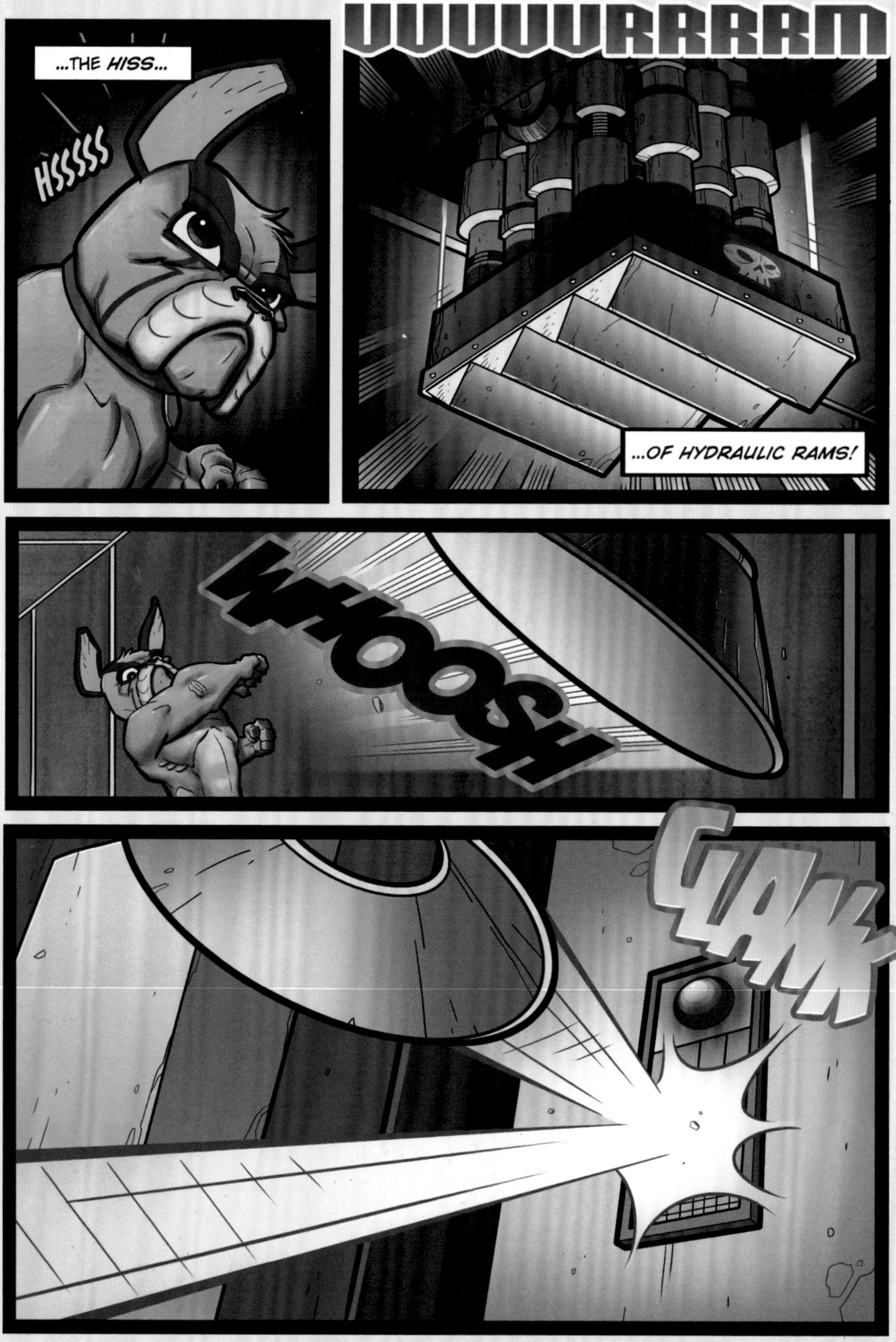
...THE *HISS*...
HSSSSS
VVVVVVRRRRM
...OF HYDRAULIC RAMS!
WHOOSH
CLANK

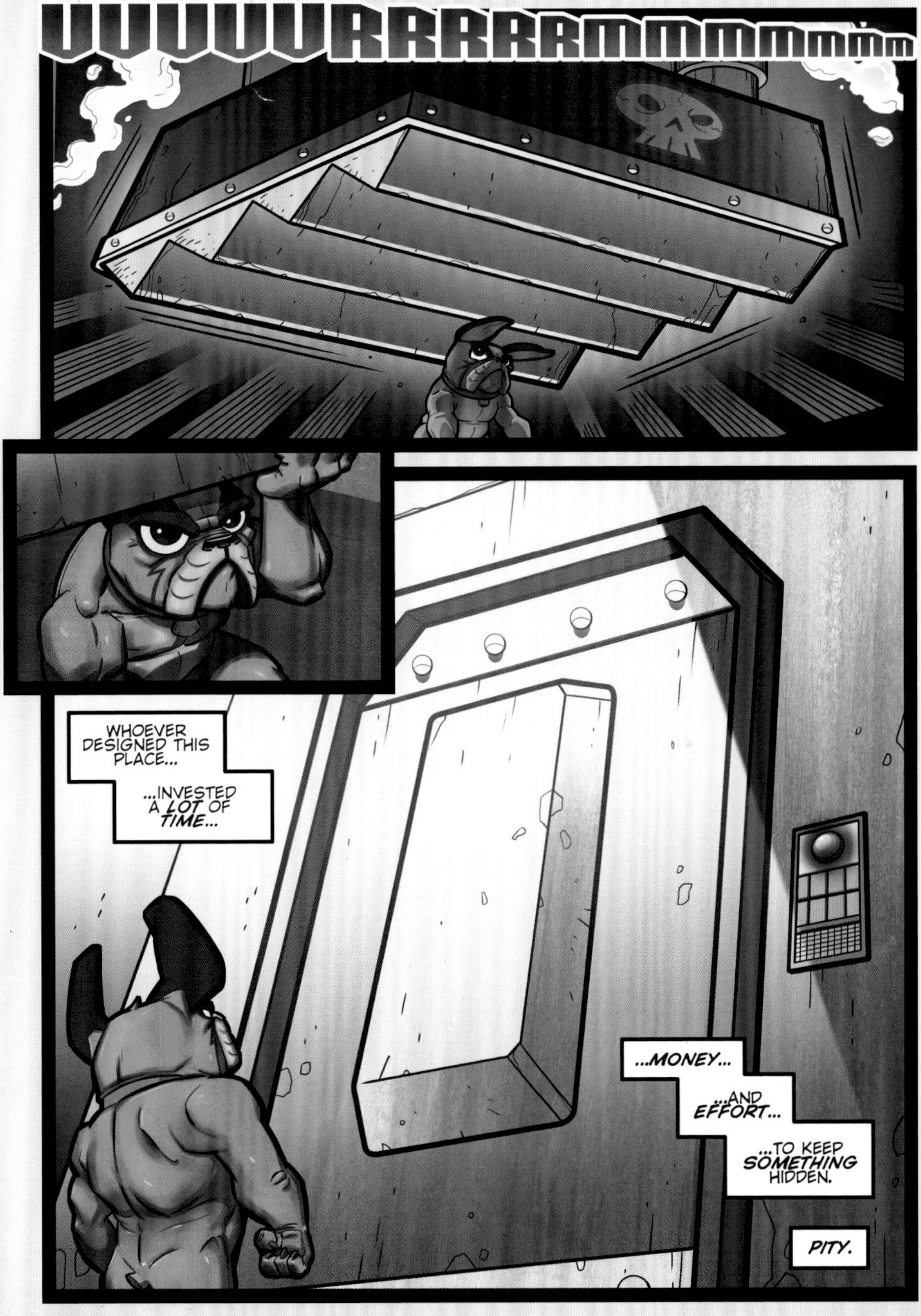
VVVVVRRRRRMMMMMmm
WHOEVER DESIGNED THIS PLACE...
...INVESTED A *LOT* OF *TIME*...
...MONEY...
...AND *EFFORT*...
...TO KEEP *SOMETHING* HIDDEN.
PITY.

This shouldn't take long, the Frenchie told himself.

OB had come to stand beside him. "That was incredible!"

"Was it really?" Kirby asked him, unfazed by the act. "To the likes of you, I imagine it would be."

He concentrated on the severe metal door before him.

"Are we gonna try to get in?" OB asked in a fear-filled whisper.

"Try?" Kirby scoffed. "Lend me your shell," he ordered OB, who promptly dropped to all fours, allowing Kirby to stand on his back.

"Can you reach it?" OB grunted, watching as Kirby studied the numeric keypad to the right of the door.

Kirby leaned in close, examining the keys, and felt his frustration grow. He was certain that he could eventually crack the code needed to give him access, but the amount of time required . . .

"Well?"

"Silence, I'm thinking," Kirby growled. He was about to begin the process of finding the correct series of numbers when . . .

Click!

Kirby reared back, unsure of what had just occurred.

"What happened?" OB asked, extending his neck to see. "You got it open already?"

"I did no such thing," Kirby said, watching as the heavy metal door swung inward with a haunting creak.

"Well, if you didn't open it . . . who . . .?" the turtle whispered.

"Let us see." Kirby stepped off of the turtle's shell and through the door without a moment's hesitation.

"Wait!" OB yelled. "You don't know what's in there!"

"Exactly," Kirby said, the lure of the mystery drawing him into the room like an electromagnet pulling metal filings.

Kirby stopped just inside the door, his round eyes attempting to understand the shapes that he could barely discern in the darkness.

"Well, what's in there?" OB asked nervously, still standing outside the door.

"I can't see," Kirby said. "It's too dark. Go back to the house and get me a flashlight," he ordered, forgetting in his eagerness how excruciatingly slowly the turtle moved—he'd be lucky to have the flashlight within a day and a half.

But it didn't matter, for no sooner had the words left Kirby's mouth than the lights came on, illuminating the mysteries of the room. The machines within came to life as well.

All Kirby could do was stare in awe.

"What is this place?" OB asked in fearful wonder, finally brave enough to enter and stand beside the Frenchie.

Kirby could not answer. He was staring at a vast chamber, a laboratory filled to the brim with technological marvels beyond even his comprehension. The machines were singing to him. These were the sounds he had heard when first arriving on the property, the ones that made him want to howl.

Ancient computers hummed and clicked as monitors turned on to relay secret information, automated systems flashing to life as if awakened by their presence.

His presence.

"Can't you see, OB?" Kirby finally addressed his turtle friend as his hungry eyes continued to find treasure after treasure in the crowded workspace.

"We are home."

All the technological marvels before him seemed to be vying for Kirby's attention. As he moved toward one, his eyes would fall on another, as if it were screaming, *Look at me! Look at me!*

But then a real shout put a damper on his awe.

"Kirby! Where are you, boy?"

OB gasped. "Did you hear that?"

The Frenchie paused, cocking a pointed ear toward the open doorway behind them. He heard a high-pitched whistle from beyond the underground chamber and the garage that hid it.

"Kirby!" a woman's voice called. "Mama's got a treat for you! *Kirrrrrrrrrrby!*"

"Oh, gosh, it's Tom and LeeAnne," OB said.

"I know who it is," Kirby said, feeling his ire begin to rise.

"They're looking for you," the turtle said nervously, looking toward the doorway. "We had better get out of here."

Kirby wanted to say something sarcastic and cutting, but in this particular instance the turtle was right. If he wanted his technological treasure trove to remain secret, he was going to need to keep it hidden from his humans.

"We had better get out of here," he said instead, finding it tortuous to turn away from the technology.

"That's what I said," OB told him, walking beside Kirby toward the open door.

"Was it? I must not have been listening."

"Kirby!" called his humans in unison. He could hear a tone of panic in their voices. *Pathetic.*

Kirby gave the secret laboratory one more glance as he took hold of the door. An old photograph suddenly dropped down from where it was taped to a bulletin board, drifting through the air to land picture-side up.

The photo was of an old, bespectacled gentleman dressed in a white lab coat with what appeared to be a large metal screw sticking out of his forehead.

How odd, Kirby thought, wondering if the strange-looking human might be the one responsible for this treasure trove of marvels.

"Kirby!" the humans wailed beyond the garage, spurring him to action.

"Soon," he promised the technological wonders, before closing the door ever so carefully so that it would not lock again.

"I will return."

♥

"Kirby!" LeeAnne called out, then cocked an ear, listening. Nothing.

"Where is that dog?" she muttered, crossing the yard toward the chain that Kirby had been tethered to.

She heard a faint call of "Kirby" coming from the direction of the driveway. It was Tom, his voice tinged with guilt and concern. She knew why, too. He was beating himself up for his outburst and for not double-checking the lock on Kirby's chain.

"This is my fault!" Tom said to LeeAnne in the kitchen shortly after. "I shouldn't have blown up like that. I flipped out, and now he's run away!"

"Tom, you don't know that," she countered. "Maybe he saw a squirrel and decided to investigate."

As soon as she said it, she realized how false it sounded. Not once on any walk or trip to the park had Kirby ever shown the slightest interest in *any* animal—not squirrels, not cats, not even other dogs. Aside from OB, animals seemed to be nothing but a bother to Kirby.

LeeAnne tried to soothe Tom as they made their way out the mudroom door to begin searching.

"I'm sure he's around here somewhere. I mean, how far could he have gone, right?"

Secretly LeeAnne *was* concerned. This was unusual even by Kirby standards. Kirby was not a runner. Not like Sparky, the dog she had had as a girl. Sparky had been an energetic dog who took every opportunity he could to make a break for it. Kirby, by contrast, was calm—almost eerily so.

She stopped at the tree that Kirby had been chained to and scanned the area. The garage—more of a converted old barn—was off to her right, while a row of trees that led into a thicker wooded area stood to her left. She glanced back and forth from one to the other.

"Flip a coin," she thought.

FOUR

Kirby and OB peeked out from behind the door to the garage.

"The coast is clear," the Frenchie said, seeing no sign of the humans.

"I've got to get back into the house," the turtle said, panic in his tone. "What will they think if they see me out of my tank?"

That is a question indeed, Kirby thought, paw coming up to stroke his hairy chin. It was a question he'd rather not have answered, for it would likely bring attention to him and the clandestine activities he would soon be launching.

"Get back to the house as quickly as you can," Kirby told him. "I'll distract them long enough to give you time to return to your reptilian habitat."

"Thanks, K," the turtle said, already making his way. "You're a pal."

"I most certainly am," Kirby grumbled, moving away from the garage.

"Kirby!" he heard Tom yelling off in the distance, farther away from the garage.

Kirby cleared his throat. "*Woof*!" he barked with a roll of his eyes. He examined the claws on one paw, while listening for his humans to respond. "*Woof! Woof!*" he announced again, just to give them an idea of his whereabouts.

Kirby heard the sound of someone approaching and immediately sat down, ready to be found.

He expected to see either Tom or LeeAnne come around the side of the rickety garage. He was not expecting . . . this.

The French bulldog recognized the child as the one from next door whom he'd partially seen over the fence.

"Well, lookie here," the homely child said, as what appeared to be an attempt at a smile spread across his doughy features. "What are you doin' out here all alone, little doggy?"

Kirby eyed the youth suspiciously, disliking the boy's tone.

The human child stepped closer, and Kirby backed up.

"Not good for such a little dog to be outside unsupervised," the boy said, his breathing growing heavier as if from exertion—or was it excitement?

"I can just imagine all the *terrible* things that could happen to a poor pup out in the cold, cruel world."

Kirby didn't like the sound of that, or the fact that the monstrous child was attempting to get within grabbing range.

"C'mere, boy," the youth said with an evil twinkle in his piggish eyes. "Let your good buddy Ogden Stempleworth take care of you."

Ogden Stempleworth? the Frenchie thought, repeating the child's name over and over in his mind. He'd never seen someone more appropriately named. This was most certainly an Ogden Stempleworth attempting to grab him.

Attempting being the operative word.

Kirby was deciding on whether a growl or an actual snap of his jaws would be best when . . .

"Kirby!" LeeAnne squealed, running around the garage from the other side.

The Stempleworth beast stepped back as LeeAnne rushed forward, Tom right at her heels.

"Kirby, where the heck have you been, boy?" his human asked.

"I found him back here by himself," Ogden interjected. "I didn't want him to get hurt, so I was going to try and bring him back to the house for you."

LeeAnne kissed the top of the Frenchie's head as she picked him up.

"Thank you so much," she said, squeezing Kirby so tightly he thought she might break something.

"Yeah, thanks," Tom said, extending his hand toward the creature. "My name's Tom by the way, and you?"

The Stempleworth thing stared at his human's offered hand and took it.

"Ogden," he said. He shook Tom's hand limply before pulling it away as if infected by a disease. "Ogden Stempleworth."

"Thank you so much, Ogden," LeeAnne said, kissing Kirby's head again. "We were beside ourselves when we saw that he'd somehow gotten free of his chain."

Ogden glared at Kirby, and Kirby glared back at him.

"Yeah, it's a good thing that I found the little rascal," the boy said, reaching out to pet Kirby's head.

Kirby snapped at his fingers, and the creature quickly pulled them back.

"Woulda hated if something nasty happened to the little guy," Ogden said with a smile that looked more like gastric discomfort than joy.

"Well, thanks again," Tom said as LeeAnne carried Kirby back toward the house.

Over his human's shoulder, Kirby stared at the Ogden-beast, who watched them with small, cruel eyes. Deep in his Frenchie gut, Kirby knew that something would have to be done about him.

🐾

It was very early morning, and Kirby lay sleeplessly between his unconscious humans, wondering what higher being he had offended to be enduring such torture.

They had dropped him on the floor in the new kitchen and scolded him for running away, then tossed him treats and heaped a sickening amount of affection on him. He'd had to endure an evening lying between them on the couch as they watched an inane comedy on television, and now he was trapped between them on the bed, as if the physical contact could keep them from losing him again. Even sweet thoughts of world domination couldn't assuage his dark mood.

Tom snored loudly in one ear, and LeeAnne wheezed and gurgled in the other. It was a symphony of nauseating noises, and he was trapped in the orchestra pit.

He closed his eyes and thought of the laboratory—a mystery that had been stirred like silt from the bottom of a stagnant pond. Why was it there? Why hide it beneath the ground? Who built it?

Kirby felt as though his brain was on fire with the mystery of it all, and opened his eyes, finding himself gazing up into the face of a . . .

Ghost.

The Frenchie did not normally believe in such supernatural folderol, but there was no other away to explain the spectral apparition that hovered above the bed, clothed only in a bath towel and holding a pillow from the couch downstairs.

How strange!

Kirby tensed, preparing to defend himself, but the ghost raised a long finger to his translucent lips, signaling the Frenchie to be silent.

What is he doing? Kirby wondered as the ghostly creature drifted closer to his humans.

The ghost moved with deft precision. He placed the pillow between Tom and LeeAnne, allowing Kirby to escape while they continued to blissfully snort and gurgle.

The ghost smiled and gave Kirby a thumbs-up signal, and suddenly the Frenchie recognized the apparition. The wild hair, the strange goggle-like glasses, the large screw sticking from his head—this was the man from the photo in the secret lab.

Cold, spectral hands picked him up from the bed and carried him downstairs, where he dropped Kirby unceremoniously on the living room floor.

The Frenchie sat and stared with his large, unblinking eyes.

"Boo!" the ghostly creature said, throwing up his hands and surging toward the dog.

Kirby took a swipe at the spirit, his tightly balled Frenchie fist of fury passing through the ghost's cold, immaterial face.

The ghost of the old man laughed, the sound like a rusty gate swinging open.

"I like you, kid," he said gleefully. "You've got spunk!"

Then he abruptly turned and floated away, motioning over his shoulder for Kirby to follow. The ghost entered the sunroom. As he passed a sleeping OB inside his tank, he pointed. "I don't know about this one," the ghost said. "Kinda gives me the creeps."

He continued on and disappeared through the outside wall, leaving Kirby standing there. The Frenchie was pondering how to get outside the house when the window slowly began to rise.

"Destiny waits for no man . . . or dog!" the ghost said, again motioning for him to follow.

Kirby considered waking OB to join him as he leapt up onto the windowsill, but thought better of it.

Dropping down to the ground outside the house, Kirby scanned the area, catching sight of the specter as he floated through the wall of the garage.

"Of course that's where you're taking me," Kirby muttered beneath his breath as he darted across the backyard and through the door into the darkened garage.

The secret passage was already open, waiting for him.

Kirby ran to the stairs and began his descent, stopping short at the bottom when he remembered the elaborate security defenses.

"It's quite all right, Kermit," came the ghost's voice from inside the lab. "I've deactivated the security systems."

Kirby strode down the corridor and entered the laboratory.

The ghost hovered above the floor, waiting.

"Kirby," the Frenchie announced, coming to stand before the ghost.

"Come again?" the ghost asked.

"My name is Kirby," the dog said. "You incorrectly addressed me as Kermit."

The ghost stared blankly, and then smiled, his long features expanding as if made of rubber.

"You!" the ghost said, wagging a spectral finger. "You've got moxie, anybody ever tell you that?"

"Yes, moxie," Kirby answered, having no idea what the expression meant, his eyes wandering over all the wondrous devices. "Who are you and what is your connection to this place?"

"My name is . . . *was* Erasmus J. Peckinpah!"

The ghost waited, as if for some sort of reaction to his name.

"Never heard of you," Kirby said.

"Well, you are kinda young . . . and a dog, so . . ."

THE
T-19
GARBAGE
KILLER

"Why are you clothed that way?" Kirby asked, making reference to the ghost's towel.

Erasmus looked down at himself.

"It's what I was wearing when . . ." He paused, as if not wanting to say the words.

"You shuffled off the mortal coil?" Kirby suggested.

Erasmus smiled. "I like that," he said. "You got a way with words, kid!"

"Yes, I try," Kirby said, starting to wander. "What is this place?"

"This was my sanctum sanctorum," the ghost of Peckinpah said. "Where the magic happened!"

"Magic," Kirby repeated, strolling amongst the strange technology. "Tell me of your magic."

The ghost of Erasmus brightened, flying through the air toward a metallic object in the corner covered in dust and cobwebs. It resembled a high-tech trash barrel merged with some sort of primitive automaton.

"The T-19 Trash Killer," Erasmus said, waving his hand above its lid. "It would have made Strasburg the cleanest city in all the world. If only I'd been able to iron out the bugs," he added almost dreamily.

"Bugs?" Kirby asked as he approached the T-19 Trash Killer. "What kind of bugs?" The Frenchie leaned in for a closer examination of the robotic contraption.

"Just some minor issues with the mechanical brain's ability to differentiate between what was trash and what wasn't."

"Problematic," Kirby agreed, clasping his paws behind his back and strolling toward another apparatus.

"You would have been able to eat a five-course meal off any street in the city if . . ." Erasmus was proclaiming when Kirby interrupted.

"And this?"

The contraption was all spinning blades and spidery metal limbs poking through multiple ports in the device's mechanical shell.

"Ah, the Weed-a-nator 300," Erasmus said, floating over to hover beside Kirby. "Here is a device that could have revolutionized yard care for all eternity."

"Could have?" Kirby questioned.

"Hmmm, yes," Erasmus said. "If only . . ."

"You could have ironed out the bugs?" Kirby offered.

"Precisely," the ghost said, stroking the metal body with a ghostly hand. "Spinning blades and sandals are not friends."

"Words to remember." Kirby walked across the lab, stopping before a harness

THE WEED-A-NATOR

THE
BABY BOUNCER
7000

that held a child-sized test-dummy, which hung from a powerful-looking robotic arm. "And that?" he pointed.

"The Baby Bouncer 7000," Erasmus proudly announced, rubbing his ghostly hands together.

"Baby Bouncer?"

The ghost nodded.

"It bounced . . . babies?" the Frenchie asked.

Erasmus nodded, suddenly looking nervous. "Oh, yes it did."

"Bugs?" Kirby asked.

Erasmus nodded again. "Bounced them a bit too hard."

"Moving on," Kirby said, walking farther back into the cluttered space. It was dark back there, the shadows hiding even more technological treasures.

"This," he heard Erasmus say.

Kirby turned as a light went on.

Click!

A single bulb illuminated the space, and the Frenchie stared with intense curiosity at what had been revealed.

He had no idea what it was, or what its purpose might have been . . . but something deep down inside him told him that it had the potential for something great.

"Tell me," Kirby commanded the ghost of Erasmus Peckinpah.

The spirit drifted closer. "It is the future, Kareem," the ghost whispered into one of the Frenchie's ears. "Most specifically, *your* future."

It was a helmet with a braid of multicolored wires leading from the top of the helm to a complex-looking bank of machinery behind it.

Fascinating, Kirby thought, reaching up to stroke his hairy chin with a paw. He could not take his eyes off of the bizarre mechanism.

"What is it for?" he asked. He reached a paw out and caressed the roundness of the helmet.

"It was to be the ultimate source of learning—providing a vast amount of information in the shortest amount of time," Erasmus said. "Want to learn Swahili, or how to dismantle and reassemble a thermonuclear device, or how to prepare the perfect cherries jubilee? The atomically powered InfoMatic 6000 would download everything you need directly into your coconut." Erasmus pointed to his ghostly skull.

Kirby turned his eyes from the wondrous device, pinning the ghost with their intensity. "Directly into the brain, you say?"

Erasmus nodded. "Right into the ole pine nut," he said.

"Bugs?" Kirby asked.

Erasmus shrugged as he admired his craftsmanship.

"*Bugs?*" Kirby asked again, much louder.

"A few," Erasmus answered. "There were . . . side effects."

"Side effects," Kirby repeated. "What kinds of side effects?"

"Headaches," Erasmus began. "Eye strain, vertigo . . . oh, and oily brown discharge."

Kirby wrinkled his face. "From where?"

Erasmus looked just as disgusted. "The less said about that the better."

"Is that it?" Kirby asked.

"Yes . . . no," Erasmus said, changing his mind.

"There's more?"

Erasmus nodded. "Cranial expansion with a chance of brain detonation."

"*Brain detonation?*" Kirby repeated, just to be certain he had heard correctly.

Erasmus nodded, bringing his spidery fingers up to the sides of his head and wiggling them on either side while making an explosion sound.

"Brain detonation," the ghost repeated.

"Unfortunate," Kirby said.

"Yes, it was. I made some minor adjustments to the device right before I . . . *ahem* . . . shuffled off this mortal coil, but I never had the opportunity to test it."

"So it could be fine now," Kirby stated.

"Yes, it could."

"It still needs to be tested," Kirby continued, staring intently at the device.

"It does."

"I know just the test subject," Kirby said. "Allow me to return to the house and fetch OB . . ."

"That won't do at all," Erasmus said as he shook his head sadly. "A superior brain like mine is required for the InfoMatic to work correctly."

Kirby stroked his hairy chin. "That would most certainly leave OB out of the running. Perhaps one of my humans would do?"

Erasmus shook his head. "No, sorry. Barely one average brain between the pair. It would leave them drooling vegetables."

Kirby remained silent, lost in intent thought. The Frenchie knew that his intelligence was beyond reproach, but there was still so very much he could learn. How long had he plotted and planned with little success? Perhaps this was the answer to the question of world domination that he had waited so long for. It was not long before he knew what must be done. "I'll do it," Kirby announced.

"You?" Erasmus asked, floating backward, spectral eyes wide behind his goggles.

"Yes, me," Kirby said. "You said that a superior intellect is needed, and I am most certainly in possession of that."

Erasmus smiled a crooked smile. "Yes, you are indeed," the ghost said.

"Then I will test it," Kirby said, reaching up to take the large helmet down.

"Do we dare?" Erasmus asked, already beginning the process of activating the long-dormant machine.

"I say yes," Kirby said, placing the overly large helmet onto his blocky Frenchie head.

"And what shall we learn today?" Erasmus asked, turning a succession of knobs. The invention lit up like a winning slot machine.

"Everything," Kirby announced.

"Excuse me?" Erasmus asked, mid switch flip.

"Everything," Kirby repeated, adjusting the helmet so that it would not crush his large ears. "I want to learn everything."

Erasmus brought a crooked finger to his mouth, and then shrugged. "Everything it is, then," he proclaimed happily, floating around to twist some knobs all the way to the right, and then to pull a lever down in the center of the great machine.

"Open wide!"

The InfoMatic 6000 came alive; hums, clicks, beeps, and boops filled the air of the secret laboratory as all the information in its vast computer memory banks came together . . .

And downloaded into the brain of one little French bulldog.

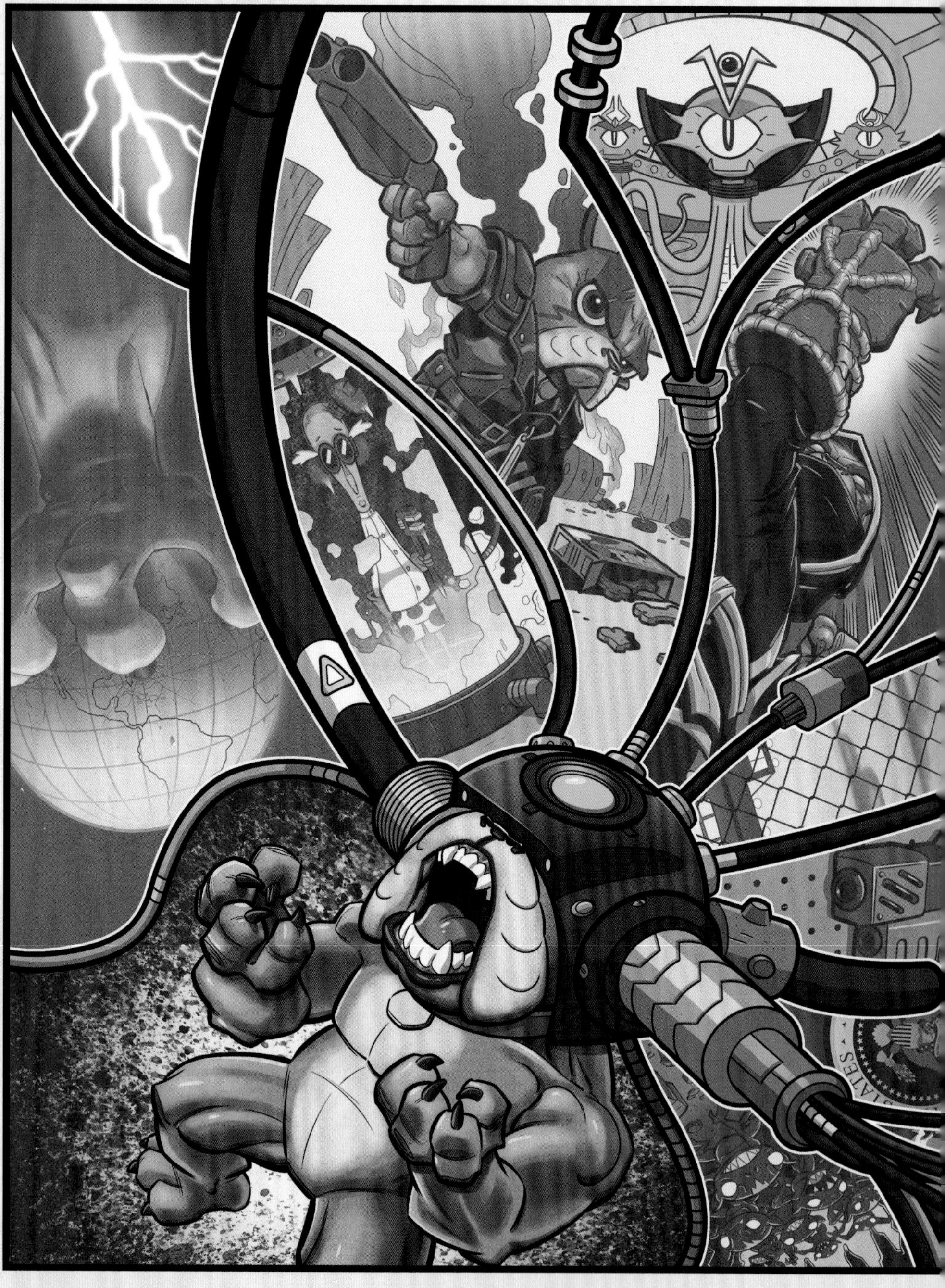

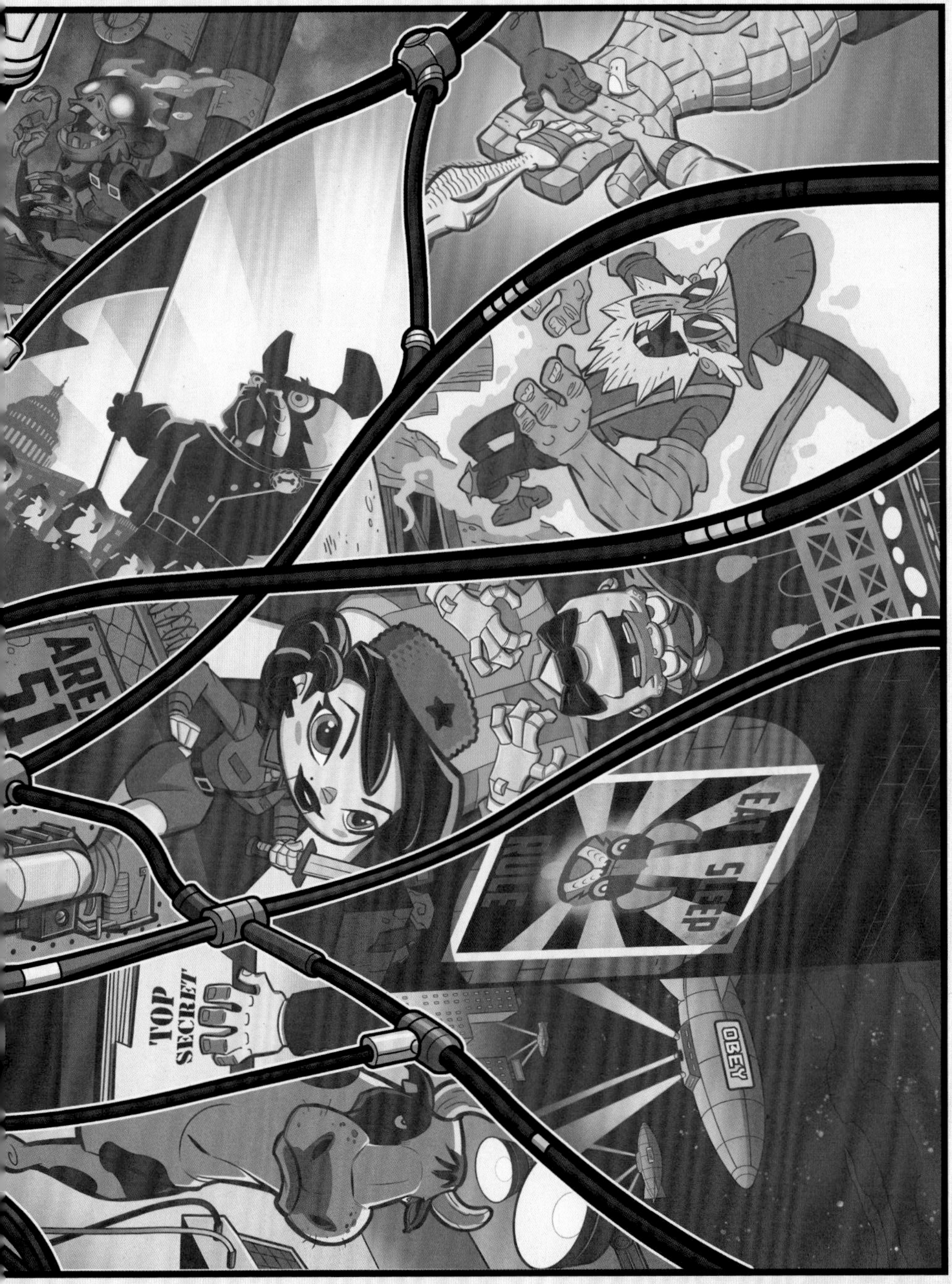
ARE
51
TOP SECRET
EAT
SLEEP
RULE
OBEY

FIVE

It was as if the planet's entire nuclear arsenal had been detonated inside Kirby's skull, but instead of devastating atomic fire there was wave after wave after wave of something far more powerful.

Information.

Information of all kinds, of all sizes and shapes—important and not so important.

Harmless, and oh-so dangerous.

Kirby thought his skull was about to split, but with his furious Frenchie will, he kept it together.

Kept all that information trapped inside.

The vast computer banks of the InfoMatic 6000 finally emptied, and the machine automatically shut down.

Kirby removed the helmet to see the ghost of Erasmus hanging in the air, watching him with a scientist's eye.

"Well?" Erasmus asked.

Kirby just stared, rendered speechless by the magnitude of knowledge that now packed his canine cranium.

Erasmus snapped spectral fingers in front of Kirby's face. "Hello? Mission control to Kirkwood! Are you in there, or did your brain take the last bus to Puddingville?"

"I . . ." Kirby began. ". . . I'm here."

"You're here?" Erasmus asked excitedly, bringing his ghostly hands together. "You're *here* here?"

The information inside his head roiled in an enormous stew of untapped potential.

"I am," Kirby said, this time more forcefully.

"It worked!" Erasmus cried out, floating up to the ceiling and happily spinning around. "It worked . . . at last, something worked! I knew you had it in you somewhere, Erasmus old boy!"

Kirby's brain felt as though it was on fire. He began to sway as an overwhelming wave of fatigue washed over him.

"What is it?" Erasmus asked, stopping his spinning but remaining close to the ceiling. "Your head isn't going to explode, is it?"

Kirby shook his head.

"Good," Erasmus said. "Wouldn't want me to look bad, would you?"

In all honesty, Kirby couldn't have cared less. "I need to lie down," he said, moving toward the door.

"Good idea," Erasmus said. "You go lie down, and I'll stay right here basking in the glow of my superior genius."

"You do that," Kirby growled, dragging himself across the lab toward the door, escorted by the whooping cackle of the ecstatic ghost scientist.

♉

The sun had risen, chasing away the concealing shadows, and Kirby moved as quickly as he could across the yard toward the house.

The blast of an air horn lifted him up from his feet and made him yelp in surprise. He landed in a frazzled heap on the ground, then spun around to face the perpetrator of this sudden, startling insult.

Ogden Stempleworth, clad in ill-fitting *Star Wars* pajamas and a bathrobe, hung over the fence between yards, air horn clutched in a pudgy hand. His sorry excuse for a canine sniffed around at the bottom of the fence once again.

"Morning, ugly," the evil boy said with a giggle. "How's *that* for a wake-up call?"

Kirby started toward the fence, but stopped. His mind was a swirling maelstrom of facts and now wasn't the time. But the Ogden beast would pay.

Soon.

Kirby turned away and headed back toward the side of the house where he'd left the window to the sunroom open.

"Catch ya later, puppy dog," the boy cackled as Kirby disappeared around the corner.

Very soon.

♥

"Hey! Hey, Kirby!"

The Frenchie dropped to the floor of the sunroom from the open window as OB peered out through the glass of his aquarium.

"Are you okay?" the turtle asked. "You look like you got hit by a bus!"

"Are you aware that the only bird that can fly backward is the hummingbird?" Kirby asked, the piece of knowledge dropping from his mouth as easily as a crumb from a treat.

"Oh yeah? I didn't know that. Are you all right, Kirby?"

Kirby nodded, the movement causing another fact to spill from his skull.

"The only food that does not spoil is honey."

OB climbed a plastic bridge, threw himself over the side of the tank, and tucked into his shell as he hit the floor. He rolled a foot or two, then popped out of his shell and ran—as fast as a turtle is able—over to his friend.

"Is that really true about honey?"

Kirby nodded. "And Iceland consumes more Coca-Cola per capita than any other nation."

OB just stared. "Hey, you think you might wanna lie down?"

Kirby's vision was growing blurred, and he attempted to focus on the face of the reptile. "Yes," he said. "That might not be such a bad idea."

OB left his side, running across the sunroom to fetch a circular dog bed. Using all the strength that he could muster, OB slid the bed across the hardwood floor to where Kirby swayed.

"Here ya go, Kirby," OB said. "Take a little snooze before . . ."

Kirby did not hear the last of his compatriot's words; he had already fallen asleep where he stood. He fell forward into his bed . . .

And into the arms of darkness.

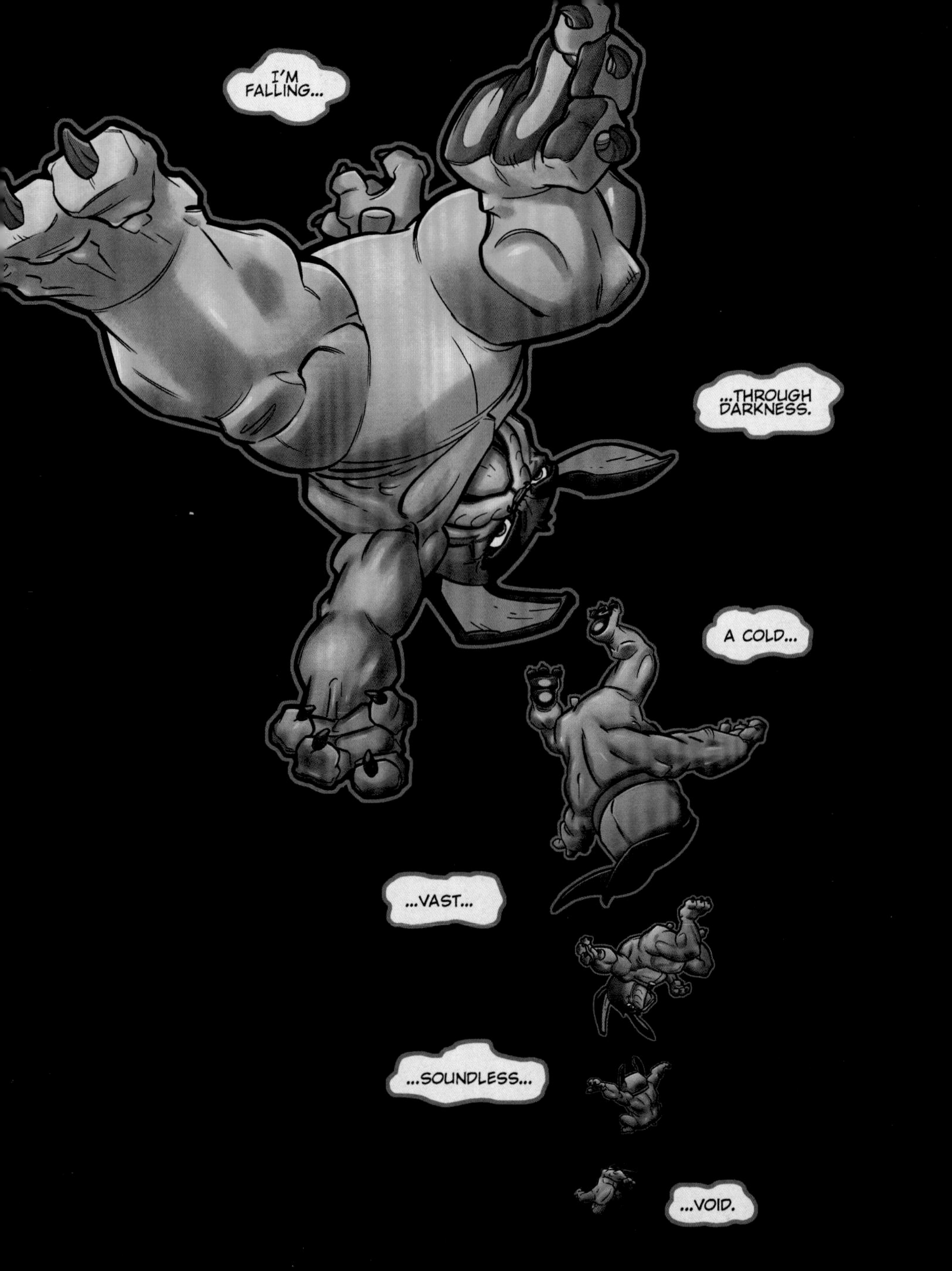
I'M FALLING...
...THROUGH DARKNESS.
A COLD...
...VAST...
...SOUNDLESS...
...VOID.

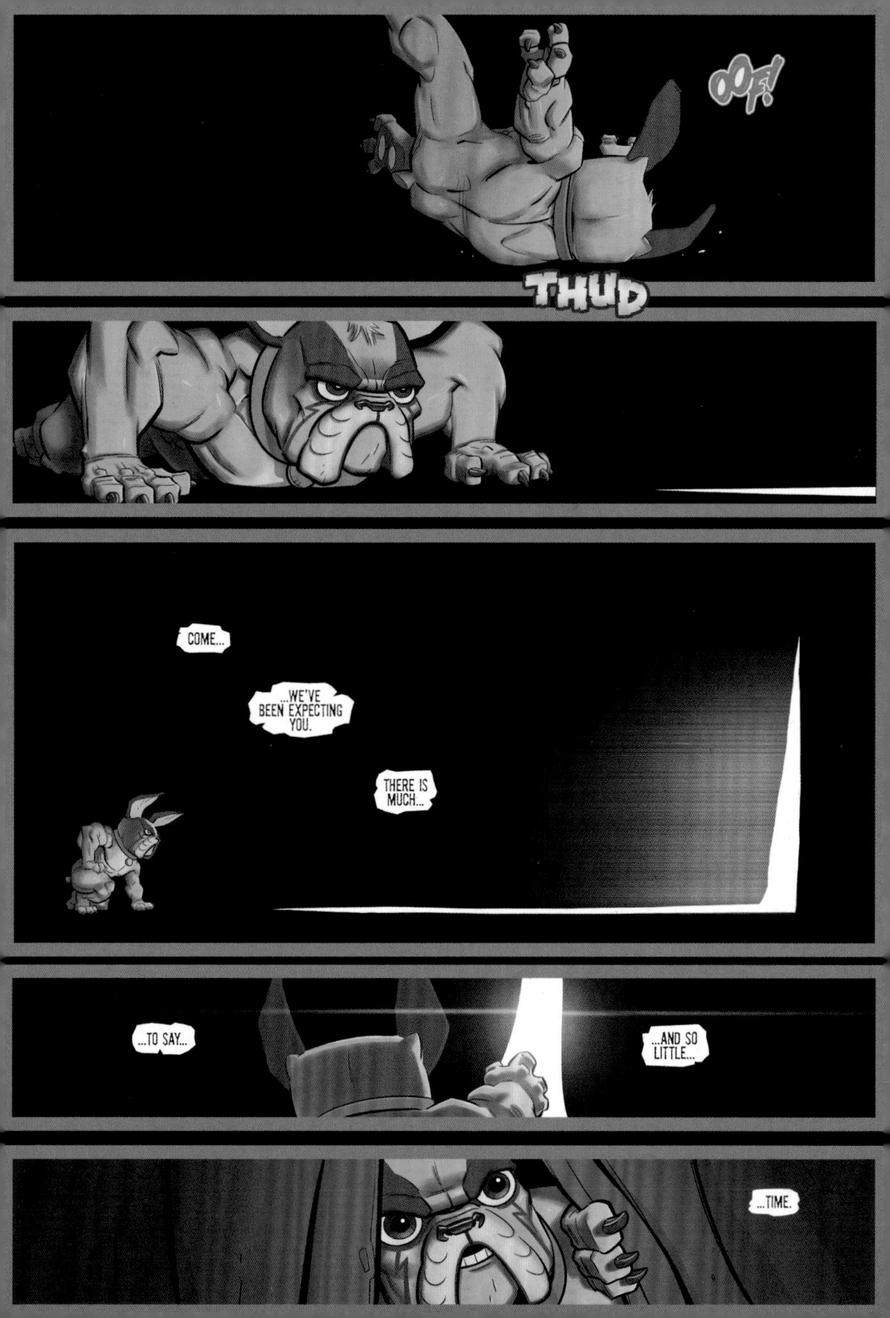
OOF!
THUD
COME...
...WE'VE BEEN EXPECTING YOU.
THERE IS MUCH...
...TO SAY...
...AND SO LITTLE...
...TIME.

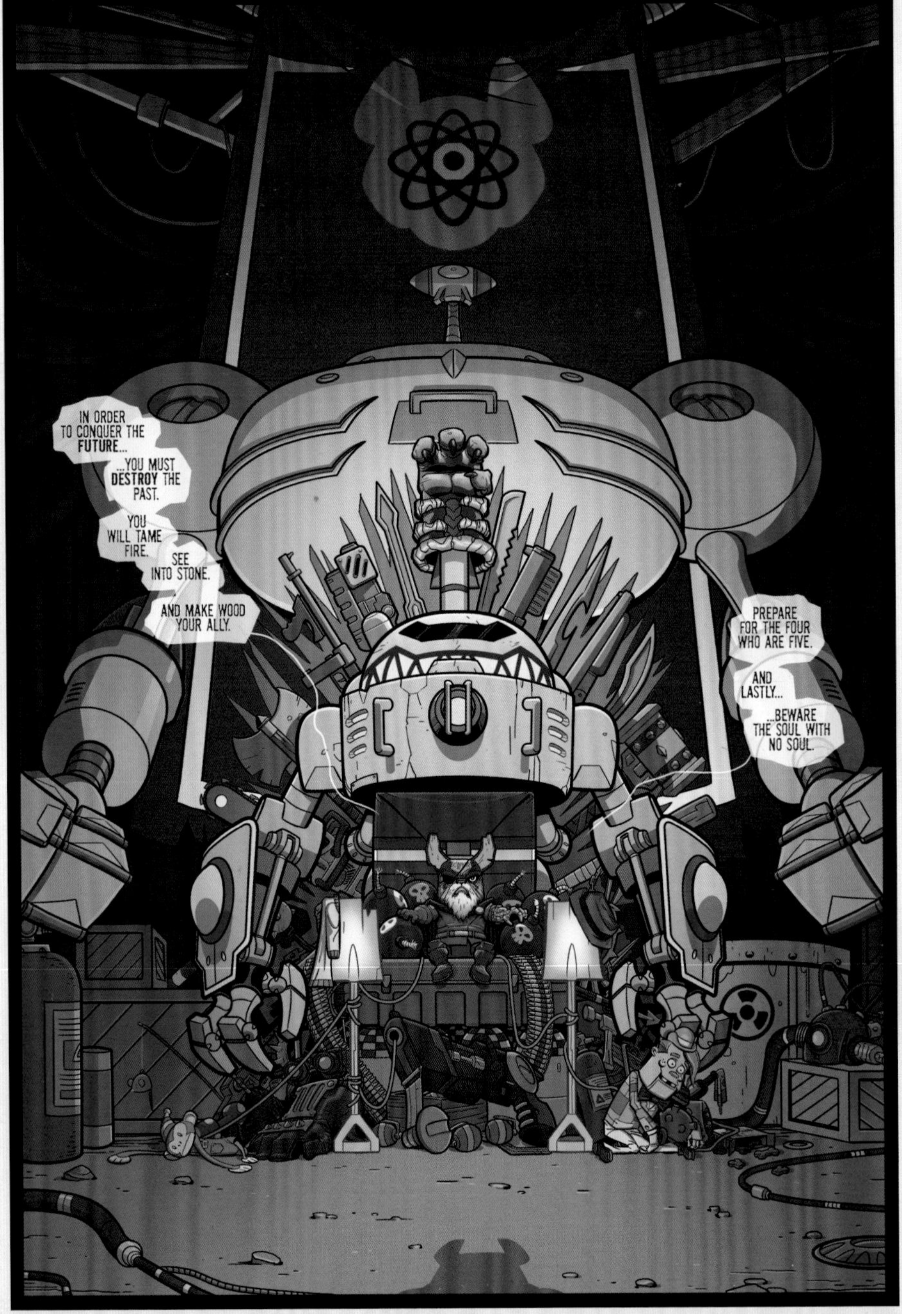
IN ORDER TO CONQUER THE FUTURE...
...YOU MUST DESTROY THE PAST.
YOU WILL TAME FIRE.
SEE INTO STONE.
AND MAKE WOOD YOUR ALLY.
PREPARE FOR THE FOUR WHO ARE FIVE.
AND LASTLY...
...BEWARE THE SOUL WITH NO SOUL.

It was if he'd been born anew.

Such an odd dream, he thought. *Or was it something more?*

A vision of some kind, perhaps?

With the memories of what he had seen already beginning to fade to the recesses of his mind, Kirby opened his eyes and realized that something had dramatically changed. No longer did his brain hum, sputter, and spark with all the things he had to accomplish, a confusing miasma of steps to fulfill his destiny.

Those things were still there, yes.

But now there was an order, a pattern that he could see as clearly as if the brightest spotlight were shining upon it.

A pathway to greatness. And all he had to do was walk it.

Kirby leapt up from his bed, filled with the sense of being reborn—revitalized. Glancing over to OB, he saw that the turtle was sound asleep in a warm patch of sun. He decided to leave the little terrapin to his respite, choosing instead to embrace this important moment in his evolution alone.

It's a new day, Kirby thought, puffing out his chest as he pushed the screen door open and stepped out into the backyard. The sun was shining; the air smelled especially sweet. *No, it's a new era,* he corrected himself. *An era that I will carve from the very earth with my own two paws!*

He stood in the center of the yard and turned his face toward the warmth of the sun.

An era in which the world will know my greatness! An era of—

The blast of water struck him hard, hurling him backward to the ground. Kirby had no idea what was happening, but it all became clear when he heard it.

The laughter of his enemy.

The indignity, though only seconds long, seemed to last for hours. It was made all the worse by the raucous amusement of the perpetrator.

And then something happened inside of Kirby. Something dark and sinister.

There are moments in time when history becomes irrevocably altered, when the wheels of fate turn, the tumblers drop, and the cosmic forces click into place. Sometimes these moments are cataclysmic, and other times they are invisible. This was one of these moments. This seemingly harmless prank by a cruel boy galvanized the Frenchie's purpose, hardened his spirit, and forged him like steel.

He stared at his tormentor, the Mega-Splasher 4500 Deluxe still in the creature's fat-fingered hands, and thought of the future—*his future*. Historians would dub this "The Stempleworth Incident," the moment that a dog and the world were changed forever.

Oh yes, Kirby thought as the water from the Mega-Splasher 4500 Deluxe trickled down his face.

It is time for the Stempleworth insect to pay.

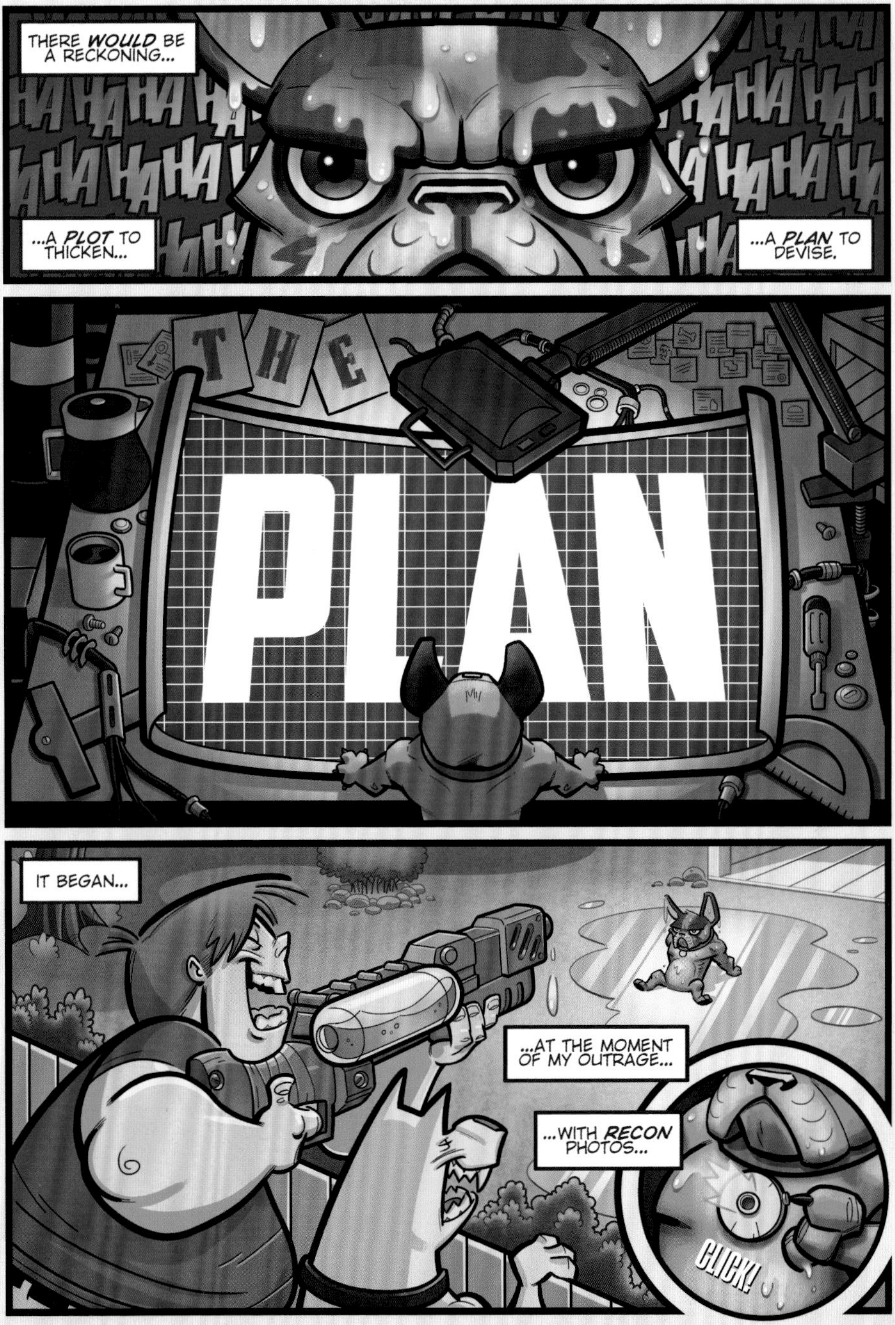
THERE WOULD BE A RECKONING...
HA HA HA HA HA HA
...A PLOT TO THICKEN...
...A PLAN TO DEVISE.
THE
PLAN
IT BEGAN...
...AT THE MOMENT OF MY OUTRAGE...
...WITH RECON PHOTOS...
CLICK!

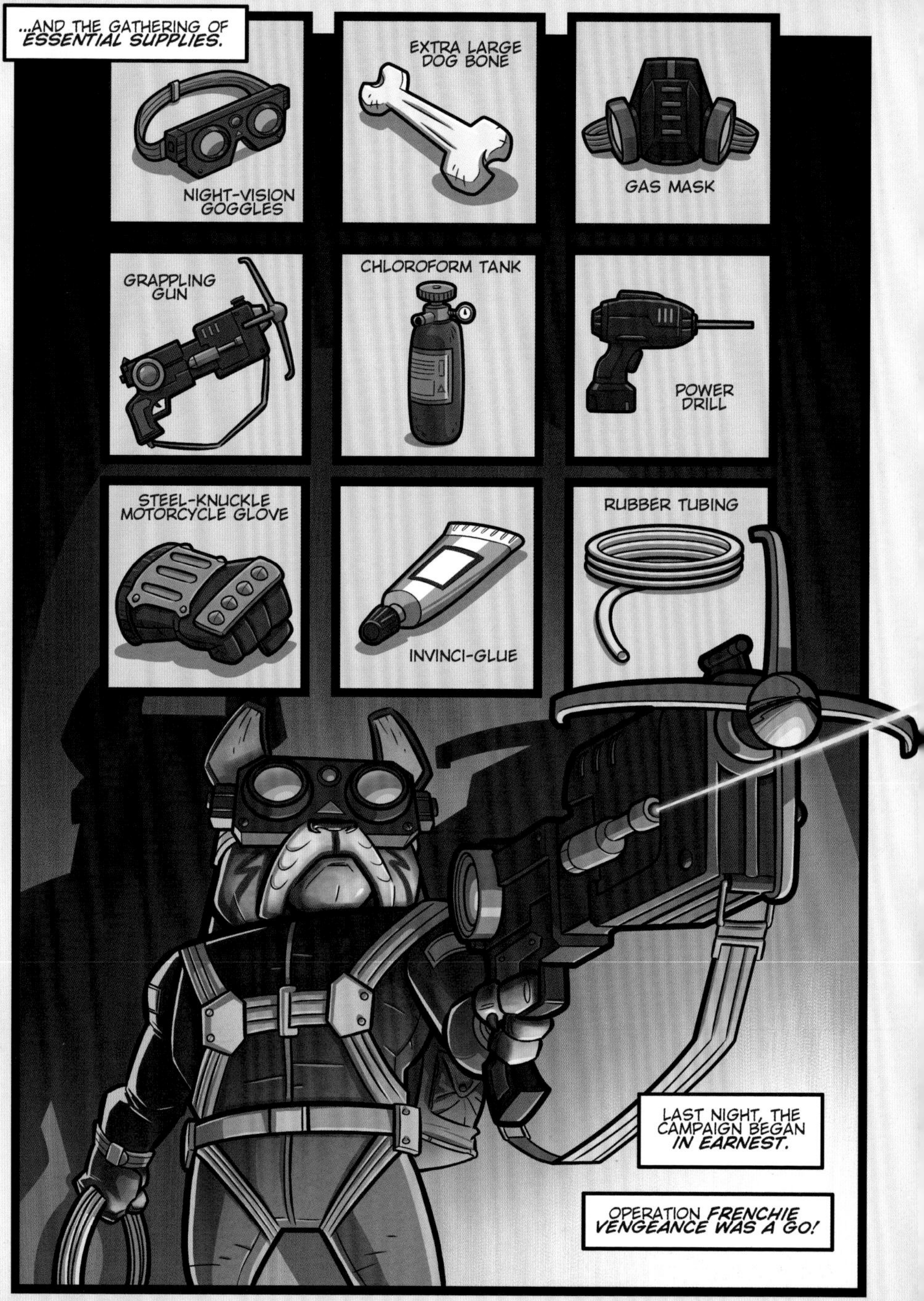
...AND THE GATHERING OF *ESSENTIAL SUPPLIES.*
NIGHT-VISION GOGGLES
EXTRA LARGE DOG BONE
GAS MASK
GRAPPLING GUN
CHLOROFORM TANK
POWER DRILL
STEEL-KNUCKLE MOTORCYCLE GLOVE
INVINCI-GLUE
RUBBER TUBING
LAST NIGHT, THE CAMPAIGN BEGAN *IN EARNEST.*
OPERATION *FRENCHIE VENGEANCE WAS A GO!*

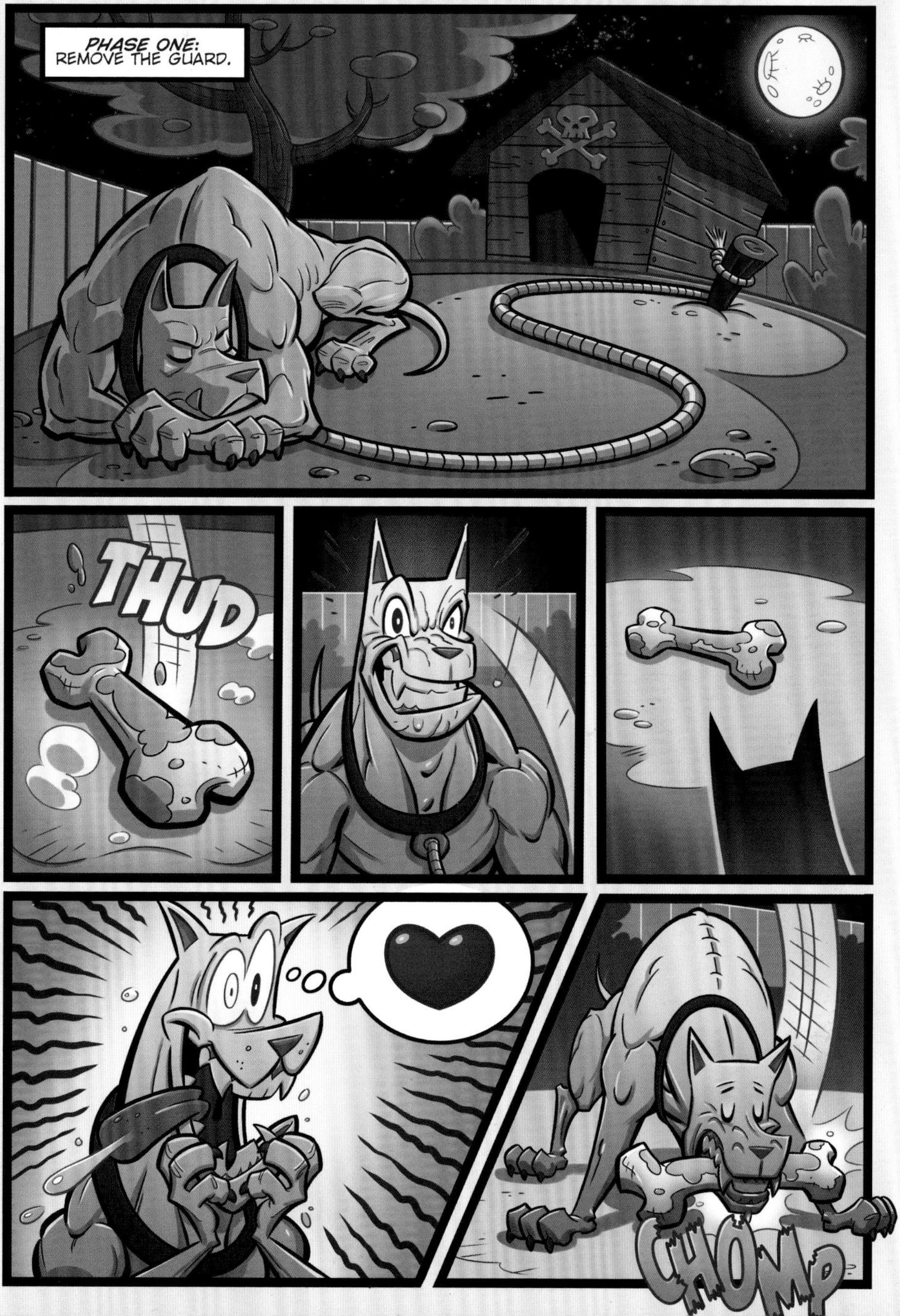
PHASE ONE:
REMOVE THE GUARD.
THUD
CHOMP

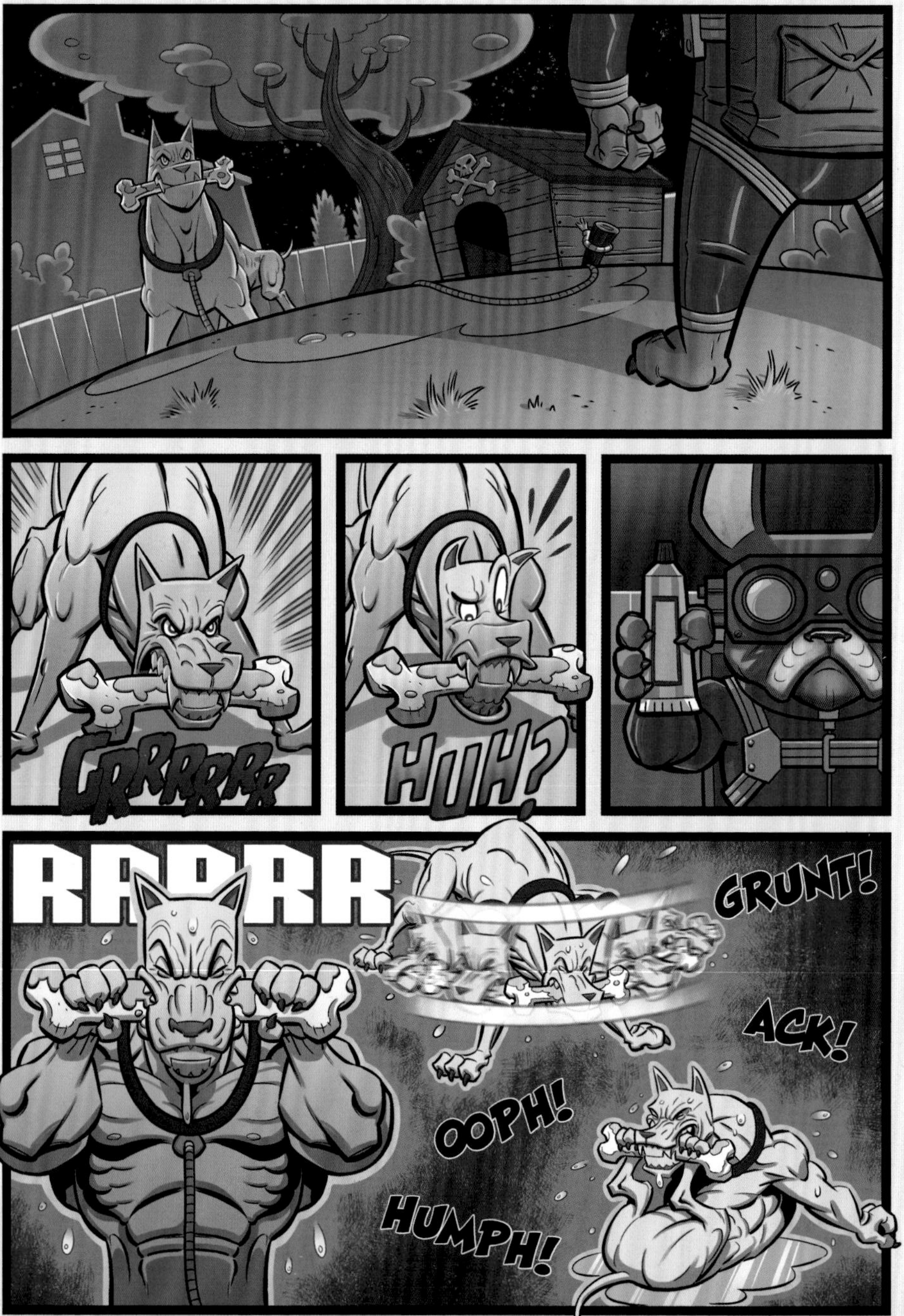
GRRRRRR
HUH?
RARRR
GRUNT!
ACK!
OOPH!
HUMPH!

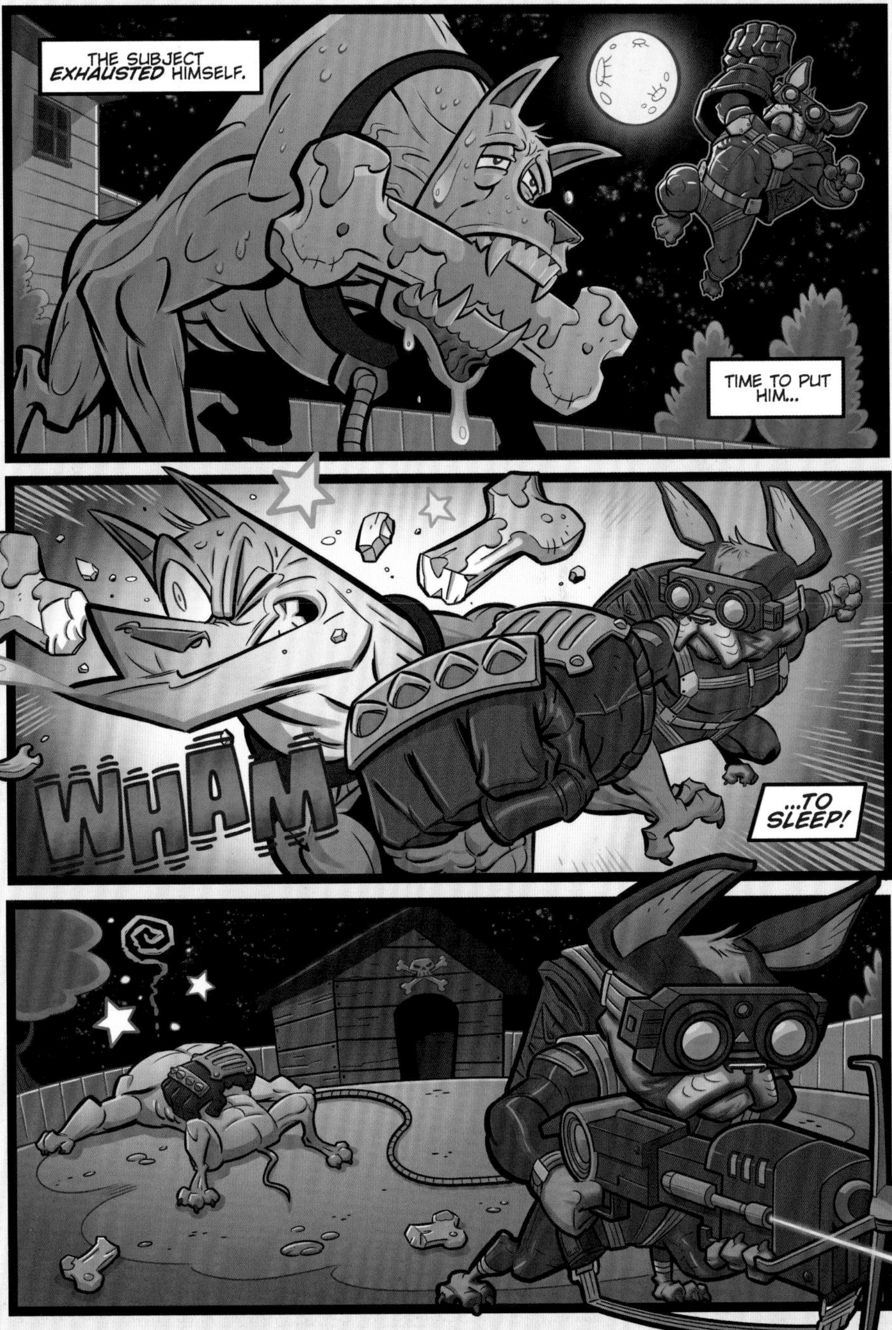
THE SUBJECT *EXHAUSTED* HIMSELF.
TIME TO PUT HIM...
WHAM
...TO SLEEP!

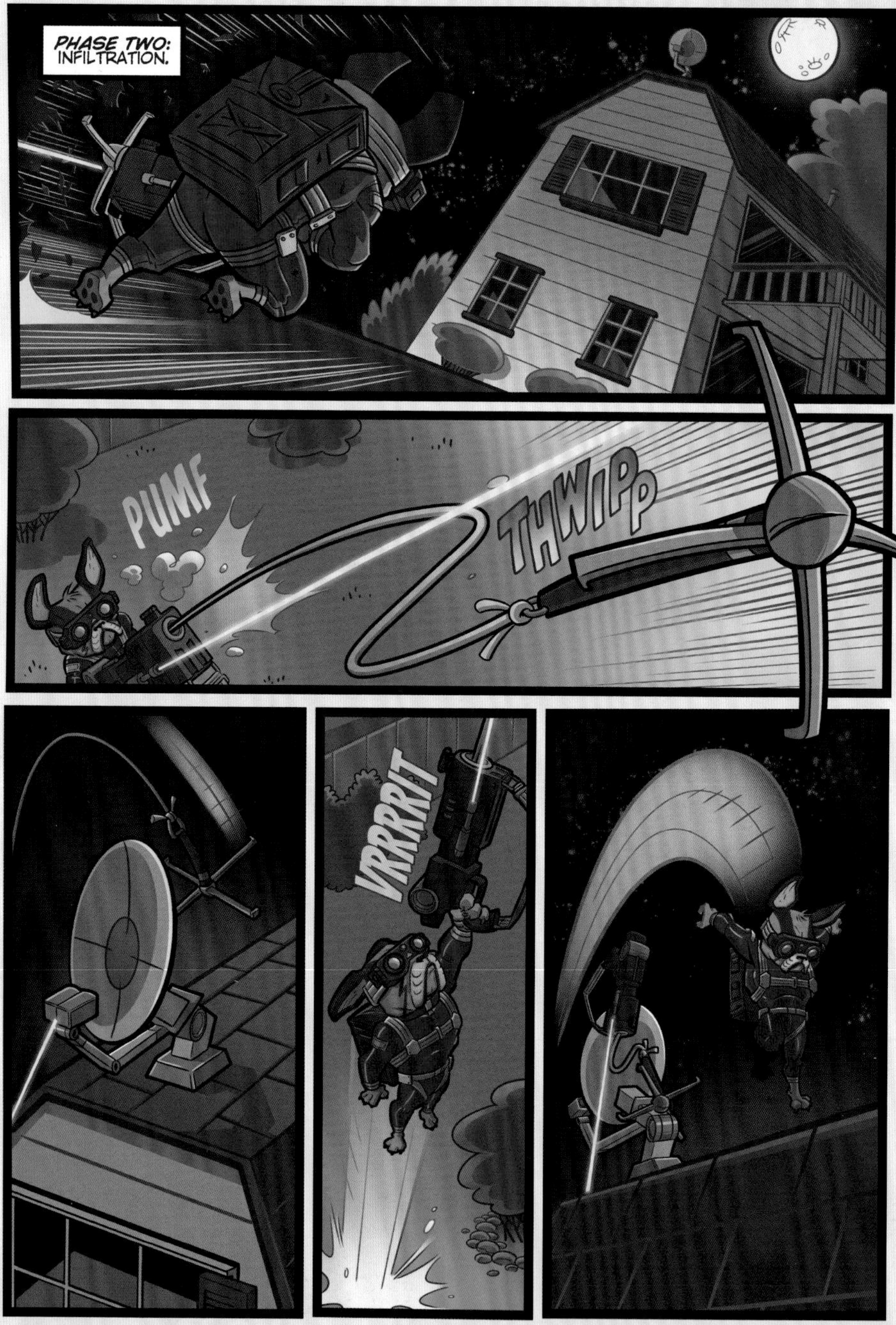
PHASE TWO:
INFILTRATION.
PUMF
THWIPP
VRRRRIT

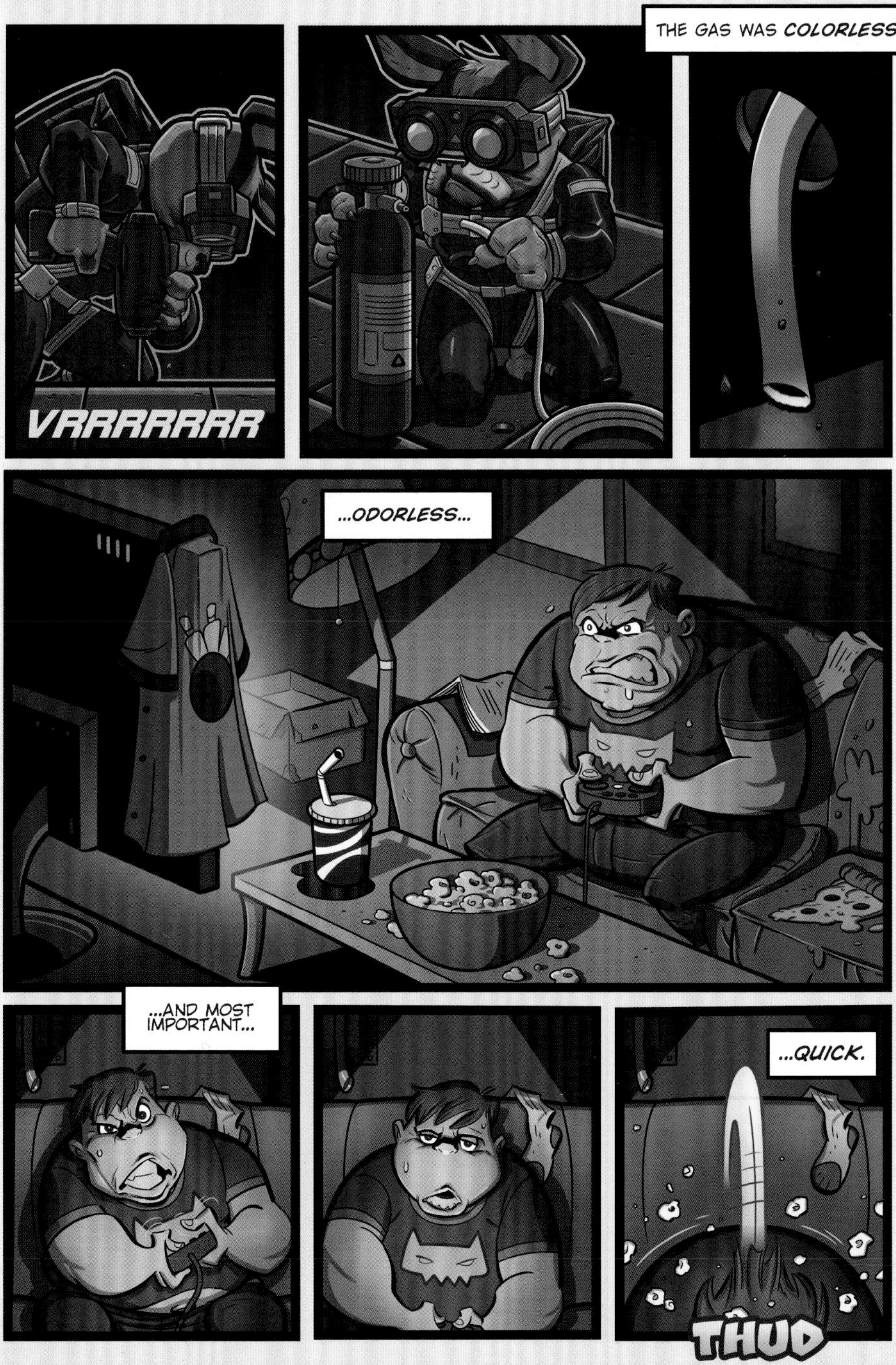

VRRRRRRR
THE GAS WAS COLORLESS...
...ODORLESS...
...AND MOST IMPORTANT...
...QUICK.
THUD

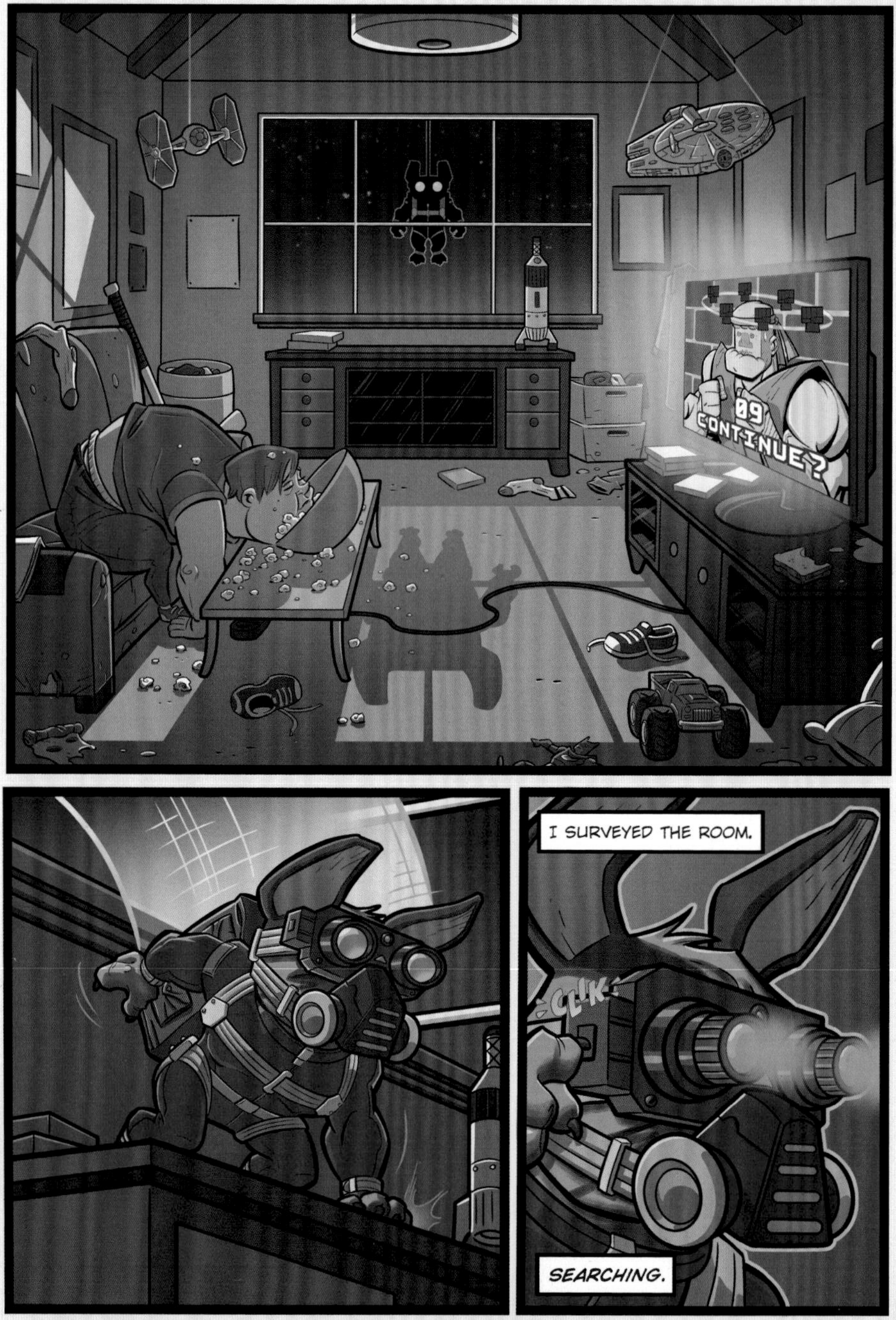
09
CONTINUE ?
I SURVEYED THE ROOM.
CLIK!
SEARCHING.

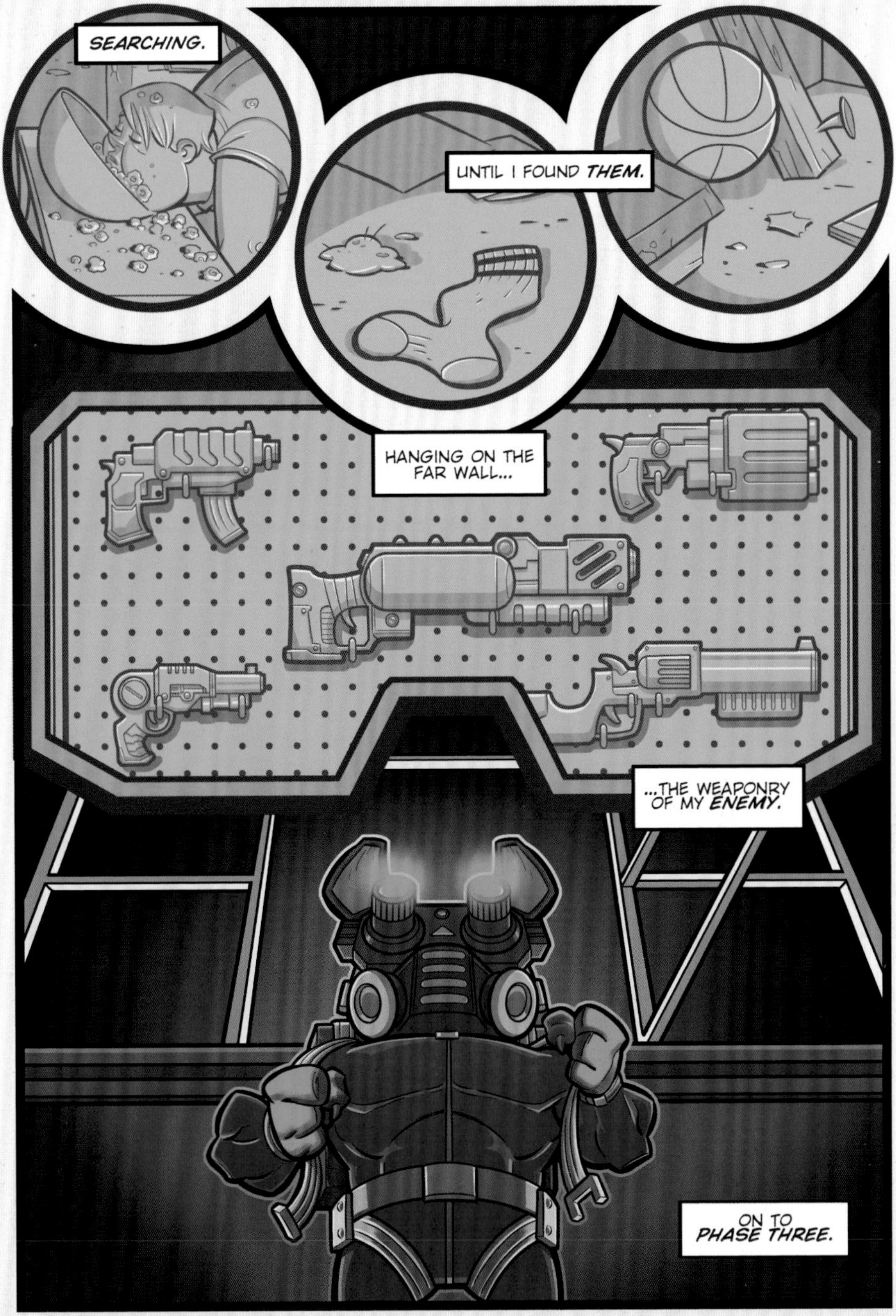
SEARCHING.
UNTIL I FOUND THEM.
HANGING ON THE FAR WALL...
...THE WEAPONRY OF MY ENEMY.
ON TO PHASE THREE.

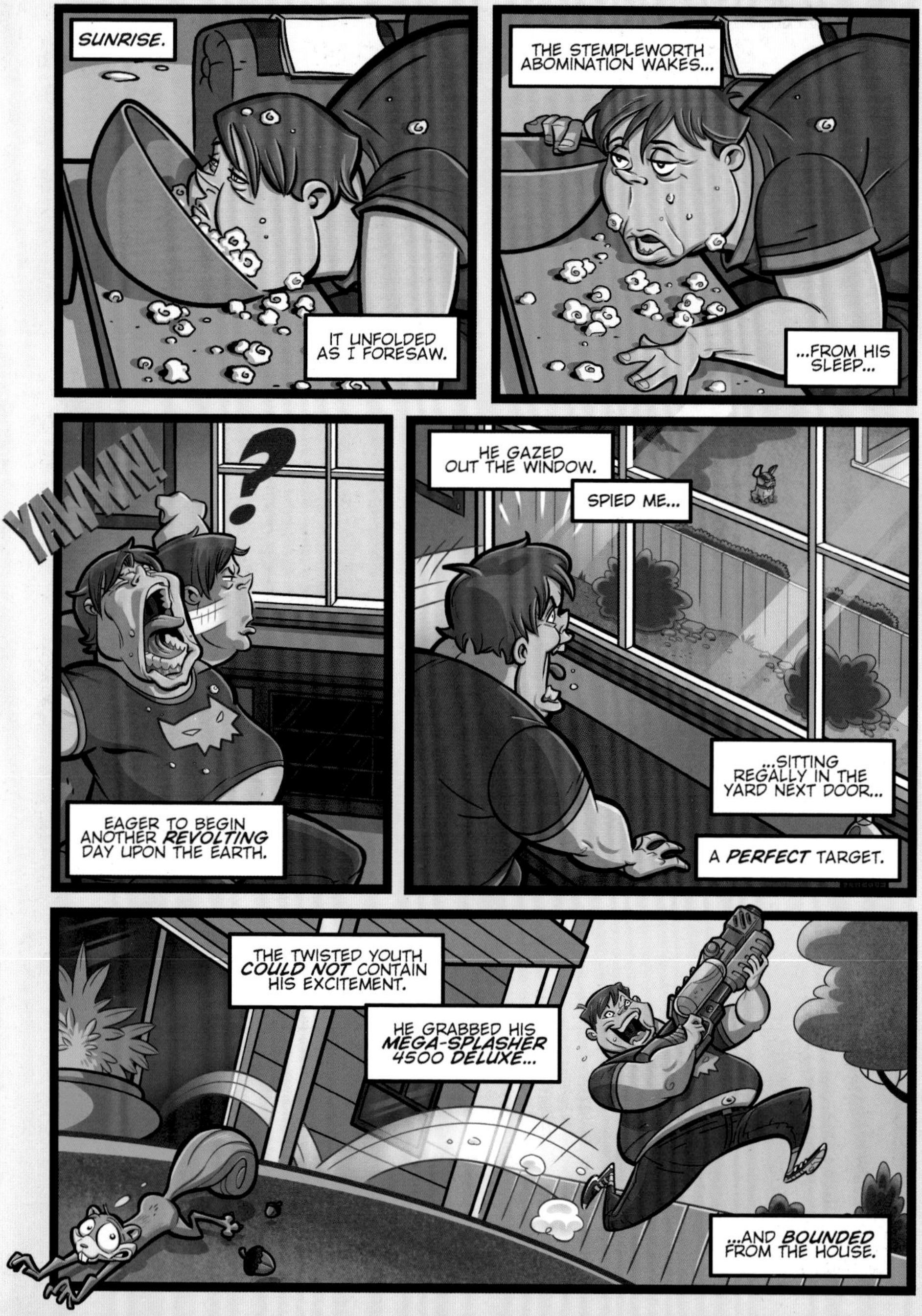
SUNRISE.
IT UNFOLDED AS I FORESAW.
THE STEMPLEWORTH ABOMINATION WAKES...
...FROM HIS SLEEP...
YAWWN!
EAGER TO BEGIN ANOTHER REVOLTING DAY UPON THE EARTH.
HE GAZED OUT THE WINDOW.
SPIED ME...
...SITTING REGALLY IN THE YARD NEXT DOOR...
A PERFECT TARGET.
THE TWISTED YOUTH COULD NOT CONTAIN HIS EXCITEMENT.
HE GRABBED HIS MEGA-SPLASHER 4500 DELUXE...
...AND BOUNDED FROM THE HOUSE.

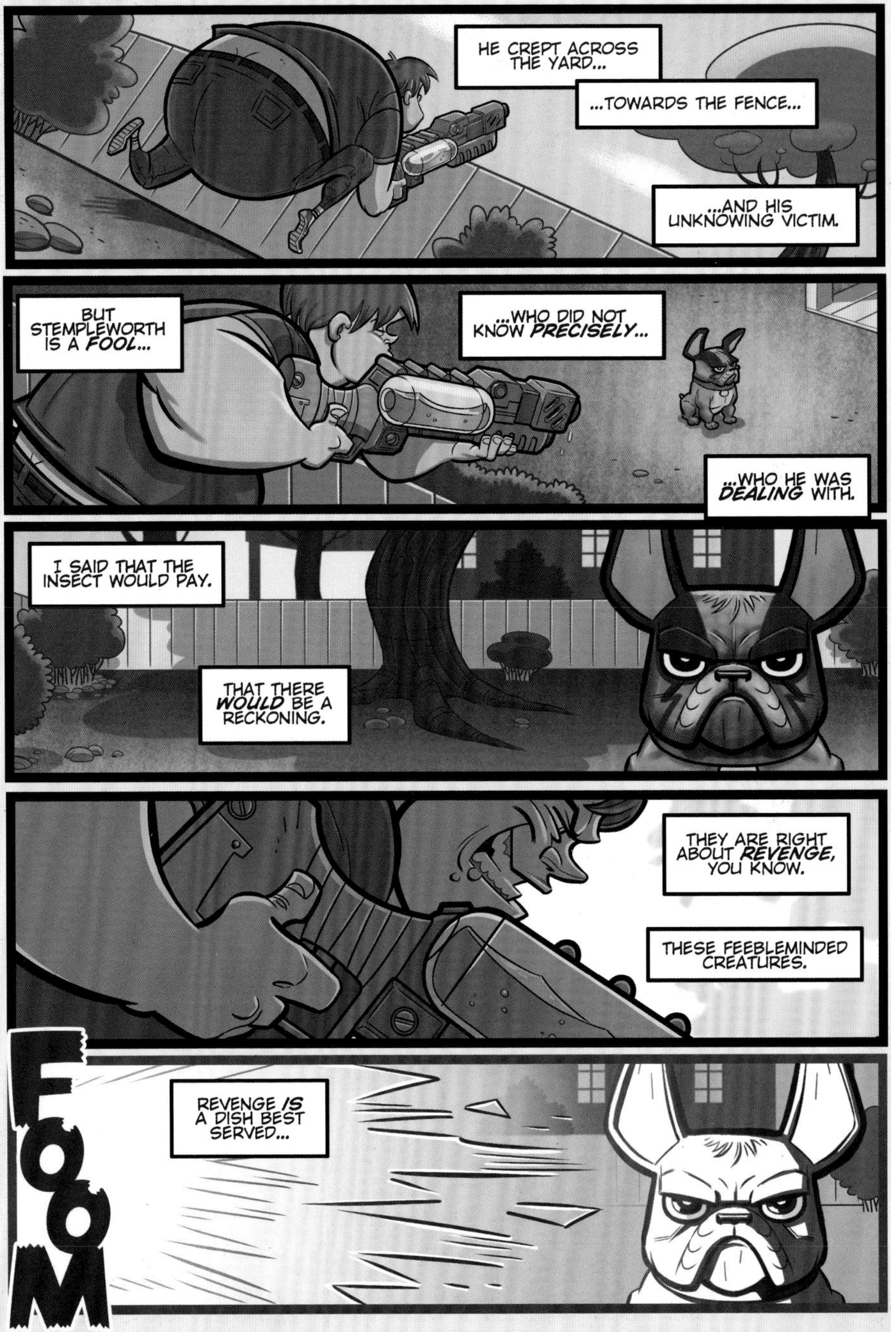
HE CREPT ACROSS THE YARD...
...TOWARDS THE FENCE...
...AND HIS UNKNOWING VICTIM.
BUT STEMPLEWORTH IS A *FOOL*...
...WHO DID NOT KNOW *PRECISELY*...
...WHO HE WAS *DEALING* WITH.
I SAID THAT THE INSECT WOULD PAY.
THAT THERE *WOULD* BE A RECKONING.
THEY ARE RIGHT ABOUT *REVENGE*, YOU KNOW.
THESE FEEBLEMINDED CREATURES.
FOOM
REVENGE *IS* A DISH BEST SERVED...

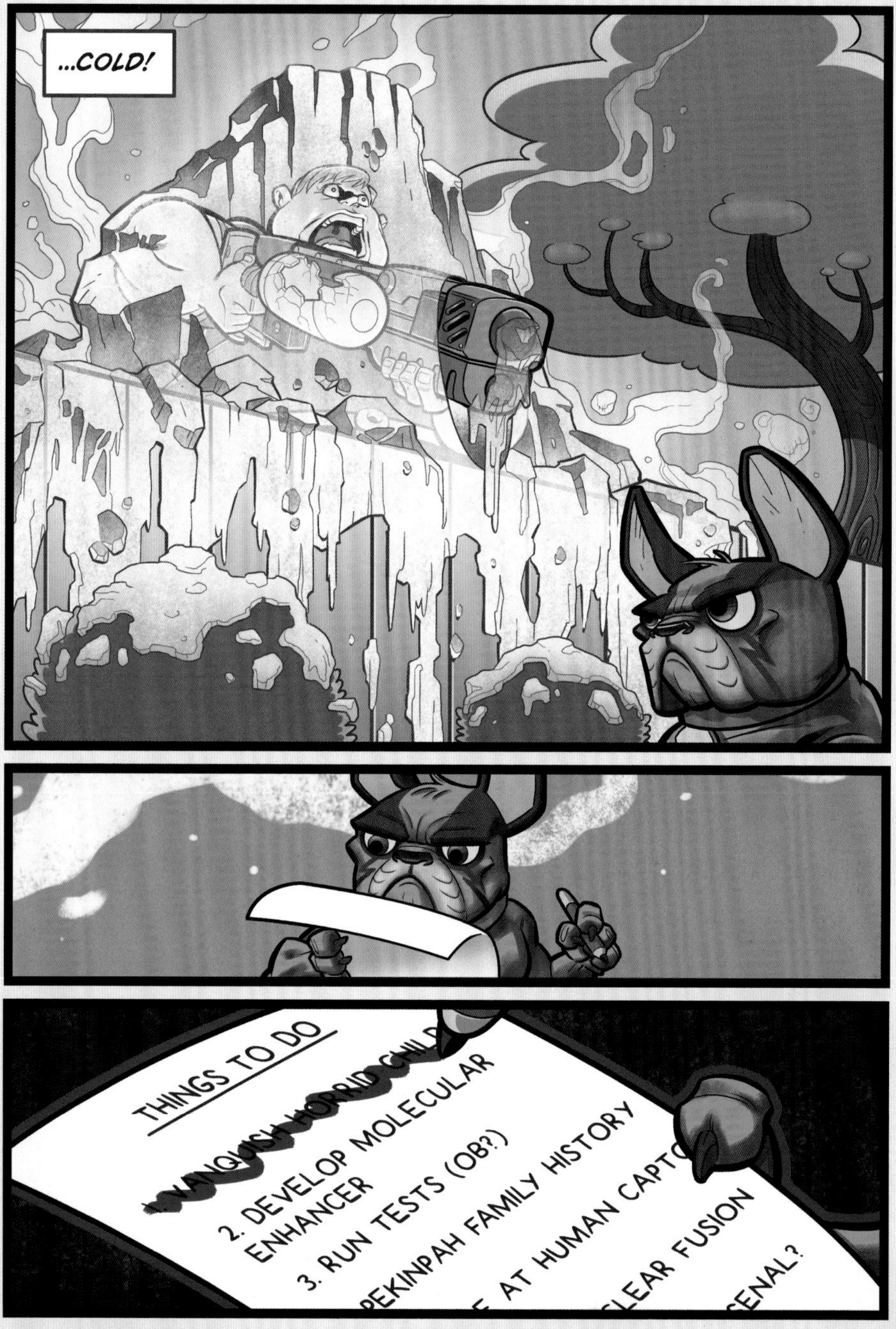
...COLD!
THINGS TO DO
VANQUISH HORRID
2. DEVELOP MOLECULAR ENHANCER
3. RUN TESTS (OB?)
PEKINPAH FAMILY HISTORY
AT HUMAN
CLEAR FUSION
SENAL?

SIX

Kirby and OB trotted across the backyard unhindered, the fear of being tormented by their next-door neighbor no longer a concern.

Ogden Stempleworth was no more.

He hadn't been permanently dispatched—just removed, to a place where he could no longer make a nuisance of himself. From what Kirby understood, overhearing Tom and LeeAnne talking about the bizarre squirt gun malfunction in hushed whispers, the loathsome child had been sent to some place called Happydale Sanitarium where his severe case of frostbite could be properly treated.

Good, Kirby thought as he and OB continued on their way to the garage.

"Did you figure out what all that mechanical stuff was for, Kirb?" OB asked, hustling to keep up with the Frenchie.

"Every visit reveals something new and wondrous," Kirby said, entering the garage and triggering the secret passage.

"Wow, how lucky are we?" OB said excitedly. "Out of all the places Tom and LeeAnne could have brought us to live, we ended up at the place with a secret laboratory. It's almost like . . ."

"*Fate* was somehow involved," Kirby finished the sentence. The two descended the stairs to the corridor below.

"Yeah," OB said, hopping down from each step. "Fate."

"It would seem that way, I presume, to those of a more superstitious nature," Kirby said, giving the door a push and striding inside the laboratory with purpose. "But I believe only in the cold, calculating reality of facts."

Erasmus slowly appeared in all his spectral glory.

"Kirby!" OB squeaked.

The Frenchie stopped midway across the room and turned.

"Yes?"

The turtle pointed wildly. "I think . . . I think I see a . . . a . . ."

"A ghost," Kirby finished, turning back to head across the room. "You are correct. Erasmus, OB; OB, Erasmus," he tossed over his shoulder by way of introduction.

"Hey," the ghost said, staring down at the turtle from where he floated.

"*Gulp*," the turtle said, staring up in terror.

"What's he here for?" Erasmus asked. "Doesn't look like the sharpest crayon in the box, if you know what I mean."

Kirby took a white lab coat from a box and studied it. It was far too large to fit his smaller size.

"I know exactly what you mean, but for my purpose he will serve. Intelligence is not a necessary factor."

Kirby dragged the lab coat over to a bank of machines, standing before one in particular. It was square with a circular window in the front, resembling a front-loading washing machine. He opened the hatch and tossed the lab coat inside.

"You know that's a miniaturization apparatus, correct?" Erasmus asked.

"I do," Kirby said, slamming the door closed and flipping some switches.

"Miniaturization apparatus?" OB questioned.

"A shrinking machine, if the big words are eluding you," Erasmus said condescendingly.

The machine hummed and shook, and then a bell rang. Kirby opened the door and removed the lab coat, which had now shrunk to *his* size. He slipped it on.

"Nice fit," Erasmus said.

"Spiffy," OB added.

"Thank you," Kirby said, walking toward them. "As I was saying, the reason OB was brought here has little to do with his level of intelligence."

"Okay," Erasmus said. "Spill the beans. Why is he here?"

"Loyalty," Kirby said.

"Loyalty?" Erasmus asked.

"Loyalty?" OB repeated.

"Precisely," Kirby answered. "If my plans for this world are to succeed, I must have loyal minions who dare not question my commands, whatever they may be."

"And you think he's one of those?" Erasmus asked, hooking a thumb in the turtle's direction.

"OB," Kirby said. "I'm feeling a tad peckish. Return to the house and make me a sandwich."

"Oh, okay!" the turtle said, turning away from them and starting toward the door. He stopped midway and turned.

"Peanut butter and jelly good?"

"That will be fine."

The turtle started to leave again.

Kirby looked to the ghost and tilted his head to one side.

"Guess you made your point," the ghost said, adjusting his ghostly bath towel.

"Of course I did," Kirby said. "Cancel that sandwich order, OB," he said. The turtle stopped at the door.

"You sure, Kirb? I don't mind."

"That's quite all right, OB."

"Suit yourself," the little turtle said, coming back into the lab.

Erasmus crossed his scrawny ghost arms. "Still don't know how useful a turtle can be."

Kirby pushed a step stool over to a filing cabinet and pulled open one of the drawers. He looked through the paperwork stored there.

"Of course you wouldn't," he said, perusing a document before putting it back and grabbing another. "OB's single-minded loyalty will be an asset to my approaching ascension, but not in his current state."

Erasmus drifted down to hover above the turtle, the two of them looking eye to eye.

"In this state, he'd be an awesome paperweight . . . or maybe a doorstop."

"Thank you?" OB said, obviously still frightened of the ghost.

"Which is why his current state must be changed to something more useful."

"And how exactly do you plan on doing that?" Erasmus asked, extending a long, bony finger to poke at the turtle's head.

"Through experimentation, of course," Kirby announced, jumping down from the step stool and rolling up the sleeves of his lab coat. "We will see if he can develop any special talents."

Both Erasmus and OB looked to Kirby.

"Special talents?" the pair questioned in unison.

"Superpowers," Kirby said with a nod of his blocky Frenchie head.

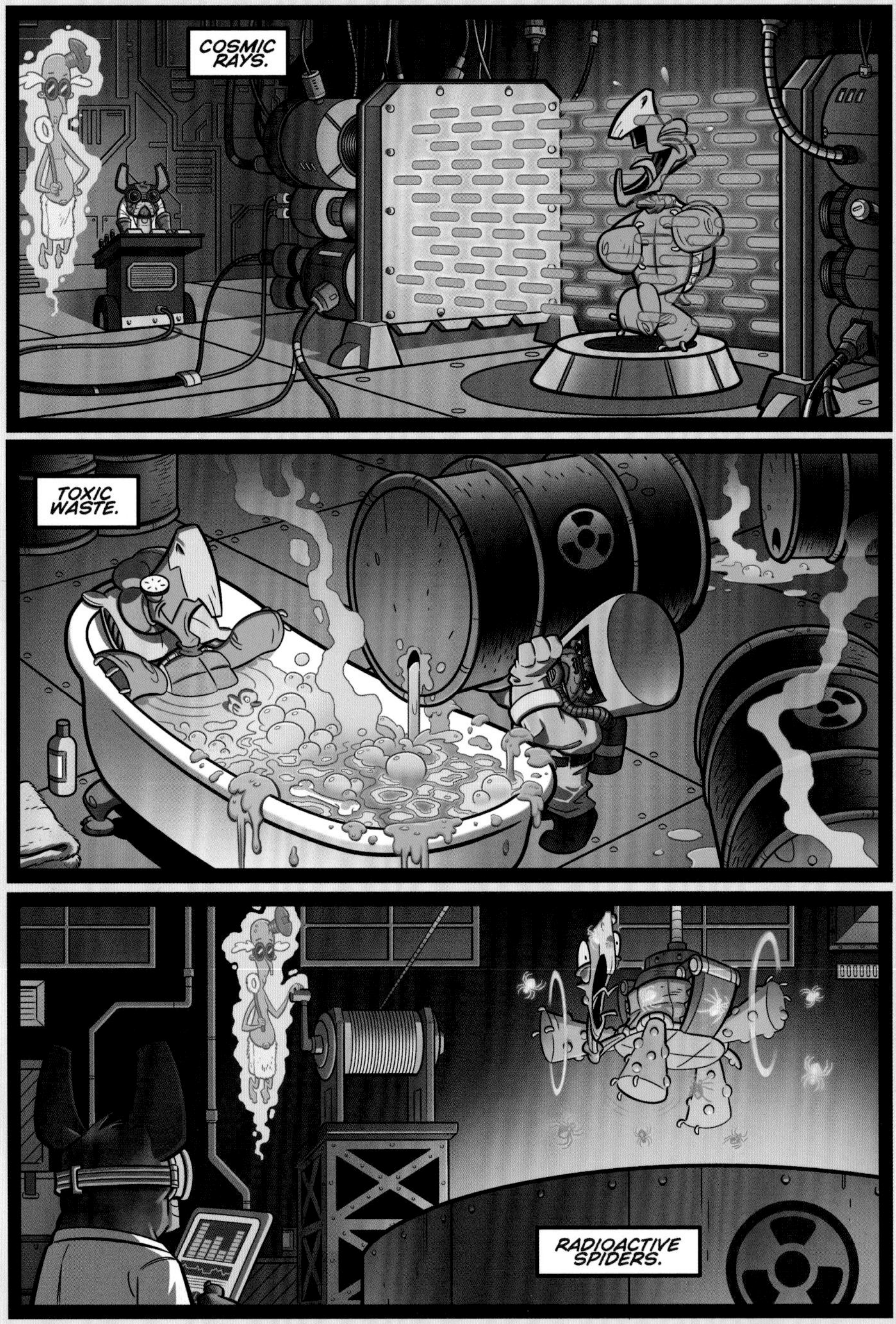

COSMIC RAYS.
TOXIC WASTE.
RADIOACTIVE SPIDERS.

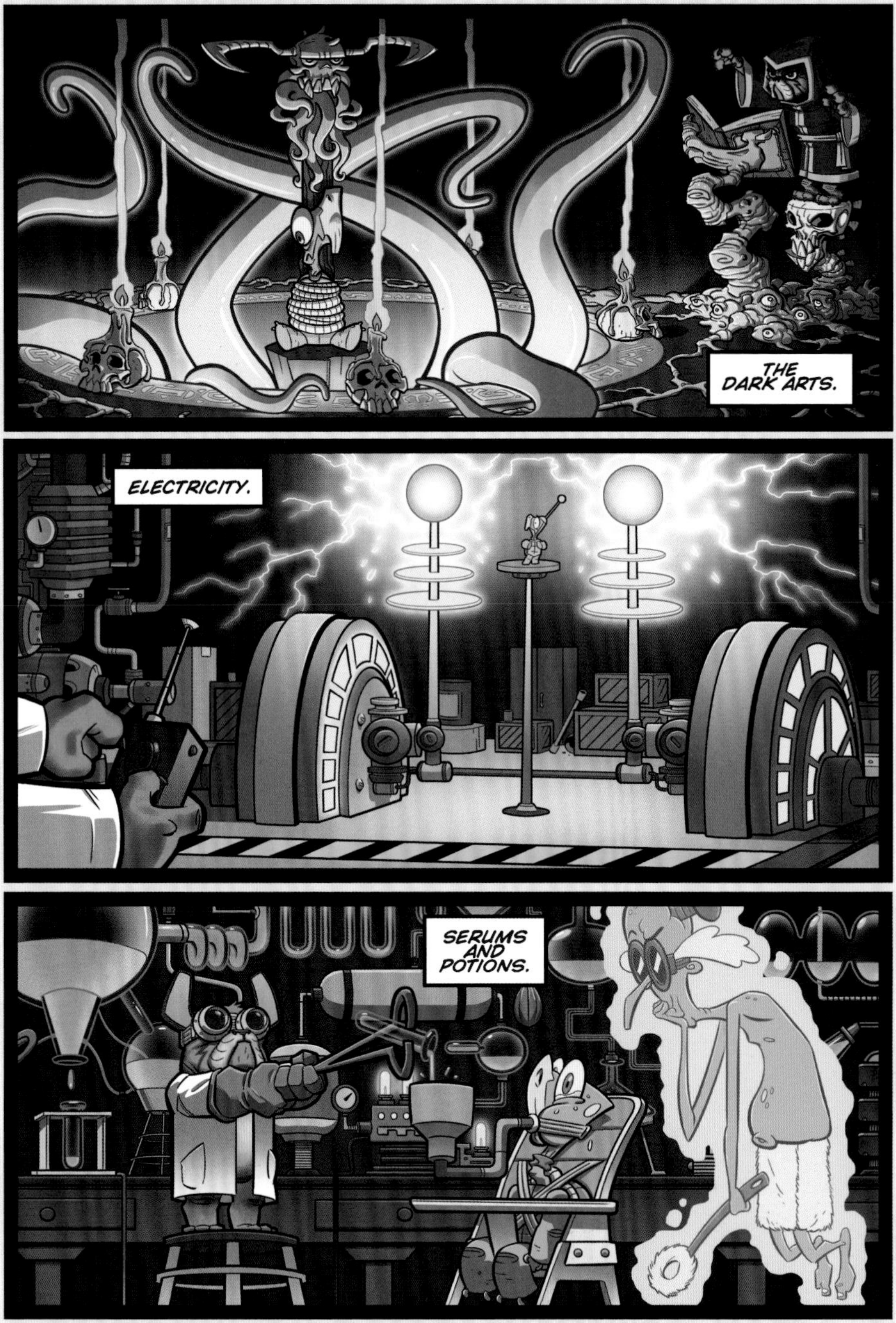
THE DARK ARTS.
ELECTRICITY.
SERUMS AND POTIONS.

Kirby held a clipboard in one hand, a pen poised to write in the other. Erasmus hovered by his side.

"How do you feel?" Kirby asked the little turtle, who sat on a stool across from him.

"Fine . . . I think," OB said. "How should I be feeling?"

"You tell us," Erasmus said. "Any sensation of genetic mutation or transdimensional metamorphosis?"

"Unnh," OB answered.

"Do you feel different in any way?" Kirby asked.

"I'm a little tired," the turtle began. "Oh, wait . . ." He suddenly went rigid.

"Yes?" Kirby asked with growing interest. "Are you starting to experience something?"

"I . . . I think I am!" OB squeaked.

"Go on!" Kirby urged.

"Something . . . something is happening inside me!" The turtle rubbed at his shelled belly.

"Yes!"

OB's eyes suddenly grew wide, his entire form starting to shake. Kirby stepped back and away.

"What do you think is happening?" Erasmus asked.

"Patience, specter," Kirby commanded, eyes fixed upon the turtle. "What are you feeling, OB?" he asked the terrapin. "Tell me every detail."

"I . . . it feels funny in my tummy," the turtle said. He began to pant, sweat dripping from his shelled body.

"Go on," Kirby encouraged, scribbling madly on his clipboard.

"Somethin' spinnin' round and round and round," OB said, his voice getting higher in pitch. "Gettin' bigger and bigger . . ."

"Yes, that's it, OB," Kirby urged. "Transform into something greater . . . something better than what you are!"

"This is getting exciting," Erasmus said. Kirby noticed that he was eating from a ghostly box of popcorn as he watched the turtle twitch and sweat. The Frenchie was about to ask where the popcorn had come from when . . .

"It's happening!" OB squeaked, his head extending farther from his shell.

"Don't fight it, OB!" Kirby urged. "Just let it happen!"

"Oh . . . okay," OB said. "I'm scared, Kirb!"

"No reason to be scared," Kirby consoled.

"Well actually, I can think of about ten reasons for him to be scared," Erasmus said, throwing kernels of spectral popcorn into his maw.

"Shhh," Kirby snapped at the ghost before turning his attention back to OB. "Go on, OB," Kirby coached. "Be like a caterpillar. Emerge from your protective chrysalis, transformed into the beautiful . . ."

OB's neck stretched long and taut, his mouth opened ridiculously wide as Kirby leaned forward, anxious for the turtle's new super ability to manifest in all its amazing glory.

"BUUUUUUUUUUUURRRRRRRRRR . . ." came the sound from that yawning cavern of a mouth. It seemed to begin from the tips of the turtle's toes.

"What kind of superpower is that?" Erasmus asked, still munching on his snack.

"I . . ." Kirby began.

" . . . RRRRRRRRRRRRRRRRRRRPPPPPPP!!!" The sound ripped from the turtle, filling the lab with its thunderous rumble, before coming to an abrupt end.

OB looked at them, eyes wide with complete surprise.

Erasmus began to slowly clap. "Impressive," the ghost said. "Reminds me of a guy I knew who could fart the alphabet."

"Sorry," the turtle said sheepishly. "Must've been that pink potion you gave me earlier."

Kirby rolled his eyes, setting his clipboard down.

"Impressive, but not a superpower like we were hoping for," Erasmus said.

"Do you think you have developed any unusual or potentially destructive super ability?" Kirby asked, not bothering to hide the annoyance in his tone.

"You mean something I couldn't do before?" OB asked.

"Yes," Kirby said, picking up the clipboard again.

OB thought for a moment. "No, afraid not."

"So what now?" Erasmus asked.

Kirby said nothing, allowing his augmented brain to assess the situation and process the information. He began to wander about the laboratory in frustration.

"Is there anything else we haven't tried?" he finally asked. "Any rare element, chemical compound, or alien artifact lying about that could infuse OB with super abilities?"

Erasmus drifted behind him like a balloon at the Macy's Thanksgiving Day Parade.

"I believe we've covered all the bases," the ghost said, stroking his ghostly chin. "Maybe we should combine some of the treatments and . . ."

Kirby stopped in front of a stack of mechanical parts and boxes. There was something behind the wall of discarded machinery.

"What's that?" Kirby asked the ghost.

OB had come to stand with them. "What do you see, Kirb?"

"You don't want to see that," Erasmus said. "Why don't we head over this way? I believe I still have some gamma-irradiated bubble gum that I was going to attempt to sell to the NFL . . ."

"I want to see it," Kirby stated, beginning to move the boxes on his own. OB helped as best he could. "What is this?" the Frenchie asked as a large, mechanical man was revealed.

"My biggest achievement, and also my greatest disappointment," the ghost said sadly. "May I present to you, the Book-bot 9000."

The robot was huge—at least fifteen feet tall—and somewhat menacing even as it leaned harmlessly against the wall, covered in dust and spider webs.

"Wow, that's pretty scary looking!" OB announced.

"Scary?" Erasmus bellowed. "What do you know of scary? The Book-bot 9000 was to be the greatest aid to libraries the world had ever known!"

"I still think it looks scary," OB muttered.

"An aid to libraries?" Kirby asked. "What was its function?"

"Do you realize the astronomical late fees libraries charge for overdue books in this great nation of ours?"

"I never really gave it much thought," Kirby said dryly.

"Pfft!" Erasmus said. "Thousands upon thousands of dollars I'd think . . . never got around to getting the numbers myself," he mumbled. "But I can guarantee you the amount is likely huge!" The ghost waved a finger in the air to make his point.

"And this metallic monstrosity was to make things better?" Kirby asked.

"Better?" Erasmus asked incredulously. "It would have made *the world* better!"

The ghost drifted down beside the metal man and slid a cart forward. On top of the cart was an old-fashioned video monitor, and Erasmus fiddled with the controls.

"This is a little something I made to inform the masses," he said, floating back as the monitor came to life.

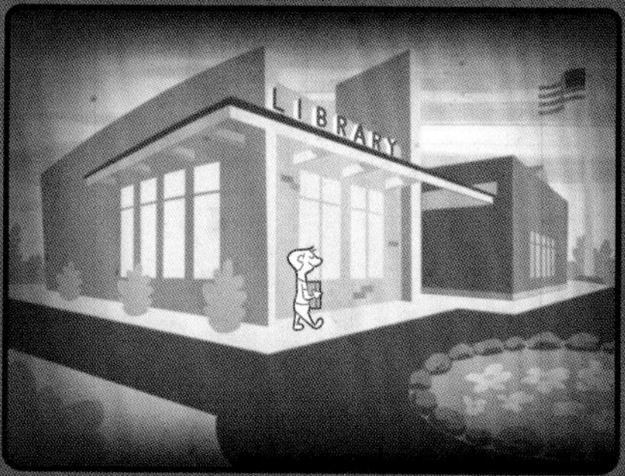
LIBRARY

WHO DOESN'T ENJOY A TRIP TO THEIR LOCAL LIBRARY?

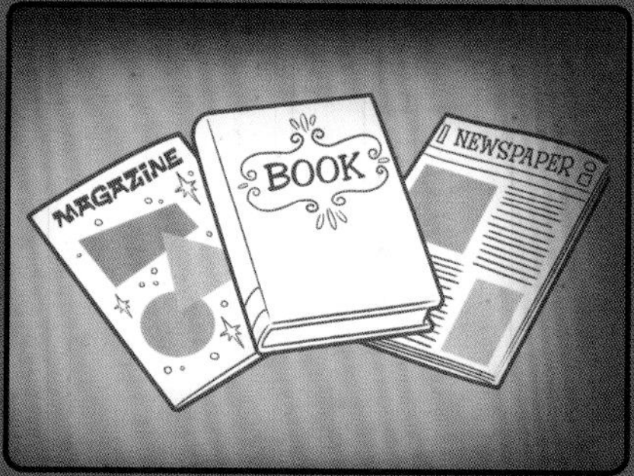
MAGAZINE
BOOK
NEWSPAPER

ALL THE BOOKS, MAGAZINES, AND PERIODICALS YOU NEED! FREE AND READY FOR YOU TO ***BORROW!***

BUT REMEMBER, WHAT YOU BORROW YOU HAVE TO ***RETURN!***

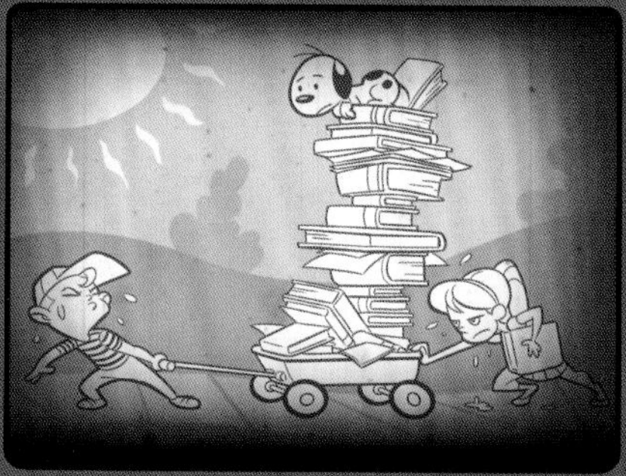

LOOK AT POOR JIMMY AND SALLY, HAVING TO BRING BACK ALL THOSE BOOKS!

NO ***PLAYTIME*** FOR THEM TODAY!

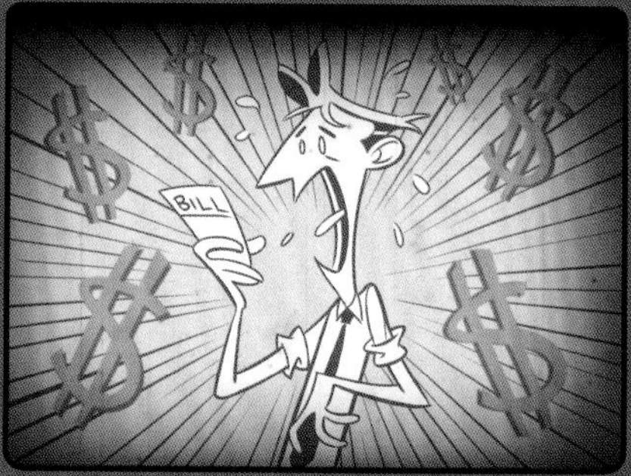
BILL

AND LET'S NOT FORGET THOSE ***LATE FEES!***

OH, MY!
THEY SURE DO PILE UP!

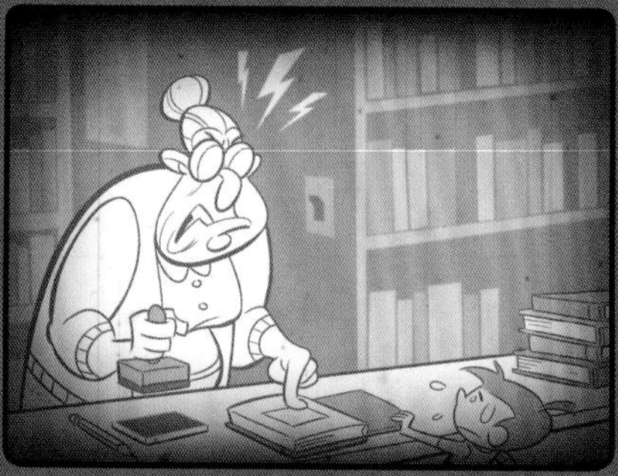

THAT ***MEAN OLD LIBRARIAN*** ISN'T HAPPY ABOUT YOUR OVERDUE BOOKS EITHER!

OH, THE SHAME!

IF ONLY THERE WAS A WAY TO MAKE USING YOUR LIBRARY FUN AGAIN...

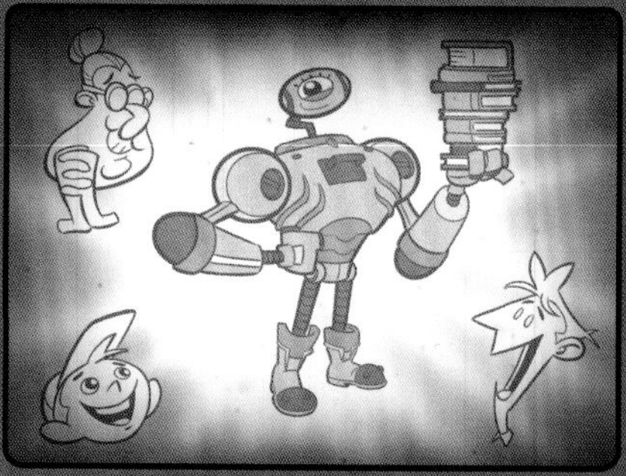

...BUT THERE IS!

INTRODUCING THE NEWEST BREAKTHROUGH IN MODERN CONVENIENCE...

THE BOOK-BOT 9000!

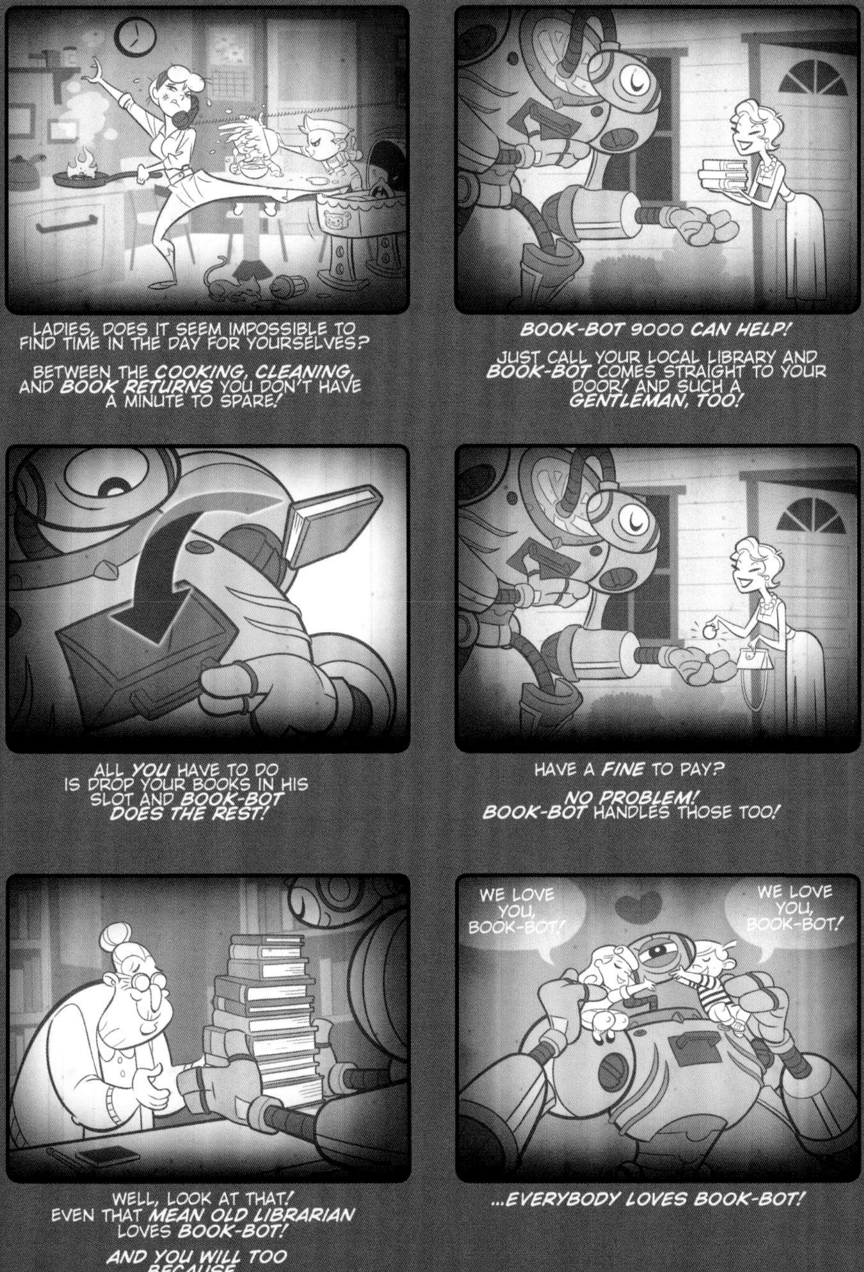
LADIES, DOES IT SEEM IMPOSSIBLE TO FIND TIME IN THE DAY FOR YOURSELVES?
BETWEEN THE COOKING, CLEANING, AND BOOK RETURNS YOU DON'T HAVE A MINUTE TO SPARE!
BOOK-BOT 9000 CAN HELP!
JUST CALL YOUR LOCAL LIBRARY AND BOOK-BOT COMES STRAIGHT TO YOUR DOOR! AND SUCH A GENTLEMAN, TOO!
ALL YOU HAVE TO DO IS DROP YOUR BOOKS IN HIS SLOT AND BOOK-BOT DOES THE REST!
HAVE A FINE TO PAY?
NO PROBLEM! BOOK-BOT HANDLES THOSE TOO!
WELL, LOOK AT THAT! EVEN THAT MEAN OLD LIBRARIAN LOVES BOOK-BOT!
AND YOU WILL TOO BECAUSE...
WE LOVE YOU, BOOK-BOT!
WE LOVE YOU, BOOK-BOT!
...EVERYBODY LOVES BOOK-BOT!

The commercial ended with a hiss of static.

"The masses just didn't get it," Erasmus snarled, popping the tape from the ancient video player. "The Book-bot 9000 performed to the highest degree of all its specifications. Once again my genius was wasted and . . ."

"What's this tape?" OB asked, picking up another dusty tape from the cart the player rested on. Kirby took it from the turtle's claws.

"Book-bot 9000 Field Test," Kirby read the label aloud.

"That's nothing," Erasmus squawked, reaching for the tape with ghostly hands.

Kirby pulled it from his reach, removing the old tape from the VCR and inserting the new. "I'll be the judge of that," the Frenchie said, hitting Play.

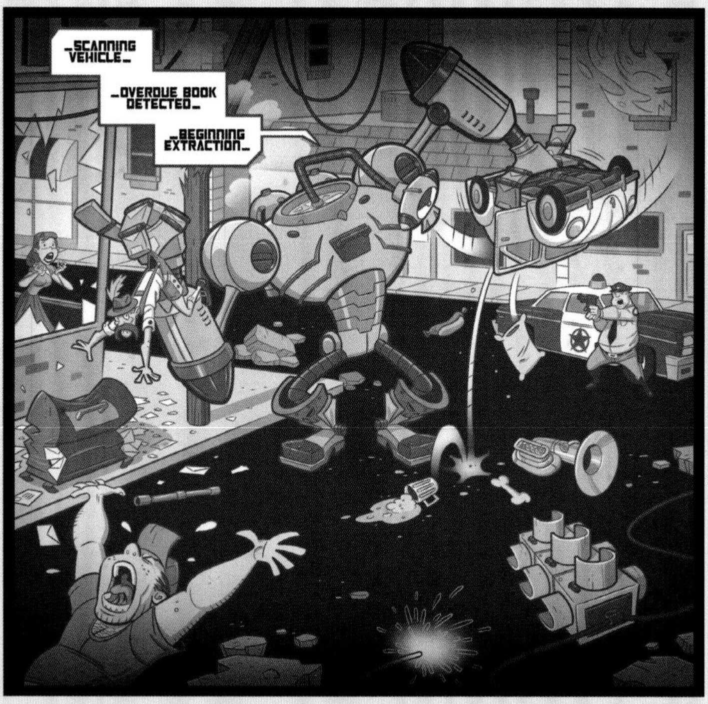
SCANNING VEHICLE
OVERDUE BOOK DETECTED
BEGINNING EXTRACTION

Erasmus quickly ejected the tape.

"That's enough of that," the ghost said, turning off the machine.

"That last part seemed a little scary," OB said, obviously shaken by what he'd just watched.

"Yes," Erasmus said with a snarl upon his ghostly face. "The fools couldn't see past the Book-bot 9000's over-enthusiasm and rejected the project."

"I can't imagine," Kirby said sarcastically.

"They squandered my genius yet again, never realizing how much of myself I'd put into this . . . my greatest creation!"

Erasmus's ghostly arms flailed, hitting a control panel that suddenly lit up. "Whoops," he said, staring at the blinking lights and ticking gauges.

"What did you do?" Kirby asked.

The Book-bot 9000 began to move.

SEVEN

The Book-bot 9000 extended its coiled neck, looking around the laboratory with its single mechanical eye.

"Book-bot 9000 activated," it said in a booming, metallic voice.

"What have you done?" Kirby asked. "Shut it down this instant."

Erasmus's ghost hands fluttered near the control panel. "Not sure what . . . oh geez, this isn't good."

"Don't like the sound of that!" OB cried.

"What's wrong?" Kirby asked, darting over to the panel.

"The years haven't been kind to the control panel. Seems to be stuck."

"*Stuck?*" Kirby bellowed, attempting to shut the mechanical man down. "There must be some kind of failsafe to . . ."

The Book-bot 9000 started forward, pushing the things stacked in front of it out of the way.

"Proceeding with prime directive!" its voice boomed.

"Ahhhhhh!" OB shrieked. He dashed out of the way of the robot before he was crushed beneath its heavy foot.

The Book-bot strode across the lab, stopping to turn its mechanical gaze on an area of the ceiling.

"Initiating prime directive," it said as two sections of the ceiling slid apart to expose a circular tunnel.

"What is this?" Kirby asked. "I thought there was only one way in and out!"

"Delivery hatch for larger pieces," Erasmus stated. "You try getting a Univac 8000 super computer through a garage door!"

Jets on the bottom of the Book-bot's feet ignited with a whoosh of dust and fire. The giant mechanical man shot up into the ceiling passage and was gone.

"Where does that lead?" Kirby asked.

"Secret opening beneath a brush pile in the far back yard," Erasmus said, drifting over to a wall of old-fashioned television screens. The ghost flicked a few switches and the monitors came to life, showing images from all over Strasburg.

"Are those live?" Kirby asked, approaching the screens. OB walked alongside him.

"What a cute little town," the turtle said happily.

Kirby looked at the turtle and snarled, before turning his attention back to the live feeds.

"There," he said, pointing to a screen in the far corner. A large pile of twigs and branches slid apart and the Book-bot 9000 emerged out into the world.

"Tell me of this prime directive," Kirby said, watching the robot as it headed down Main Street.

"It's all about the overdue library books," the ghost said. "The Book-bot 9000 will attempt to return all overdue books to the town library."

The ghost paused, eyes fixed upon the screens.

"Or else."

⚓

Kirby watched the multiple television screens and the reactions to the giant robot as it began its prime directive. Cars drove up onto curbs and people shrieked and fled in panic as the Book-bot 9000 went about its business.

"The old boy is moving pretty well for something that hasn't seen activation in over fifty years," the ghost said cheerily.

"This is not a good thing," Kirby stated flatly.

"No, of course not," Erasmus said. "Not at all. It's terrible. But look at him go."

"Yes, I'm looking," Kirby said.

"Where's he going?" OB asked, standing beside Kirby's chair.

"Wherever its prime directive is taking it," Kirby said. "Sensors tracking and zeroing in on missing library books."

"You got it," Erasmus said. "I pity the fools with late library books," he said.

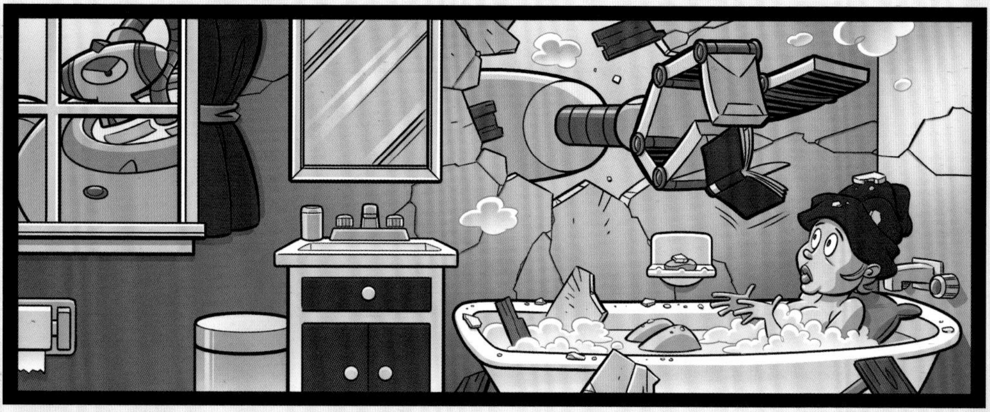

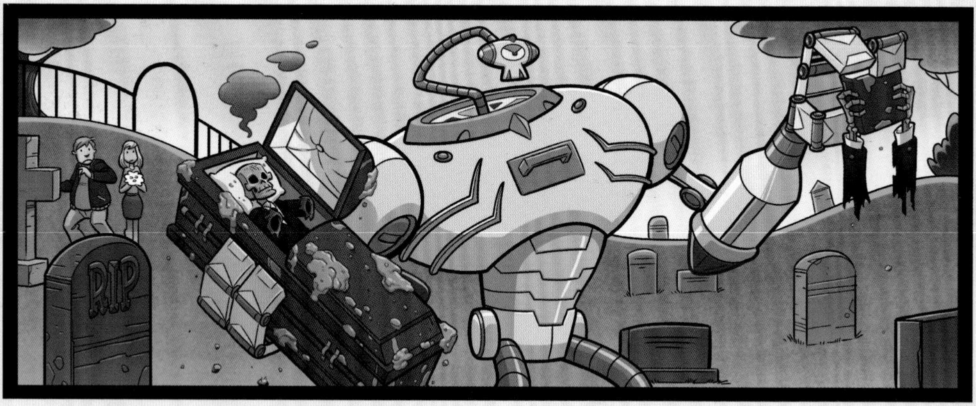
RIP

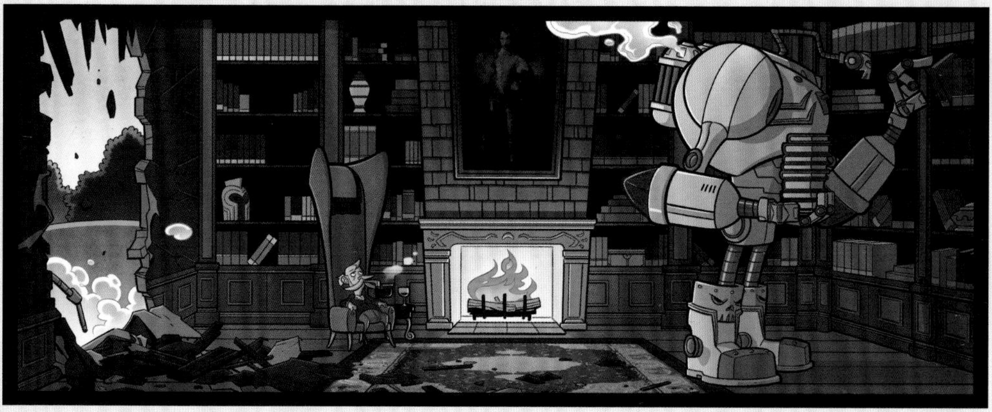

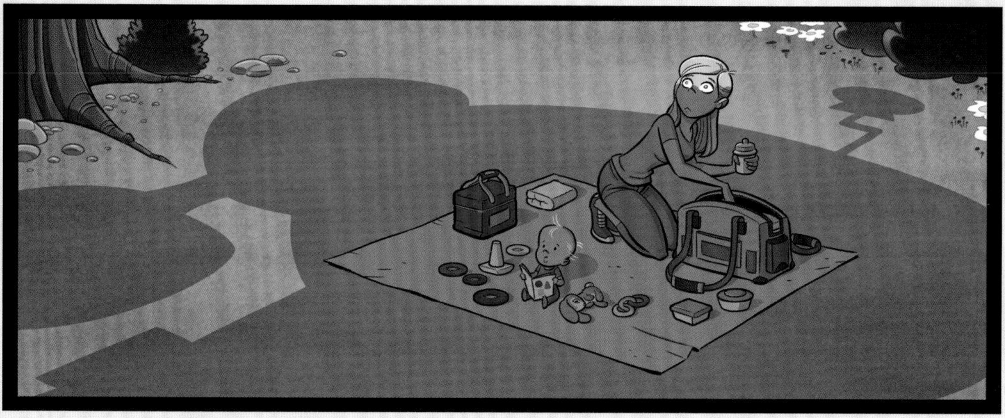

On one of the screens, the Book-bot had peeled back the roof of an ice cream truck and was rummaging through it, the contents of the vehicle spilling out onto the street.

“There!” Erasmus said pointing. “It found one!”

A book had indeed fallen out of the car, along with other items of rubbish.

“This should be good,” Erasmus said.

The robot tossed the Volkswagen aside and picked up the book. Its single mechanical eye then scanned the book's library identification card.

"*Green Eggs and Ham,*" the Book-bot 9000 proclaimed. "Overdue eight hundred sixty five days. Fine to be collected: $86.50."

A hatch opened in the robot's steel chest, and it placed the book inside. The door slid shut with a hiss, and the Book-bot turned its attention back to the man who was attempting to sneak away.

"I was going to bring that back this week!" the man cried in terror as the mechanical monster loomed above him. He tried to run, but the Book-bot snatched him up by one of his legs, holding him upside down and shaking him.

"Collection of overdue fees commencing," the Book-bot said. He shook the screaming man until change and everything else in his pockets dropped to the sidewalk.

"And we wonder why this didn't catch on," Kirby muttered beneath his breath as he watched the scene unfold.

"What?" Erasmus said defensively. "So it's a little overzealous, sue me!"

The Book-bot dropped the shaken man to the street and began to pick up the money that had fallen, even retrieving the man's wallet and helping itself to the cash inside. It tossed the empty wallet over its shoulder and pushed the money through a slot in its chest, before heading toward the center of town.

"This is not good," Kirby growled. "Not good in the least. If the authorities trace the origin of the runaway mechanical man back to this lab, it could seriously interfere with my plans for the future. Something must be done."

"But what?" OB asked. "What can we do about something like that?"

"Guess we could always wait until it runs out of atomic fuel," Erasmus said.

"And how long will that be?"

"Rough estimate? Probably another hundred and fifty years, give or take five."

"That will not do at all," Kirby said, leaping down from his chair to pace around the lab, his atomically enhanced brain reviewing a multitude of scenarios. An idea formed as he looked about the lab and all that it had to offer.

"Well?" Erasmus asked.

"Did you think of something, Kirby?" OB asked timidly.

"I have to stop it."

"You?" Erasmus asked, scoffing.

"How are you planning on doing that?" OB wanted to know.

Kirby approached the discarded T-19 Trash Killer, walking around it in a circle.

"Yes," he muttered, stroking his furry chin. "This will do."

"For what?" the ghost asked. "That's just a mechanical trash can. A very ingeniously designed trash can, but a trash can nonetheless."

"That's what it is now," Kirby said, a gleam in his dark Frenchie eyes. "But when I'm done it will be much more than that."

"What will it be?" OB asked breathlessly.

"It will be the Book-bot 9000's end," the Frenchie said, extending his paw. "Now be a good turtle and bring me an acetylene torch."

For any other, this process would have taken months, maybe even years. But for Kirby's enhanced Frenchie brain, it was a task with little more complexity than changing a light bulb.

Erasmus's lab was equipped with everything he needed—raw building materials as well as tools. It required only a Frenchie with purpose and a vision to see a failed experiment in automated trash collection transformed into a solution for the runaway Book-bot 9000 problem.

Kirby completed the final weld on his invention and removed the goggles from over his eyes.

"That should do it," he said, standing atop the ladder and admiring his work.

Not bad, he thought. *A fully functional robotic battle suit in under an hour.* Kirby wished he had time for some further improvements, but . . .

"The Book-bot has just about reached Strasburg Center!" OB announced, standing on the chair in front of the monitor screens.

"Then there is no time to waste," Kirby said.

"Are you sure this will work?" Erasmus asked, hovering beside the ladder and mechanical suit.

"It has to," Kirby said. He lowered himself into the seat within the body of the robot armor. "I will not allow my chance for world supremacy to be snatched away by a library book–collecting mechanical monstrosity."

"A little harsh, don't you think?" Erasmus asked.

"Not quite enough, actually," Kirby said, snapping his seatbelt in place. Gripping the battle suit's controls, he activated the servomechanisms and it began to move.

"Okay then," Erasmus said. "Me and the turtle will stay here and watch the monitors."

Kirby clomped by in the heavy battle armor, stopping beneath the ceiling hatch.

"Good luck, Kirb!" OB shouted, waving.

"Knock 'em dead, Krispin!" the ghost yelled, raising his ghostly scrub brush in salute.

Without another moment of hesitation, the French bulldog activated the rockets on his back and blasted up into the tunnel.

The Book-bot 9000 knew that it had a purpose.

Sensitive instruments throughout its mechanical body scanned the area before it, searching for the items that gave the mechanical man its reason to exist.

The Book-bot stopped in the center of downtown Strasburg, zeroing in on its objective.

Books. Overdue books. Fines to be collected.

The Book-bot 9000 scanned as chaos erupted. People ran and screamed in panic at the sight of it, but that did not hinder the Book-bot 9000.

In a matter of minutes its instruments were registering objectives . . . *The Care and Feeding of a Wombat*—overdue three months. *Turn on Anything, You'll Get It: An Amateur's Guide to Indoor Plumbing*—overdue eighteen months. *Mommy Cries Because You Are Bad*—overdue two weeks, three days . . .

The Book-bot fixed upon the overdue books' locations.

It had a job to do.

A purpose.

The Mailman handed Mr. Douglas Greevley of Greevley's Hardware Store his afternoon mail.

"Morning, Lucas," Greevley said, taking the mail just outside the store's front door. "Beautiful day."

"Certainly is, Douglas," the Mailman said. "Though I hear there might be some rain coming in for the weekend."

"Good for the grass, I guess," Greevley said as he perused the mail. "Nothing all that interesting today."

"And sometimes that's a good thing," the Mailman said with a smile, already taking the next delivery from his satchel.

"You're probably right," Greevley said, about to head back into the store. "You have a great . . ."

The cries of surprise froze them both in their tracks.

"Wonder what that's all about?" Greevley said, starting to wander farther from his store.

The Mailman was already reacting, his super Mailman vision already locating the source of the screams.

There was a giant robot coming down the street.

"There's something you don't see every day," the Mailman muttered beneath his breath. "Think it might be wise for you to go into your store," he advised Mr. Greevley.

"Yeah, I think you might be right," Greevley agreed, quickly ducking into the store and flipping the sign from OPEN to CLOSED.

The robot moved closer, crushing cars and smashing through buildings as the people of Strasburg fled in total panic. By its actions, it appeared that the mechanical menace was looking for something. *But what?* Mailman wondered.

And would there be any town left by the time it was finished searching?

The Mailman knew that he couldn't deal with this threat alone. Maybe it was time to make a call.

"We've got an emergency in the center of town," he said. "Looks like our special talents are needed."

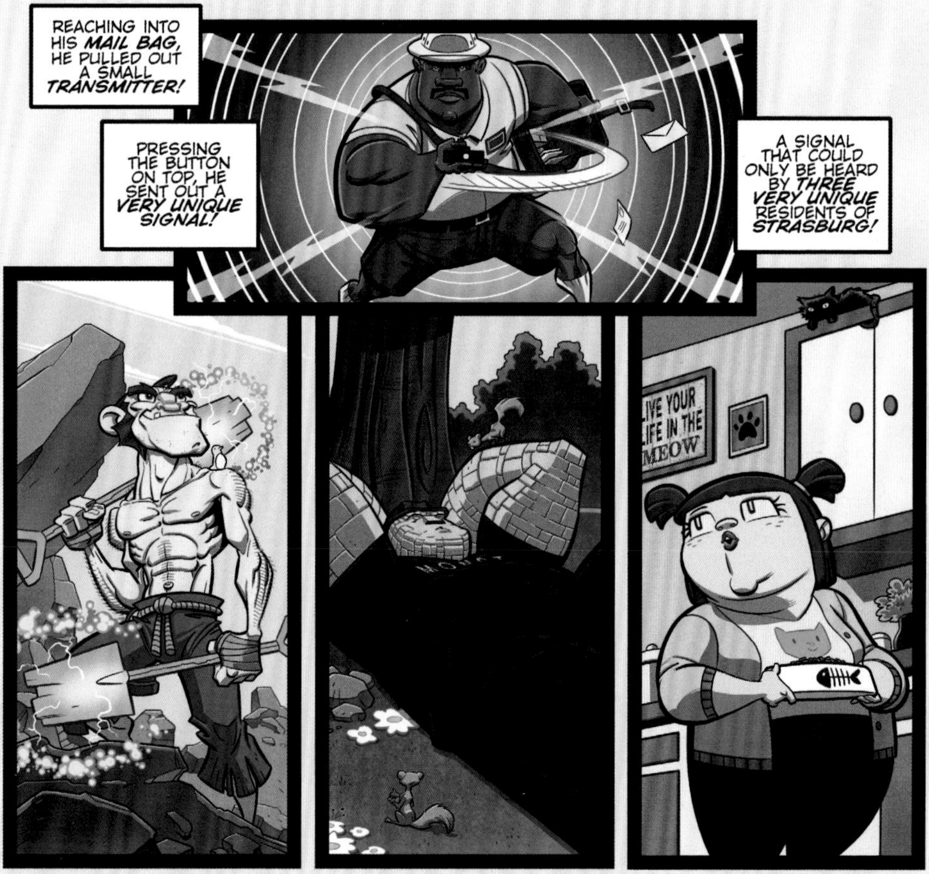
REACHING INTO HIS MAIL BAG, HE PULLED OUT A SMALL TRANSMITTER!
PRESSING THE BUTTON ON TOP, HE SENT OUT A VERY UNIQUE SIGNAL!
A SIGNAL THAT COULD ONLY BE HEARD BY THREE VERY UNIQUE RESIDENTS OF STRASBURG!
LIVE YOUR LIFE IN THE MEOW

EIGHT

Kirby rocketed over Strasburg.

Looking through the cockpit visor to the streets below, he followed the trail of wreckage that would lead him to the Book-bot 9000.

Adjusting the controls and checking his instruments, Kirby prepared for the conflict that he knew would come. He doubted very much that the Book-bot would allow its programming to be interrupted without a fight, and he wanted to be prepared.

He cursed the fact that he hadn't had time to include some more advanced tactical weaponry, but he would just have to get by with what was available to him.

Through the cockpit windshield, Kirby watched an '85 Toyota Corolla fly up into the air before crashing down to the street below.

The Book-bot emerged from a cloud of smoke, seeking out overdue books with a vengeance.

Manipulating the controls, the Frenchie brought the armored suit earthward. It was time for the Book-bot 9000's rampage to end, before any unwarranted attention was brought to his activities.

It was time for battle.

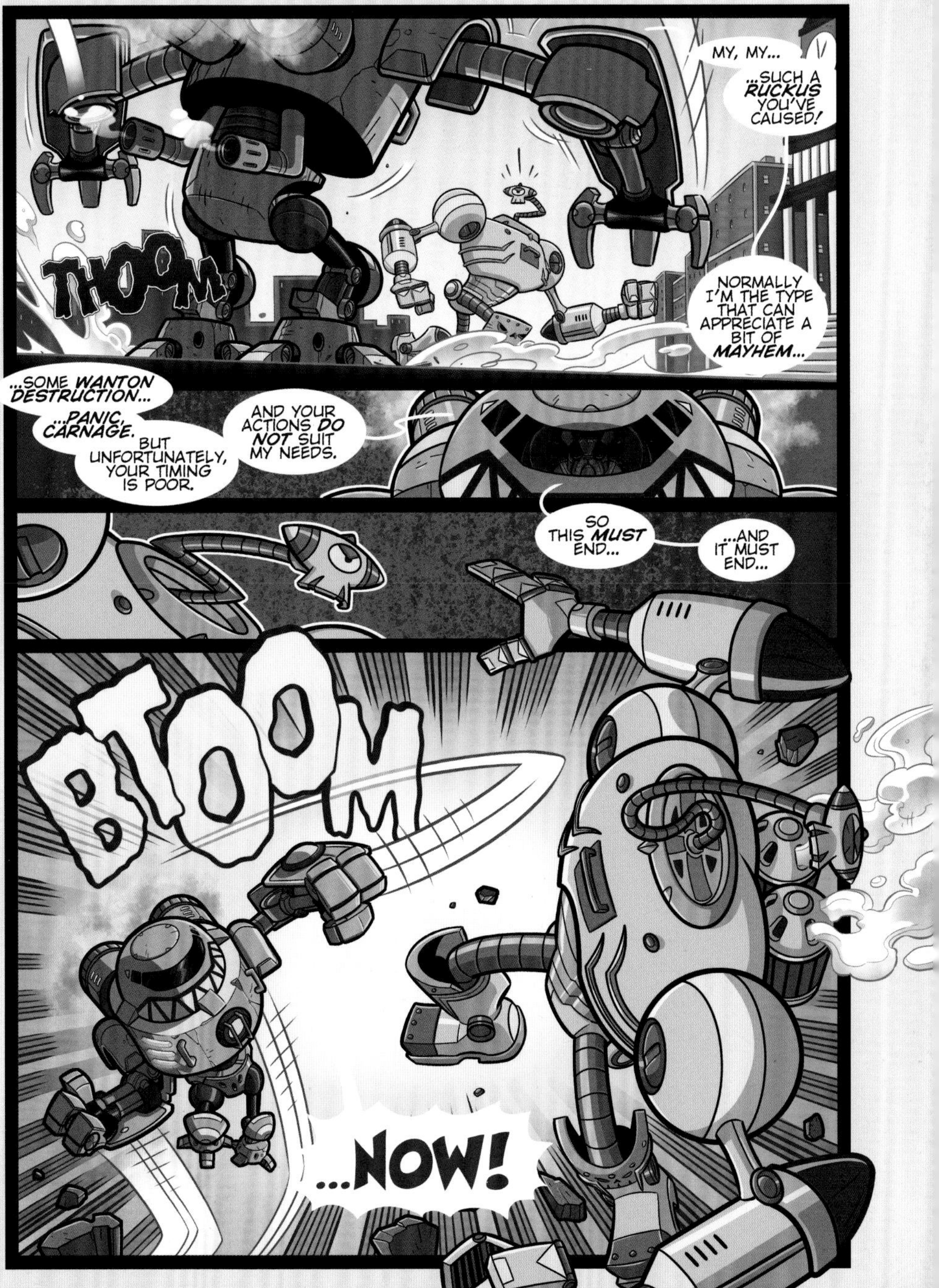

MY, MY...
...SUCH A RUCKUS YOU'VE CAUSED!
THOOM
NORMALLY I'M THE TYPE THAT CAN APPRECIATE A BIT OF MAYHEM...
...SOME WANTON DESTRUCTION...
...PANIC, CARNAGE.
BUT UNFORTUNATELY, YOUR TIMING IS POOR.
AND YOUR ACTIONS DO NOT SUIT MY NEEDS.
SO THIS MUST END...
...AND IT MUST END...
BLOOM
...NOW!

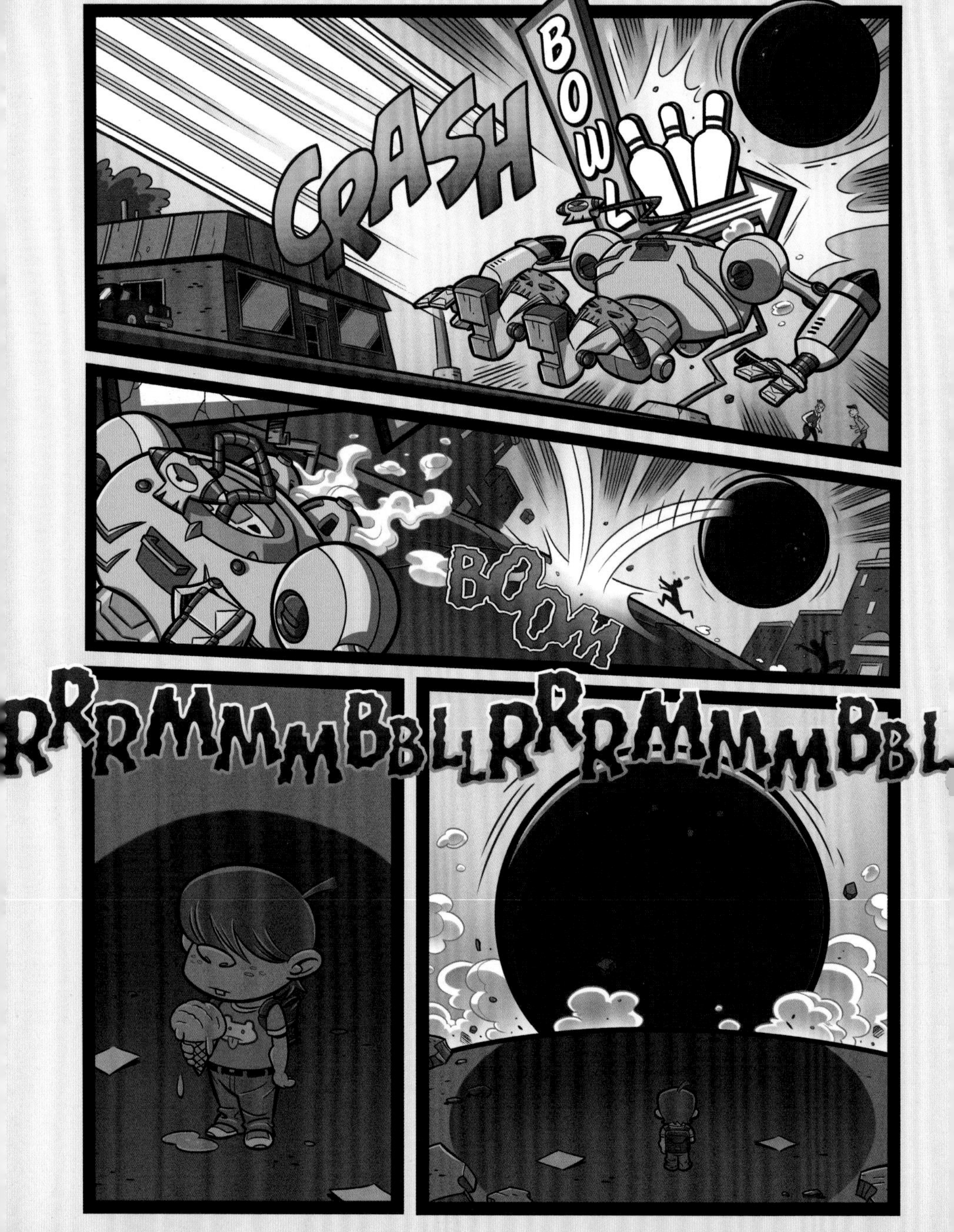
CRASH
BOWL
BOOM
RRRMMMMBBLLRRRMMMMBBL

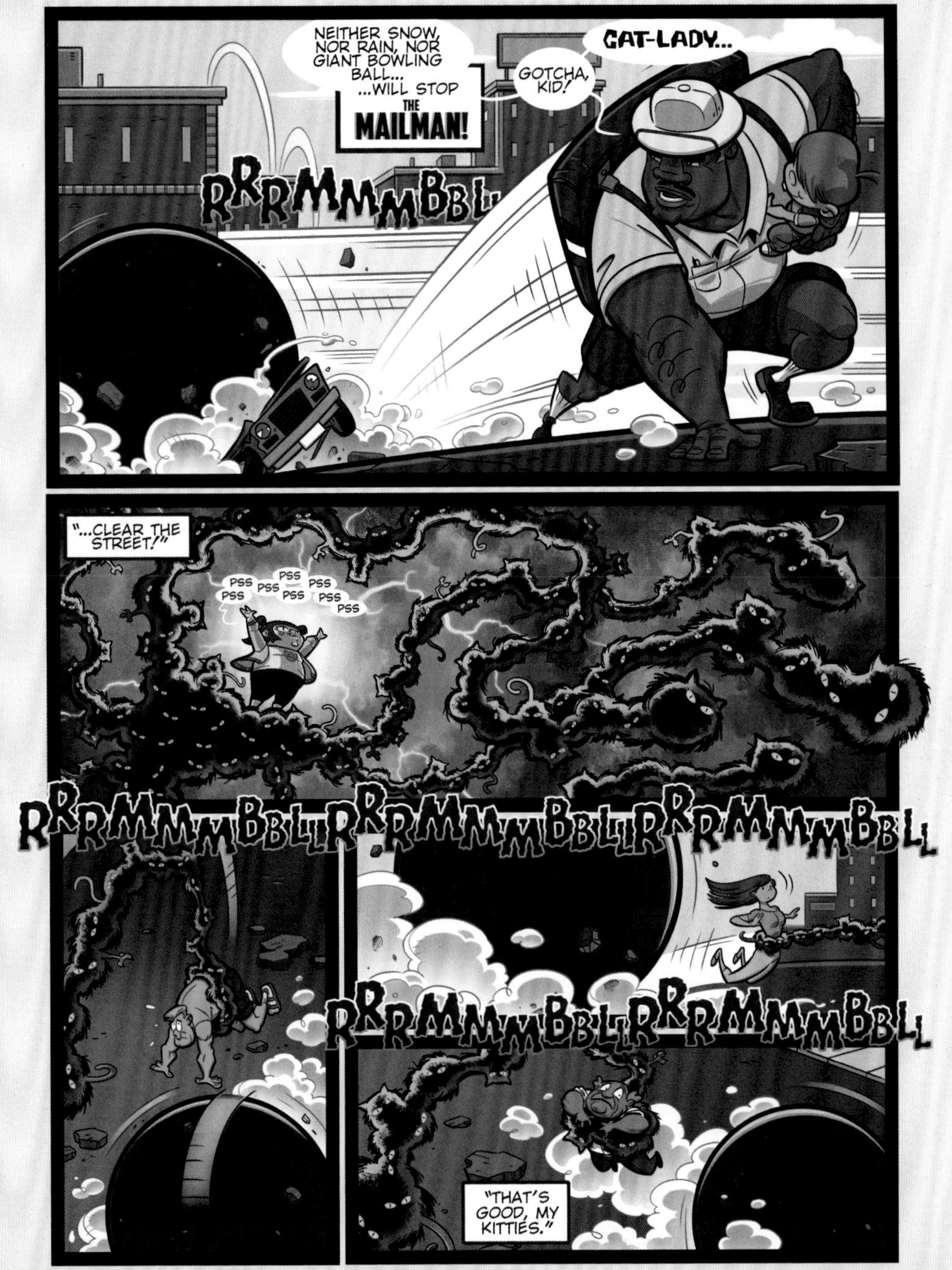
NEITHER SNOW, NOR RAIN, NOR GIANT BOWLING BALL... ...WILL STOP
THE MAILMAN!
CAT-LADY...
GOTCHA, KID!
RRRMMMMBBLL
"...CLEAR THE STREET!"
PSS PSS PSS PSS PSS PSS PSS PSS
RRRMMMMBBLLRRRMMMMBBLLRRRMMMMBBLL
RRRMMMMBBLLRRRMMMMBBLL
"THAT'S GOOD, MY KITTIES."

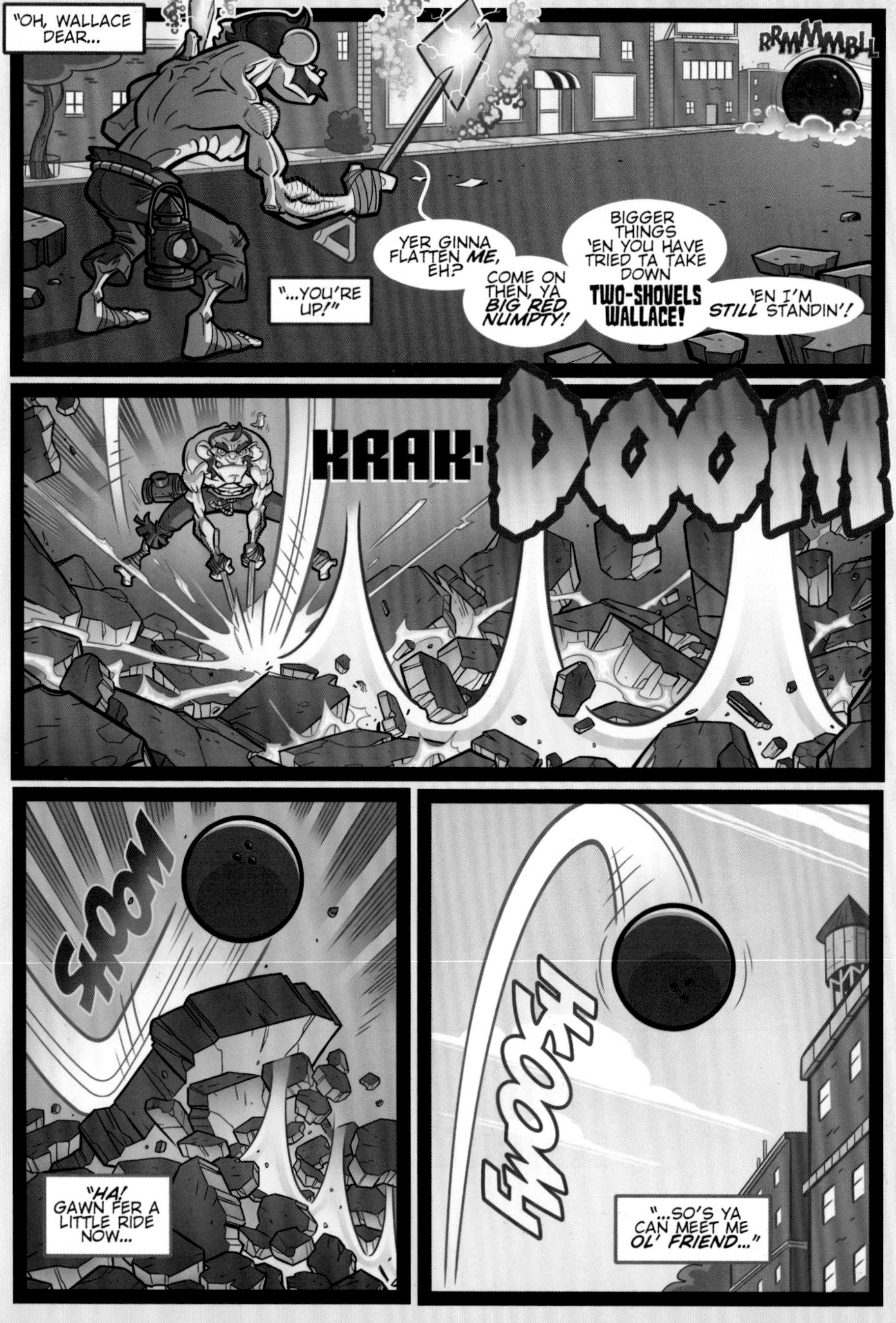
"OH, WALLACE DEAR...
RRMMMBLL
"...YOU'RE UP!"
YER GINNA FLATTEN *ME*, EH?
COME ON THEN, YA *BIG RED NUMPTY!*
BIGGER THINGS 'EN YOU HAVE TRIED TA TAKE DOWN **TWO-SHOVELS WALLACE!**
'EN I'M *STILL* STANDIN'!
KRAK-DOOM
SHOOM
"*HA!* GAWN FER A LITTLE RIDE NOW...
FWOOSH
"...SO'S YA CAN MEET ME *OL' FRIEND...*"

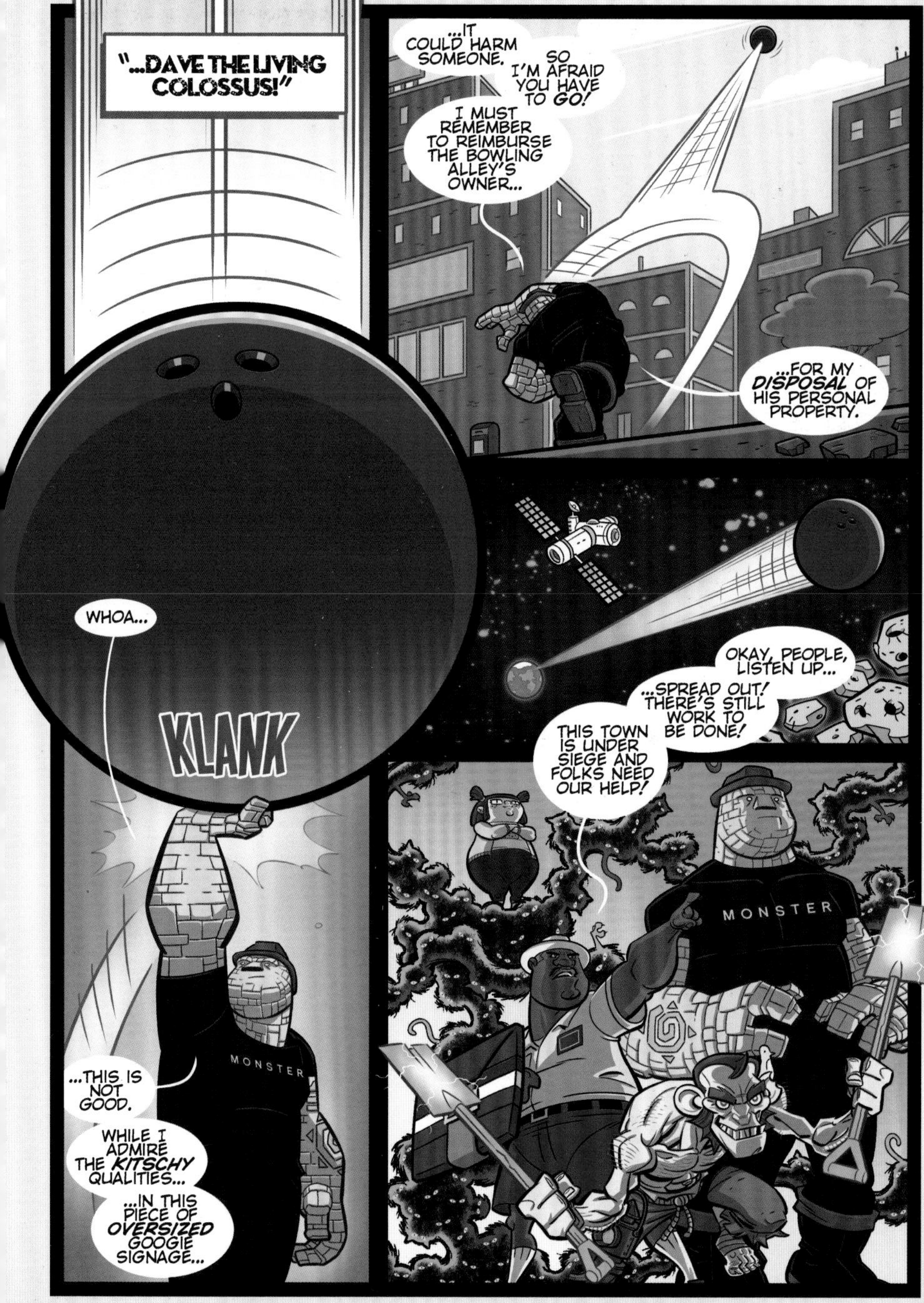
"...DAVE THE LIVING COLOSSUS!"
...IT COULD HARM SOMEONE.
SO I'M AFRAID YOU HAVE TO GO!
I MUST REMEMBER TO REIMBURSE THE BOWLING ALLEY'S OWNER...
...FOR MY DISPOSAL OF HIS PERSONAL PROPERTY.
WHOA...
KLANK
MONSTER
...THIS IS NOT GOOD.
WHILE I ADMIRE THE KITSCHY QUALITIES...
...IN THIS PIECE OF OVERSIZED GOOGIE SIGNAGE...
OKAY, PEOPLE, LISTEN UP...
...SPREAD OUT! THERE'S STILL WORK TO BE DONE!
THIS TOWN IS UNDER SIEGE AND FOLKS NEED OUR HELP!
MONSTER

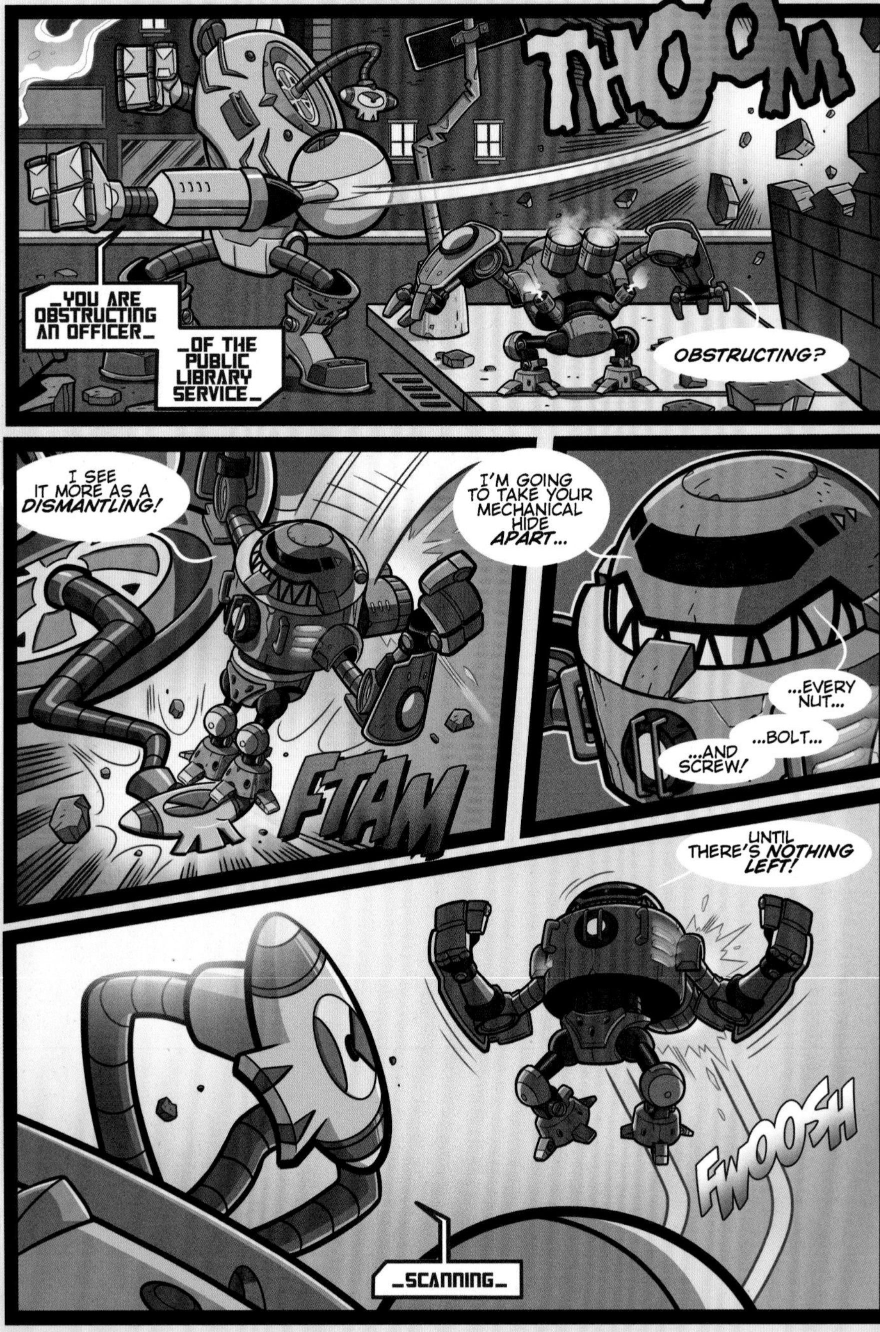
THOOM
YOU ARE OBSTRUCTING AN OFFICER
OF THE PUBLIC LIBRARY SERVICE
OBSTRUCTING?
I SEE IT MORE AS A *DISMANTLING!*
FTAM
I'M GOING TO TAKE YOUR MECHANICAL HIDE *APART*...
...EVERY NUT...
...BOLT...
...AND SCREW!
UNTIL THERE'S *NOTHING LEFT!*
FWOOSH
SCANNING

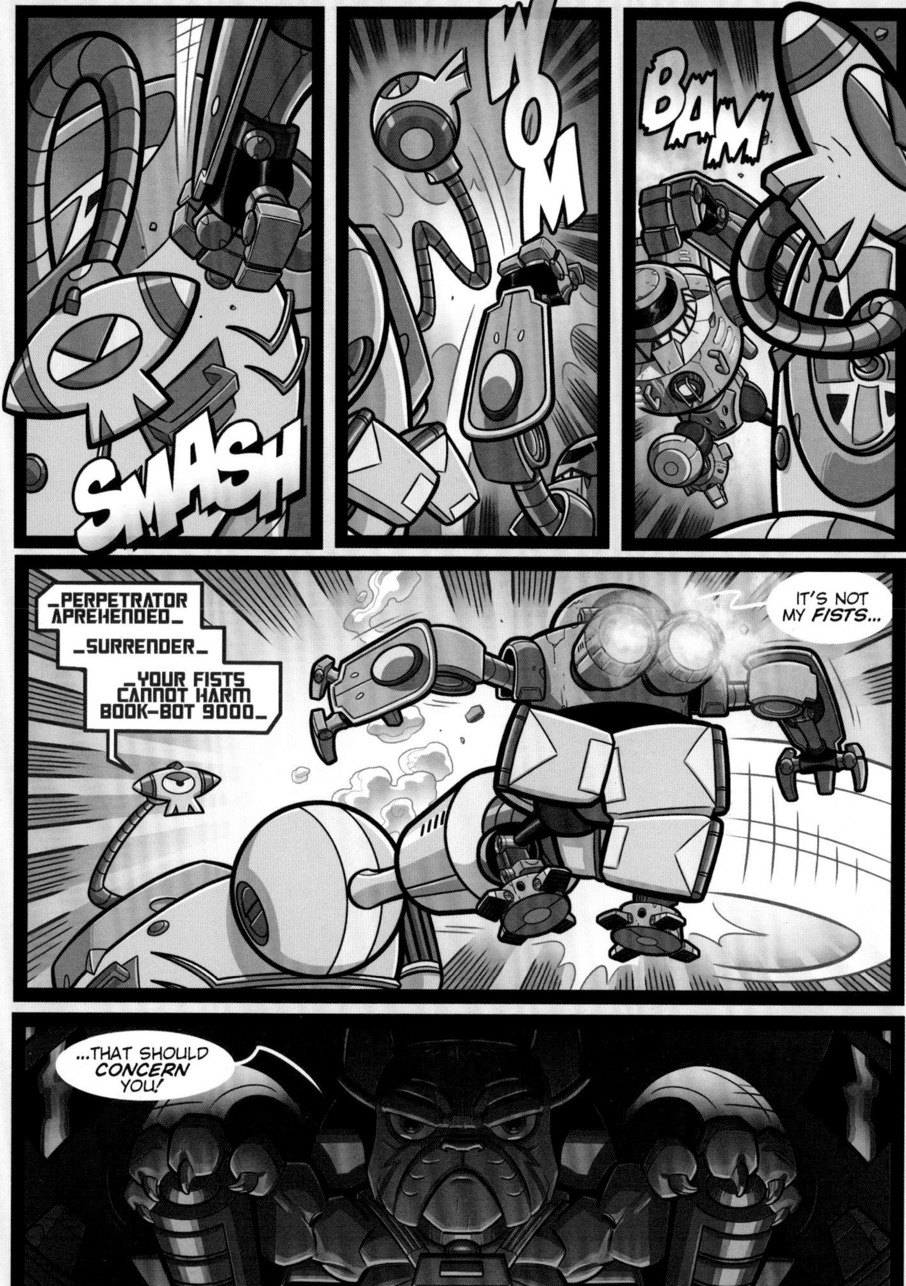
SMASH
WOM
BAM
PERPETRATOR APREHENDED
SURRENDER
YOUR FISTS CANNOT HARM BOOK-BOT 9000
IT'S NOT MY FISTS...
...THAT SHOULD CONCERN YOU!

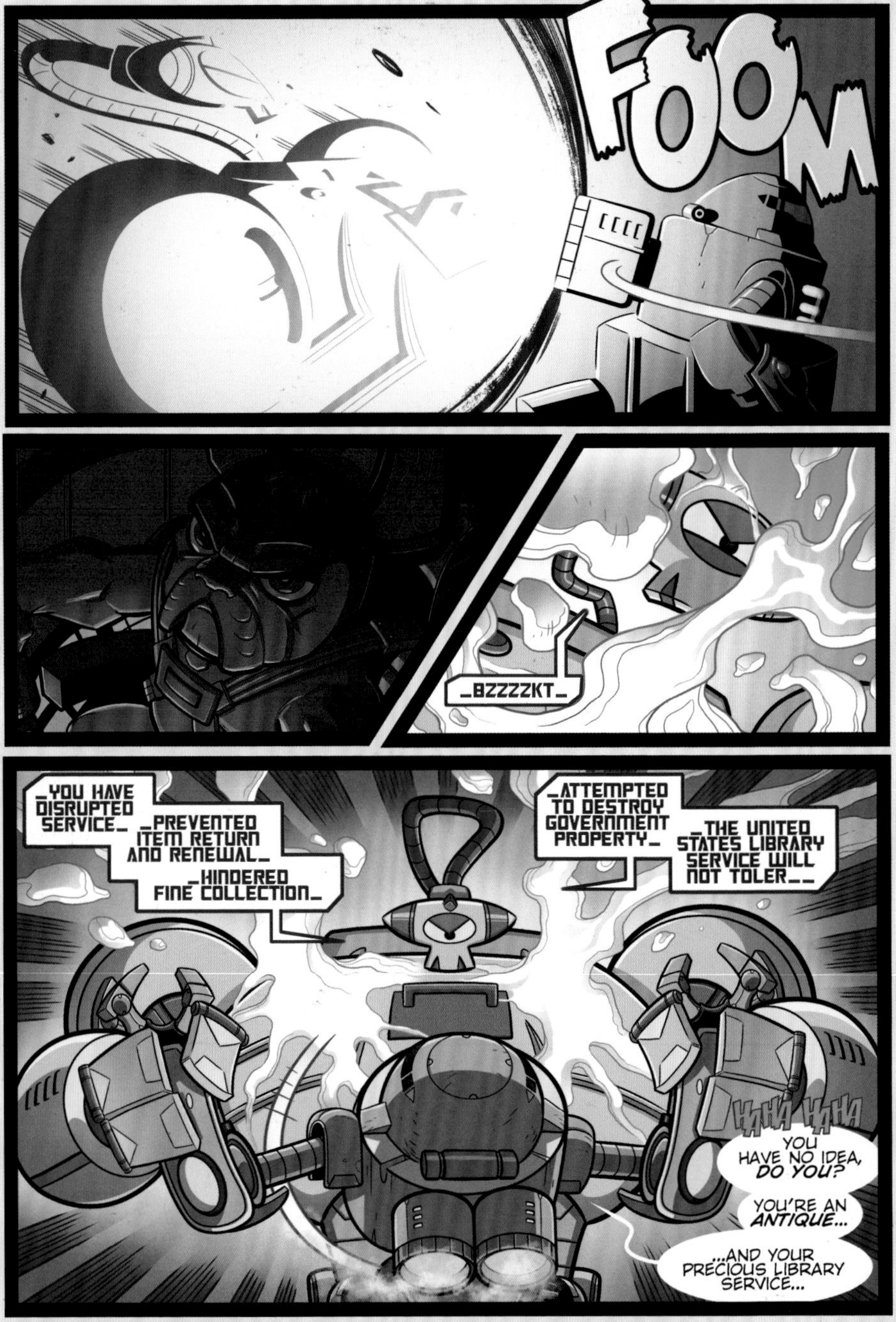
FOOM
BZZZZKT
YOU HAVE DISRUPTED SERVICE
PREVENTED ITEM RETURN AND RENEWAL
HINDERED FINE COLLECTION
ATTEMPTED TO DESTROY GOVERNMENT PROPERTY
THE UNITED STATES LIBRARY SERVICE WILL NOT TOLER _
HAHA HAHA
YOU HAVE NO IDEA, DO YOU?
YOU'RE AN ANTIQUE...
...AND YOUR PRECIOUS LIBRARY SERVICE...

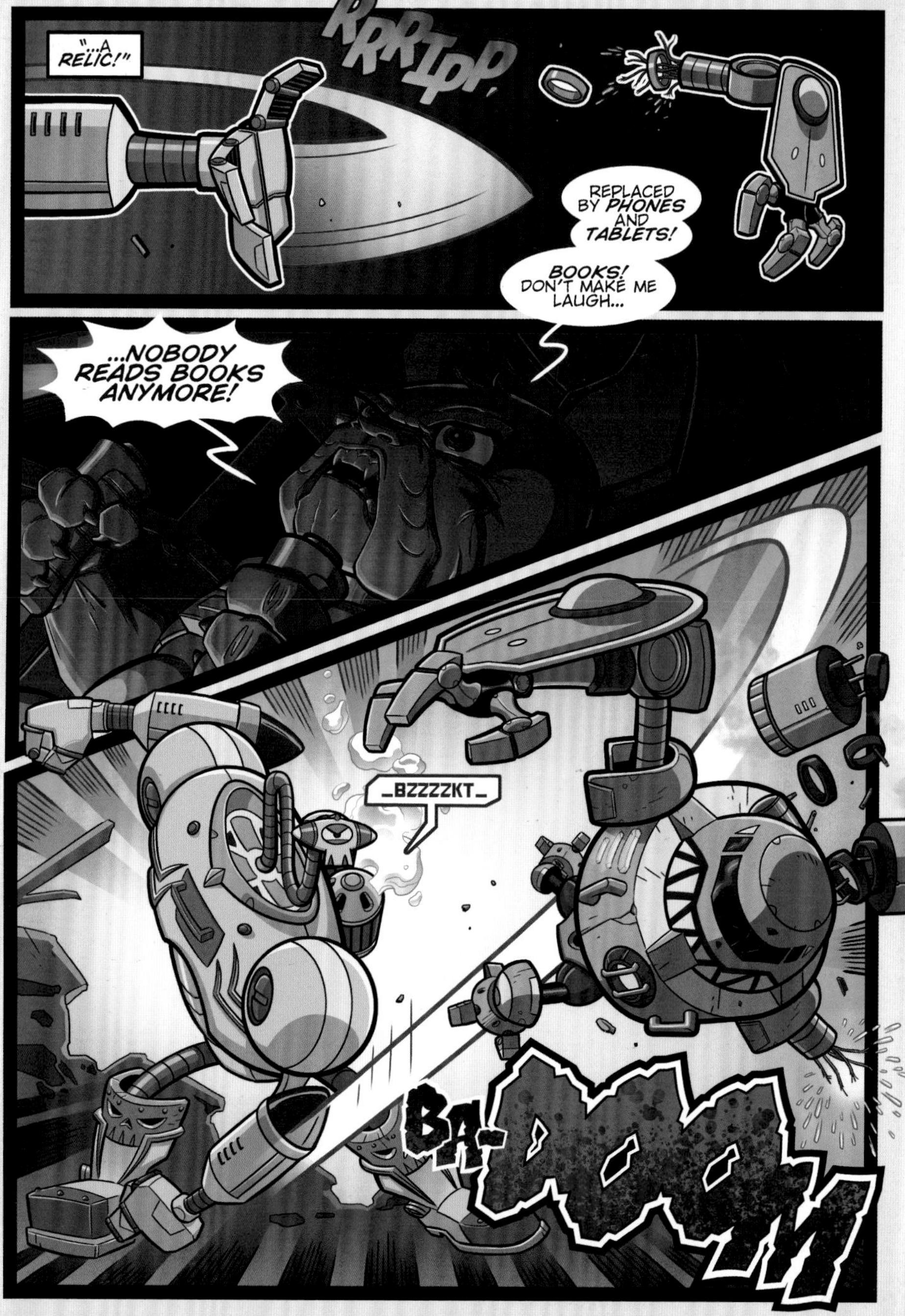

"...A RELIC!"
RRRIPP
REPLACED BY PHONES AND TABLETS!
BOOKS! DON'T MAKE ME LAUGH...
...NOBODY READS BOOKS ANYMORE!
BZZZZKT
BA-DOOM

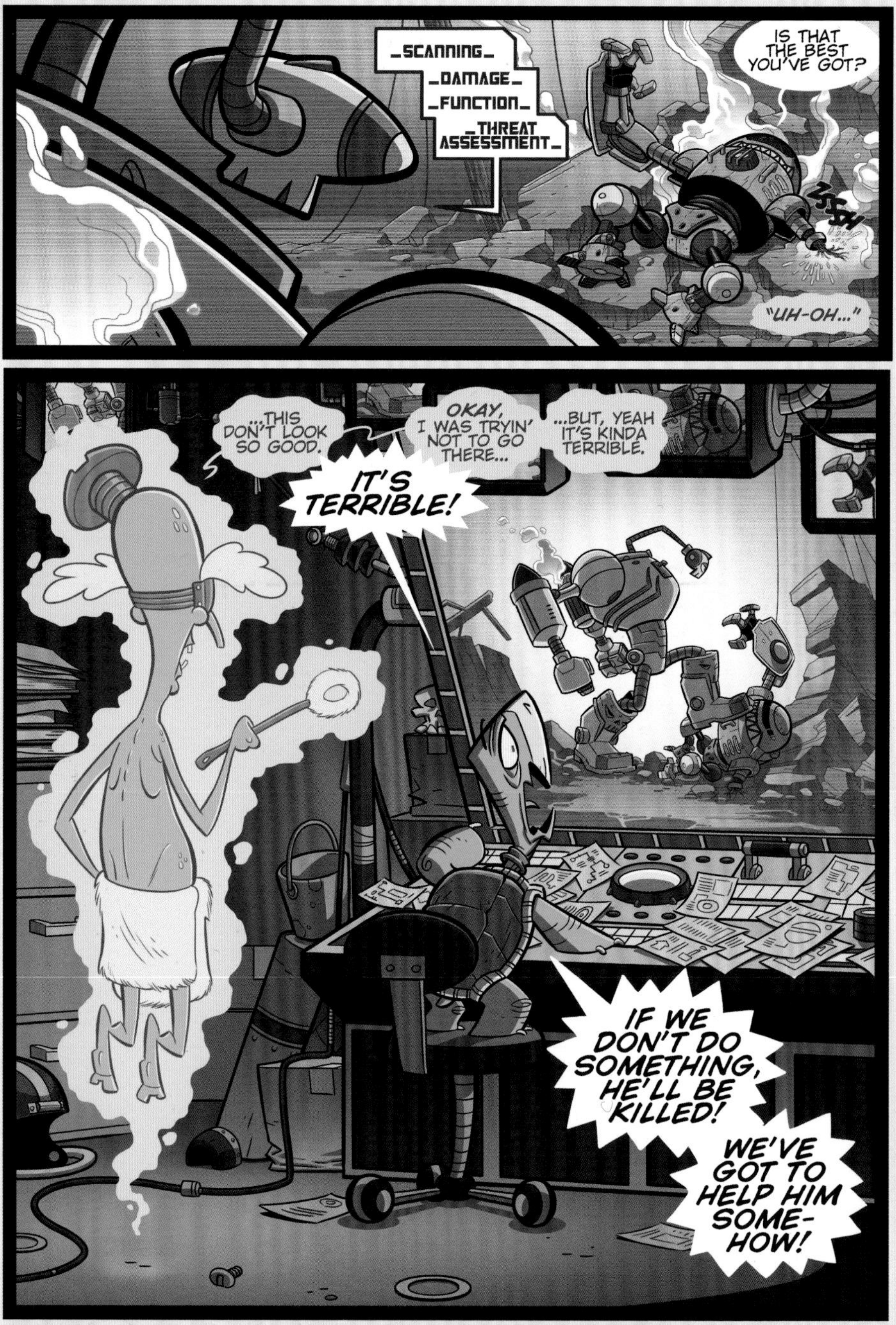

SCANNING
DAMAGE
FUNCTION
THREAT ASSESSMENT
IS THAT THE BEST YOU'VE GOT?
"UH-OH..."
...THIS DON'T LOOK SO GOOD.
OKAY, I WAS TRYIN' NOT TO GO THERE...
...BUT, YEAH IT'S KINDA TERRIBLE.
IT'S TERRIBLE!
IF WE DON'T DO SOMETHING, HE'LL BE KILLED!
WE'VE GOT TO HELP HIM SOME-HOW!

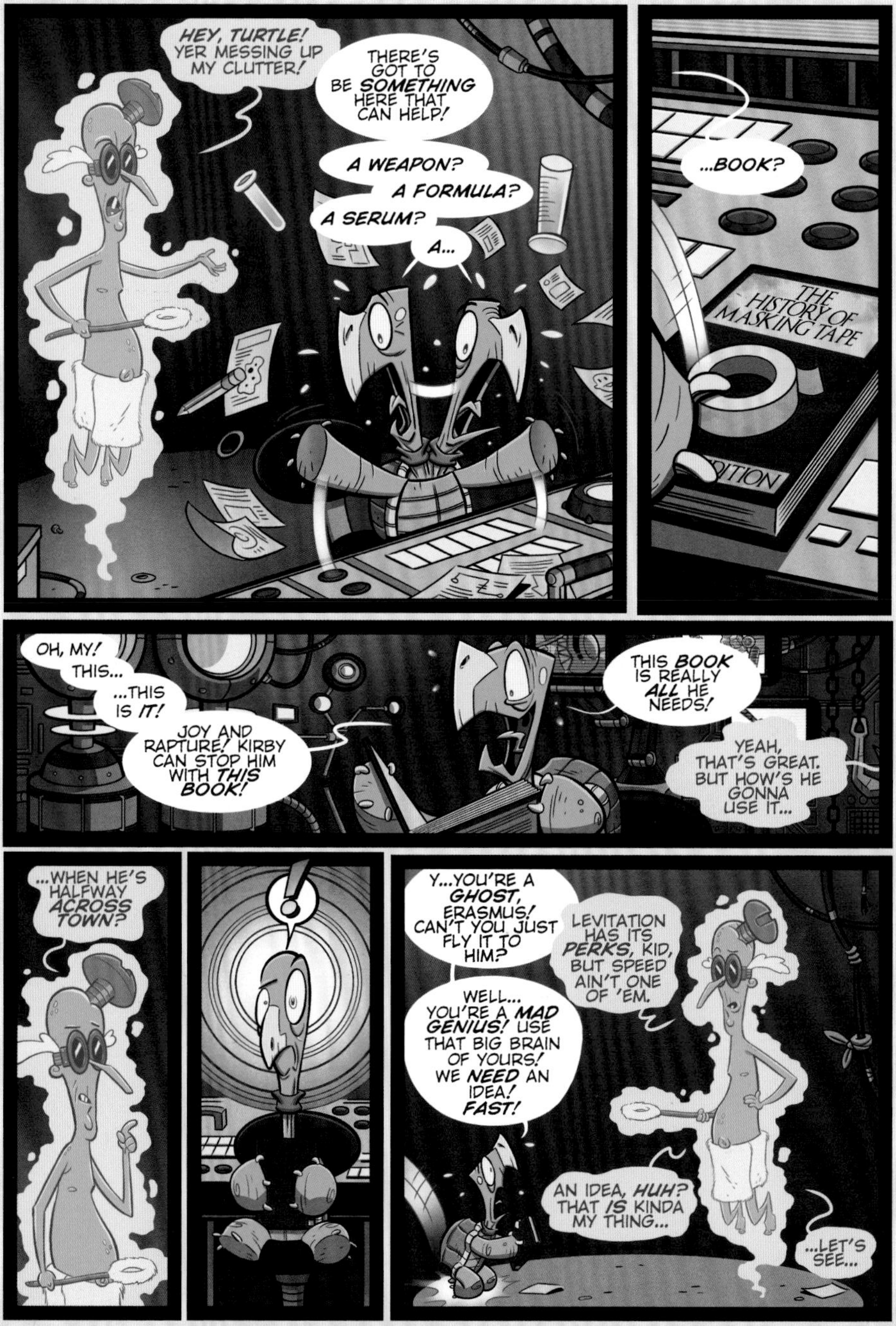
HEY, TURTLE! YER MESSING UP MY CLUTTER!
THERE'S GOT TO BE SOMETHING HERE THAT CAN HELP!
A WEAPON?
A FORMULA?
A SERUM?
A...
...BOOK?
THE HISTORY OF MASKING TAPE
OH, MY!
THIS...
...THIS IS IT!
JOY AND RAPTURE! KIRBY CAN STOP HIM WITH THIS BOOK!
THIS BOOK IS REALLY ALL HE NEEDS!
YEAH, THAT'S GREAT. BUT HOW'S HE GONNA USE IT...
...WHEN HE'S HALFWAY ACROSS TOWN?
Y...YOU'RE A GHOST, ERASMUS! CAN'T YOU JUST FLY IT TO HIM?
LEVITATION HAS ITS PERKS, KID, BUT SPEED AIN'T ONE OF 'EM.
WELL... YOU'RE A MAD GENIUS! USE THAT BIG BRAIN OF YOURS! WE NEED AN IDEA! FAST!
AN IDEA, HUH? THAT IS KINDA MY THING...
...LET'S SEE...

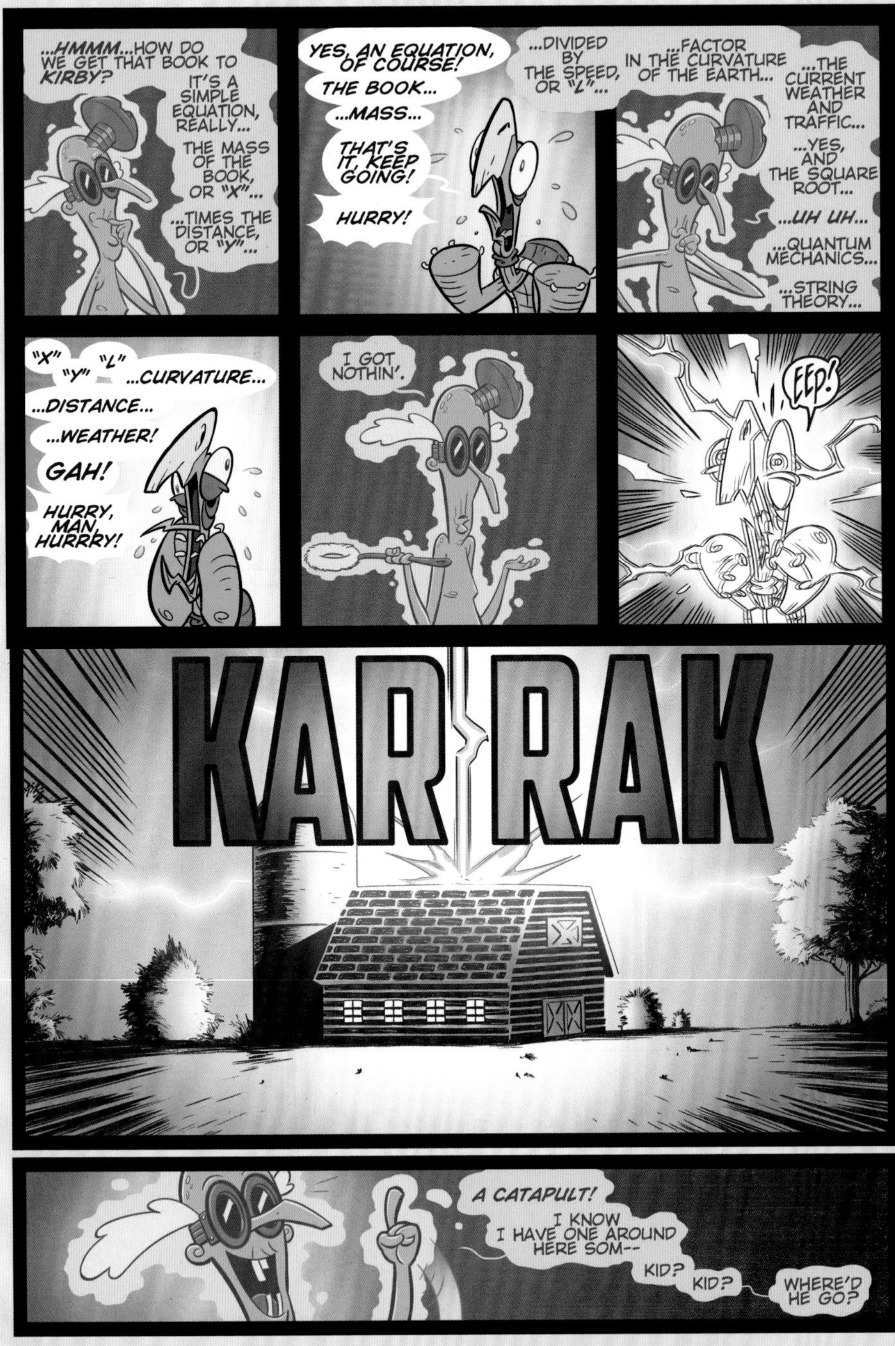
...HMMM...HOW DO WE GET THAT BOOK TO KIRBY?
IT'S A SIMPLE EQUATION, REALLY...
THE MASS OF THE BOOK, OR "X"...
...TIMES THE DISTANCE, OR "Y"...
YES, AN EQUATION, OF COURSE!
THE BOOK...
...MASS...
THAT'S IT, KEEP GOING!
HURRY!
...DIVIDED BY THE SPEED, OR "L"...
...FACTOR IN THE CURVATURE OF THE EARTH...
...THE CURRENT WEATHER AND TRAFFIC...
...YES, AND THE SQUARE ROOT...
...UH UH...
...QUANTUM MECHANICS...
...STRING THEORY...
"X" "Y" "L" ...CURVATURE...
...DISTANCE...
...WEATHER!
GAH!
HURRY, MAN, HURRRY!
I GOT NOTHIN'.
EEP!
KAR RAK
A CATAPULT!
I KNOW I HAVE ONE AROUND HERE SOM--
KID?
KID?
WHERE'D HE GO?

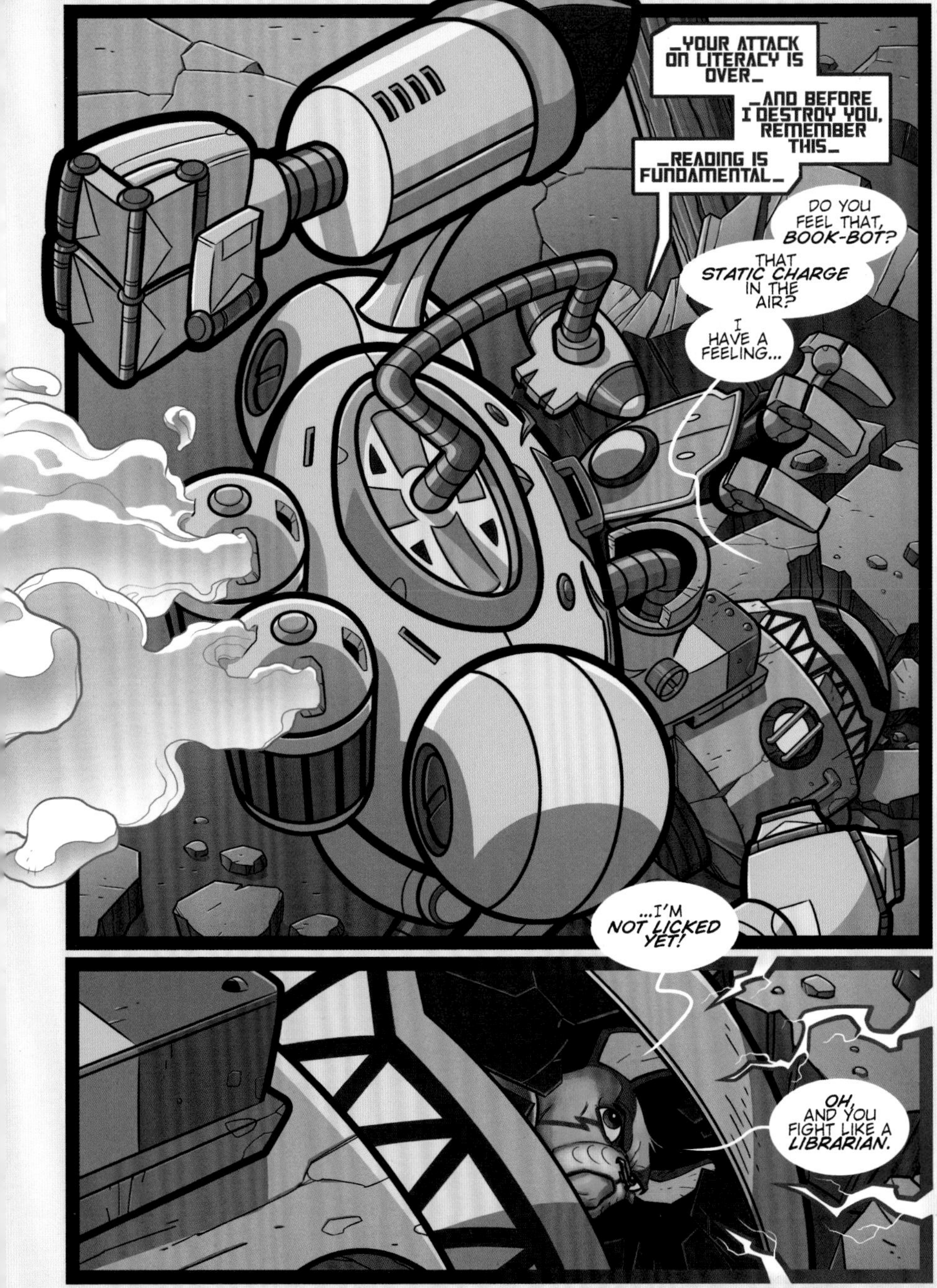
YOUR ATTACK ON LITERACY IS OVER
AND BEFORE I DESTROY YOU, REMEMBER THIS
READING IS FUNDAMENTAL
DO YOU FEEL THAT, BOOK-BOT?
THAT STATIC CHARGE IN THE AIR?
I HAVE A FEELING...
...I'M NOT LICKED YET!
OH, AND YOU FIGHT LIKE A LIBRARIAN.

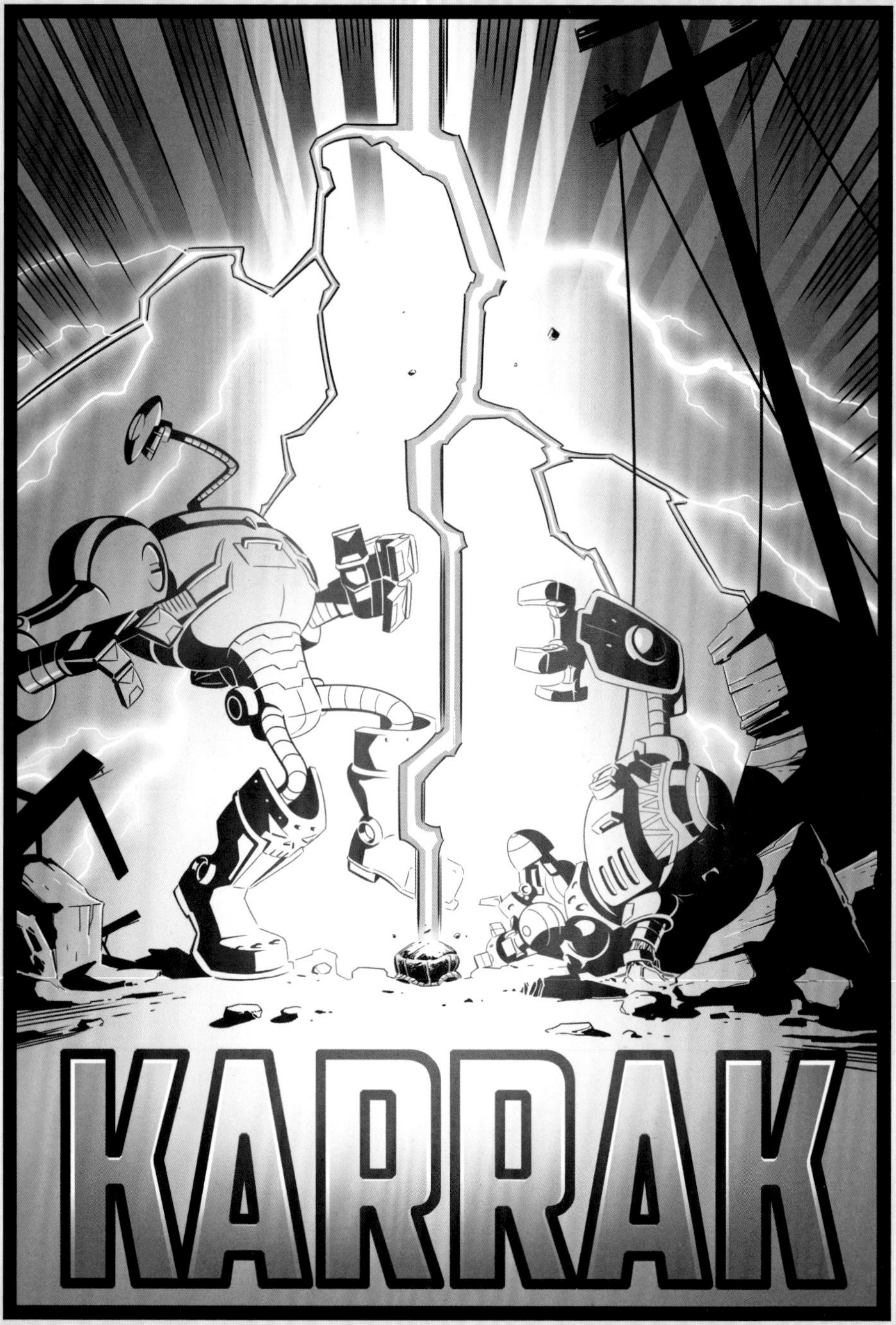
KARRAK

NINE

Kirby didn't have the slightest idea what had just occurred.

Gazing out through the cracked visor screen of the damaged battle suit, he blinked his eyes repeatedly, attempting to rid his vision of the bothersome colored dots that floated there.

The Book-bot 9000 appeared as stunned as he was, driven back by the mysterious discharge of electrical energy. The sensors within Kirby's armor had been damaged in the battle, so the Frenchie had to rely on his own sight to determine what had transpired.

On the singed ground before him rested a familiar shell.

Kirby leaned closer to the visor to make certain that his eyes were not deceived.

How? he wondered as the shell began to move, and . . .

"Kirby!" OB shrieked. His head and limbs shot out from inside his protective covering.

The Frenchie was about to demand to know what was going on when he noticed the book clutched in the turtle's claws . . .

And that the Book-bot was resuming its attack.

Kirby popped the top off of the battle suit and climbed out from the damaged armor.

"Kirby, take this!" OB cried, running at him and shoving the book into his paws.

"Are you mad, terrapin?" Kirby asked. "A book isn't going to save us. We need to flee before . . ."

The cold shadow of the rampaging Book-bot washed over them, and Kirby had no choice but to act. OB had brought him this book for a reason, and for lack of anything else, he decided might as well use it.

Kirby pushed the turtle aside as the Book-bot raised one of its large, metal fists.

"Nothing must interfere with the prime directive," the robot announced, ready to strike. "Hindrance to the Directive must be eliminated."

Kirby's life flashed before his eyes as the mighty metal fist dropped. He had not yet achieved even a fraction of what he had set out to do.

"AH-HAAAAAAAA!" the Frenchie exclaimed, raising the book to block the descending fist.

The Book-bot's violent blow never fell. Its fist froze in place as the automaton's cybernetic eye scanned the hardcover publication.

"Yes, that's it," Kirby said. "Take a good look."

"Scanning . . ." said the Book-bot.

The robot went suddenly rigid.

"*The History of Masking Tape,*" the Book-bot announced. "Overdue . . ."

The Book-bot tore the book from Kirby's grasp, bringing it closer to its cybernetic eye.

"Overdue . . ." it said again.

Kirby turned, preparing to flee while the robot was preoccupied. He would need to think of some other way of bringing the rampaging robot down before . . .

The Frenchie crashed into OB, and the two of them fell to the ground in a heap.

"You clumsy oaf!" Kirby proclaimed, scrambling to get up. "We need to escape before . . ."

"The book," OB said. He pointed to the Book-bot, which continued to stand rigidly, scanning the book title again and again.

"Yes, it's bought us some time, but not enough to . . ."

"The Book-bot checked it out from the library!" OB announced, and suddenly Kirby understood. "In 1962!"

Without a second thought, the Frenchie ran back to the looming robotic figure.

"My, that is overdue," Kirby said, standing in the shadow of the mechanical menace.

The robot backed up, its mechanical eye going from the book, to Kirby, and back again.

"And who is responsible for such a heinous act, I wonder?" Kirby asked his adversary. "Who could be so inconsiderate as to keep a book so long, to deny future readers the precious knowledge contained within? I wonder."

The Book-bot began to shake and rattle.

"Do you have any idea, Book-bot 9000?" Kirby asked the now smoldering robot.

"Book overdue . . . obtained by . . . obtained by . . ."

"Yes?" Kirby questioned. "Obtained by whom, Book-bot? Who was the inconsiderate soul who held onto this valuable tome for oh-so long?"

"Obtained by . . . B . . . B . . . Book-bot 9000!"

"You don't say?" Kirby said with malicious snark.

The robot continued to quiver and shake as it came to grips with the startling revelation.

"Then there is no choice!" Kirby demanded of the robot. "You must fulfill your purpose!"

The Book-bot held the book away from itself as if it were a filthy diaper.

"Perform your prime directive," Kirby growled.

The Book-bot stared at the book that it held, its metal body vibrating.

"*The History of Masking Tape*," it said, sensor eye locking upon the book. "Overdue eighteen thousand, two hundred fifty days . . ."

Kirby watched as the revelation began to damage the robot's systems. The machine man shook noisily, and smoke seeped from between its joints.

"And what would the fee on something like that be?" Kirby asked.

"Fine to be collected . . ." the Book-bot paused as sparks began to fly from his segmented joints. "Fine to be collected," it repeated more loudly. It began to pat at its body as if searching for something.

"Oh yes," Kirby growled. "A fine must be collected for you to perform your prime directive."

The large robot continued to search its body, looking for a source of income that it did not have.

"Insufficient funds!" the Book-bot proclaimed. "Insufficient funds!"

"Oh, dear," Kirby said. "Whatever will you do?"

"Insufficient funds!" the Book-bot wailed, its body smoking and sparking, quivering and quaking until . . .

"Insufficient . . . funds . . ."

The Book-bot 9000's head exploded in a shower of sparks, smoke, and fire.

"Whoa!" OB said, coming out from hiding. "What just happened?"

The Book-bot slumped to one side before crashing lifelessly to the ground.

"Exactly what I surmised would happen," Kirby said. "Its computer brain could not handle the paradox. The Book-bot was in direct violation of its own prime directive. It had no money, and could not pay the overdue fines."

"And that's what made its head explode?" OB asked.

"Precisely," Kirby answered.

"Wow," the turtle said.

There was the sound of a commotion up ahead and Kirby turned his attentions to the source.

It appeared that the Book-bot 9000, in its enthusiasm to find overdue library property, had thrown a minivan through the window of the Fitzgerald Pet Boutique. The store, no longer looking structurally sound, was being evacuated of its pet residents.

Kirby's eyes squinted as he observed the actions of those who had chosen to help. There was something . . . different about them.

"Who are those guys?" OB asked.

Kirby remained silent, reaching for the digital camera that hung on his collar.

Who are those guys, indeed, he thought, snapping photos as the individuals aided the animals of the pet store with talents that could best be described as . . .

Superhuman.

There was a man dressed as a US mail carrier. He seemed to be the one in command, ordering the other members of his group around with great authority.

Click! Kirby snapped a picture.

There was a strange little woman, her body surrounded by what could only be described a living cloud of cats. *Disgusting creatures,* Kirby thought, watching as the multitude of black-furred felines melded together to form a kind of cat-tentacle, which retrieved several tanks of tropical fish from the damaged store.

Click! Kirby took another picture.

The mailman called to a shirtless, red-haired man with a canary perched upon his bony shoulder. In each hand he held a shovel that crackled with some unknown form of energy. The shovels pierced the ground as if it was made of butter as the man dug up and spread showers of dirt with incredible speed and accuracy, extinguishing the small fires around the store.

Click!

The minivan sticking out from the front of the pet store began to move. At first Kirby believed that it was being driven out, but then he saw that the tires were no longer on the ground. Something was lifting the van and carrying it away. *Fascinating,* Kirby thought when he saw the one responsible. He was large, wearing a black T-shirt and jeans, and he appeared to be made from some sort of stone. The stone man carried the van out of the storefront with little effort.

Click! Kirby took another photo.

With the van removed, the proper evacuation of the larger animals could begin. Within moments, these unique individuals emerged from inside the shop, arms full of puppies and kittens, parrots perched upon their heads. The crowds of downtown Strasburg cheered their heroic actions.

"They look pretty cool," OB said, amused by their superhuman feats.

"No," Kirby said firmly. "No, they do not."

This is not good, the Frenchie assessed. *Not good at all.* If Strasburg had superpowered individuals lurking about, that meant there was a chance—no matter how slim—that they might wish to interfere with his plans for the world.

"We should depart," Kirby stated.

The crowds were thickening, and the Frenchie did not want to be noticed with the downed Book-bot and the remains of his battle armor.

"How are we gonna get home?" OB asked. "Your battle suit looks busted up pretty good."

The turtle's assessment, though primitive, was correct. The battle suit would not be taking them anywhere.

Kirby's atomically engorged brain immediately went to work once again, searching his surroundings for a solution to their quandary. Parking meters had been broken open during his struggles with the Book-bot, and the ground was littered with change.

"Gather up that money," Kirby ordered.

OB did as he was told, picking up as many of the dimes and quarters from the ground as he could.

"What are we going to do with it?" OB asked.

"We are going to leave this place," Kirby said. He looked one last time at the superpowered beings before heading down the street to their means of escape.

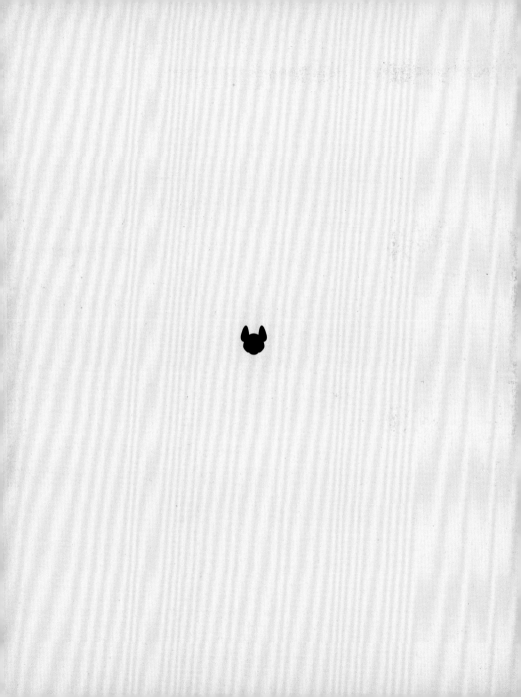

TEN

Kirby and OB got off at the bus stop closest to their home. OB waved happily at the driver as the bus pulled away from the curb and continued on its way.

"He was nice," OB said, still waving.

"You manifested a super ability," Kirby stated. He started to walk in the direction of home.

"What's that?" OB asked, walking faster to try and keep up.

"You arrived to aid me with that overdue book in a flash of electrical energy," Kirby explained.

OB stopped and thought. "Yeah, I guess I did."

"Could you do it again?" Kirby asked the turtle.

Again OB stopped to think hard about the question.

"I don't think I could," he said. "I have no idea what I did!"

"Interesting," Kirby said. "We will have to run some more tests once we get back to the lab."

"Great, more tests," OB muttered, shaking his head.

They were cutting through the neighbor's backyard when they saw him—sitting large and still, dressed in a heavy winter coat and hat despite the spring weather, beady pig eyes staring out from above a thick, woolen scarf. His dog was at his side, cowering at the sight of Kirby.

As he should be, Kirby thought.

It appeared that Ogden Stempleworth had returned home from his prolonged stay—but not prolonged enough as far as Kirby was concerned—at Happydale Sanitarium.

Kirby glared as they passed, a message silently passing between the Frenchie and his foe.

The war was over—for now.

For now.

"Congratulations!" Erasmus bellowed as they stepped into the secret laboratory. The ghost blew into a horn and tossed confetti into the air.

The lab had been decorated as if for a party; streamers and congratulatory balloons lay about the room.

"What is the meaning of this?" Kirby demanded, swatting balloons from his path.

"Congratulations are in order!" Erasmus announced. "You passed the test with flying colors!"

Kirby stopped and glared at the ghost.

"Test?"

Erasmus nodded. "Yes indeed, a test. And you passed."

OB clapped happily. "Hey, Kirby, you were tested, too!"

The Frenchie glowered at the turtle, who disappeared into his shell in fear of the withering look.

Kirby turned his glare back on Erasmus.

"So you're saying that everything that just transpired was some sort of *test*?"

"Yep," Erasmus said with a nod. "The Book-bot's activation was a way for me to see if you were ready for something big . . ."

Erasmus held up something in his ghostly hand.

A key.

"Something *really* big," the ghost emphasized.

"My patience is dwindling, apparition," Kirby growled. "Explain this big thing to me or incur my wrath."

"Okay, okay, don't get your panties in a bunch!"

"I don't wear panties," Kirby growled.

"It's just an expression," Erasmus tried to explain, floating across the laboratory to the far wall. A framed picture of the 1950s kids' TV show host, puppet Laughie Louie, hung there, and Erasmus slid it aside to reveal a keyhole.

Kirby watched the ghost insert the key and turn it within the locking mechanism.

Nothing happened.

The ghost looked at the Frenchie nervously, and then back to the key protruding from the hole.

"Something should have happened," Erasmus said. He pulled the key out and blew on it before sticking it inside the keyhole again.

"My patience is wearing tremendously thin, ghost," Kirby warned.

"Yeah, yeah, yeah," Erasmus said, turning the key again.

This time, the sounds of gears tumbling into place somewhere behind the wall echoed throughout the laboratory space.

"Yahtzee!" Erasmus proclaimed. A section of what seemed to be solid stone wall shook, sending pieces of broken rock and dust to the floor, before slowly sliding apart with a grinding sound to reveal a heavy metal vault door.

"Whatta you think?" Erasmus asked.

Kirby slowly approached the metal door.

"I'll need more than this," Kirby said. "Explain."

"After the initial failure of the Book-bot, I legitimately lost my marbles. I decided to stop trying to do anything good for the ungrateful public, and instead turned my attentions to *evil*."

Erasmus stroked the surface of the door with a ghostly hand. "Inside here are all of my greatest ideas and world domination plans," the ghost said. "Things way too spiffy to be left lying about a secret lab where any ingenious Tom, Dick, or Frenchie could stumble upon them."

"World domination plans, you say?" Kirby asked.

"That's it," Erasmus said with a nod.

"Open it," Kirby demanded, putting aside the fact that he had been played by the ghost. He would overlook that slight—*for now*—if something truly significant was housed behind the vault door.

"Not so fast, short-stuff," Erasmus said. "There's something very important that you're gonna have to do for me first. Then I'll be happy to open her up and let you have first crack at everything inside." The ghost of Erasmus Peckinpah paused, letting his words permeate the Frenchie's atomic mind. "You wash my back, and I'll wash yours."

Kirby looked to the ghost. He felt his annoyance rising, but quickly tromped it down. He would play along with the ghost . . .

For now.

"What do you need me to do?" Kirby asked.

Erasmus smiled, rubbing his ghostly hands together in anticipation.

"Kirkwood, I thought you'd never ask."

HEROES, VILLAINS, AND FRENCHIES

KIRBY IS TWENTY-TWO POUNDS OF FUR-COVERED *RUTHLESS AMBITION.* FREAKISHLY INTELLIGENT AND DETERMINED, HE HAS ONE GOAL: *RULE!*

THE MIND OF A CHESS *GRANDMASTER*, WITH THE *IRON WILL* OF A *FOUR-STAR GENERAL*, *KIRBY* WILL NEVER REST UNTIL HUMANITY BOWS DOWN BEFORE HIM.

PLAYING THE LONG GAME, *KIRBY* SLOWLY SETS THE WHEELS IN MOTION, ARRANGING THE PIECES, MOVING THEM AROUND, PLAYING THE ENDS AGAINST THE MIDDLE, ALWAYS TO *HIS* ADVANTAGE AND ALWAYS TO MEET *HIS ENDGAME!*

OB (OLD BOY)

TOM'S FIRST PET, *OB*, IS A
THIRTY-YEAR-OLD BOX TURTLE
AND THE CLOSEST THING *KIRBY* HAS
TO A FRIEND.

WHEN THE SURLY PUP FIRST ARRIVED,
OB GRAVITATED TO HIM MORE
OUT OF SIMPLE ANIMAL COMPANIONSHIP
THAN TRUE FRIENDSHIP. SINCE THEN HE
HAS BECOME STRANGELY LOYAL TO
KIRBY.

IS HE A *SIDEKICK*? A *LACKEY*?
A *GROUPIE*? THE ANSWER IS
"YES," ALL OF THE ABOVE.
GOOD-NATURED AND PURE OF SPIRIT
OB IS THE LIGHT TO *KIRBY'S* DARK,
SUPER EGO TO HIS *ID*,
CURLY TO HIS *MOE*.

ERASMUS PEKINPAH:

THE LATE *PROFESSOR PEKINPAH* DIDN'T ALWAYS
WANT TO BECOME A "MAD" SCIENTIST.
HE ACTUALLY STARTED OFF TRYING TO USE HIS
POWERS FOR THE *GOOD* OF HUMANITY.
HIS MOST NOTORIOUS INVENTION WAS
THE *BOOK-BOT 9000*-A ROBOT HE DESIGNED TO
MAKE SURE HIS LIBRARY BOOKS WERE
RETURNED ON TIME.

BOOK-BOT 9000 WORKED PERFECTLY,
UNFORTUNATELY, *ERASMUS* WAS
OBLIVIOUS TO THE AESTHETICS OF
HIS CREATION. THE ROBOT WAS THE SIZE
OF A TANK, SPEWED MORE EXHAUST THAN
A *BUICK*, COST MORE THAN A HOUSE
AND LOOKED LIKE SOMETHING OUT OF A
TERMINATOR MOVIE!

EXPECTING THE WORLD TO EMBRACE
BOOK-BOT 9000, ITS FAILURE IS WHAT
EVENTUALLY DROVE *ERASMUS* "MAD."
YEARS LATER *ERASMUS* WOULD ACCIDENTALLY
INVENT THE *RAINBOW WIG* AND BECOME RICH!
FINALLY, HE HAD THE MEANS TO BUILD HIS DREAM
LABORATORY.

THE ONE *KIRBY* NOW OCCUPIES.

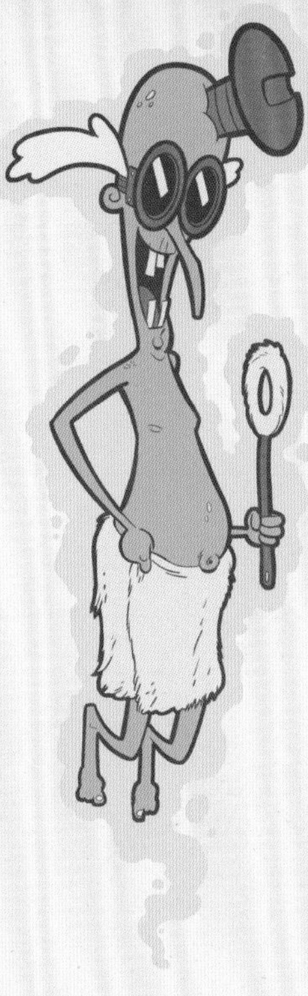
HEY! WHAT ABOUT ME?

OH, RIGHT...

GHOST ERASMUS

ERASMUS PEKINPAH IS DECEASED AND IS NOW A GHOST HAUNTING *KIRBY'S* NEW HOME.

MOST PEOPLE ASSUME THAT POOR OLD *ERASMUS* WAS KILLED IN SOME FREAK ACCIDENT INVOLVING A *CRAZY EXPERIMENT* WITH A *GIANT SCREW*, BUT NO. THE SCREW WAS EMBEDDED IN HIS HEAD YEARS AGO. SO LONG, IN FACT, THAT EVEN *HE* CAN'T REMEMBER HOW IT GOT THERE.

THE TRUTH IS THAT HIS DEATH, LIKE HIS LIFE WAS A GREAT BIG *FAIL*. HE SLIPPED WHILE COMING OUT OF THE SHOWER.

KIRBY IS INTRIGUED BY *ERASMUS*. AT FIRST GLANCE *ERASMUS* SEEMS LIKE A MORONIC LOON, AND YET HIS LABORATORY AND *BOOK-BOT 9000* SHOW THAT HE CLEARLY HAS SOME *"MAD"* INVENTING SKILLS.

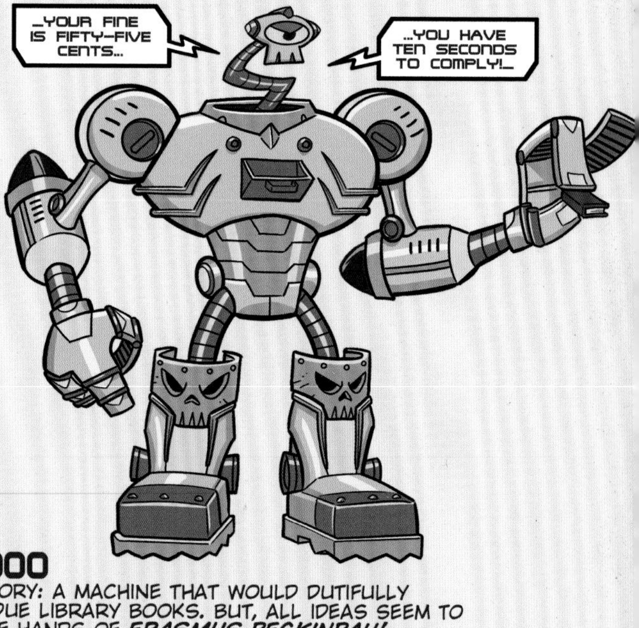
...YOUR FINE IS FIFTY-FIVE CENTS...
...YOU HAVE TEN SECONDS TO COMPLY!...

BOOK-BOT 9000

IT WAS A GOOD IDEA IN THEORY: A MACHINE THAT WOULD DUTIFULLY TRACK AND RETRIEVE OVERDUE LIBRARY BOOKS. BUT, ALL IDEAS SEEM TO GO HORRIBLY WRONG IN THE HANDS OF *ERASMUS PECKINPAH!* STANDING OVER *12* FEET TALL AND WEIGHING JUST SHY OF A TON, *BOOK-BOT 9000*, WITH HIS *MILITANT DEDICATION* TO DUTY AND *CYCLOPTIC HEAD*, INSTILLED MORE FEAR THAN LOVE.

KIRBY MECH SUIT

NEVER ONE TO BACK DOWN FROM A FIGHT, ***KIRBY*** BUILDS A SUPED-UP ***MECH SUIT*** TO STOP A RAMPAGING ***BOOK-BOT*** 9000 FROM DESTROYING HIS HOMETOWN.

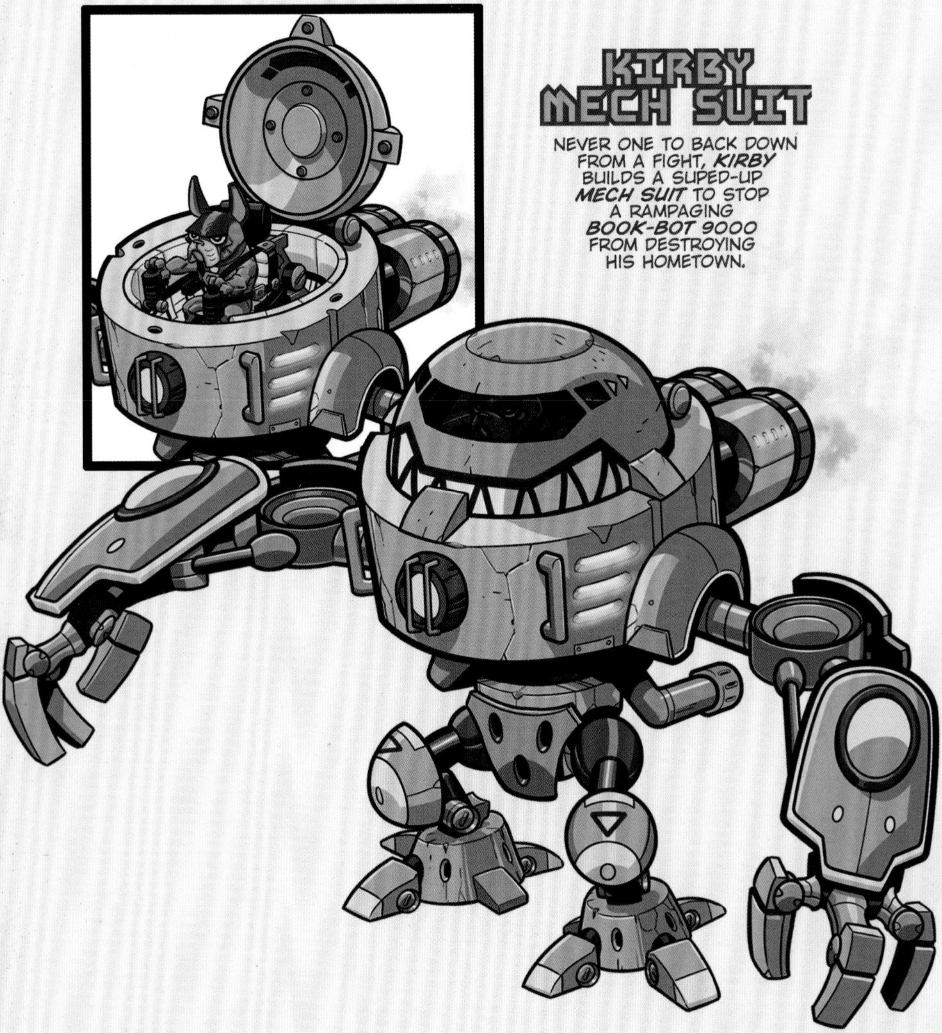

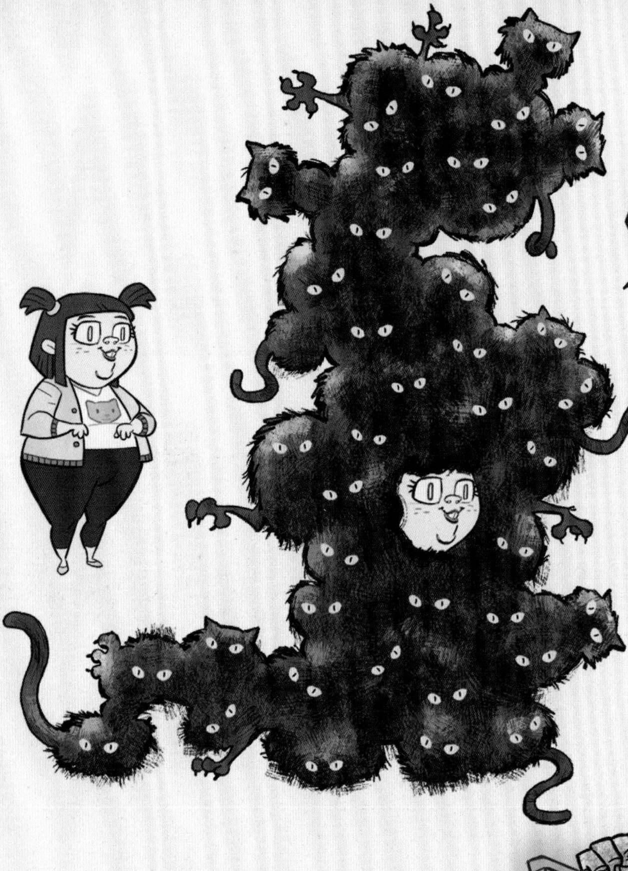

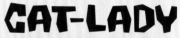

CAT-LADY

POWERS: *HAS CONTROL OVER A STRANGE, SUPERNATURAL CAT THAT CAN REPLICATE ITSELF. THE CAT-COPIES CAN MERGE INTO ONE GIANT MASS, SHAPE THEMSELVES INTO OBJECTS, AND BE WORN AS A SUIT OF ARMOR*

WEAPONS: *A SEEMINGLY INFINITE SUPPLY OF CATS*

WEAKNESS: *WATER, BALLS OF YARN*

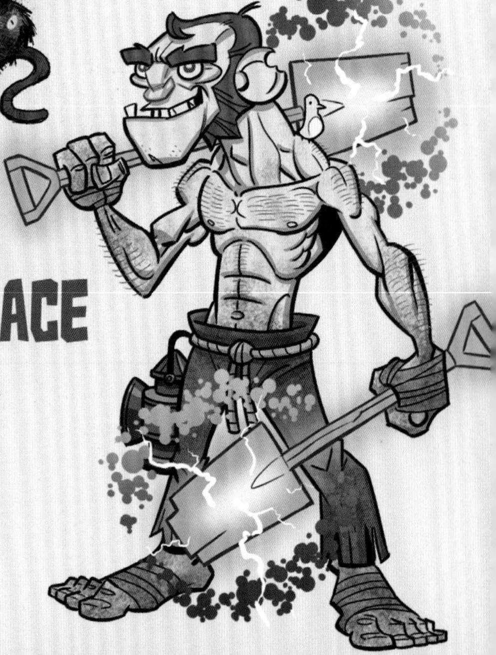

TWO-SHOVELS WALLACE

POWERS: *WALLACE HAS NO SUPERPOWERS OF HIS OWN. WHAT HE DOES HAVE, HOWEVER, ARE TWO MYSTICAL SHOVELS THAT POSSESS INCREDIBLE ABILITIES.*

WEAPONS: *HIS SHOVELS CAN DIG, CUT, OR DESTROY VIRTUALLY ANY MATTER. THEY CAN ALSO OPEN UP PORTALS TO OTHER DIMENSIONS AND TELEPORT HIM AND HIS TEAMMATES TO SAFETY.*

WEAKNESS: *A SHORT FUSE AND LOUD MOUTH*

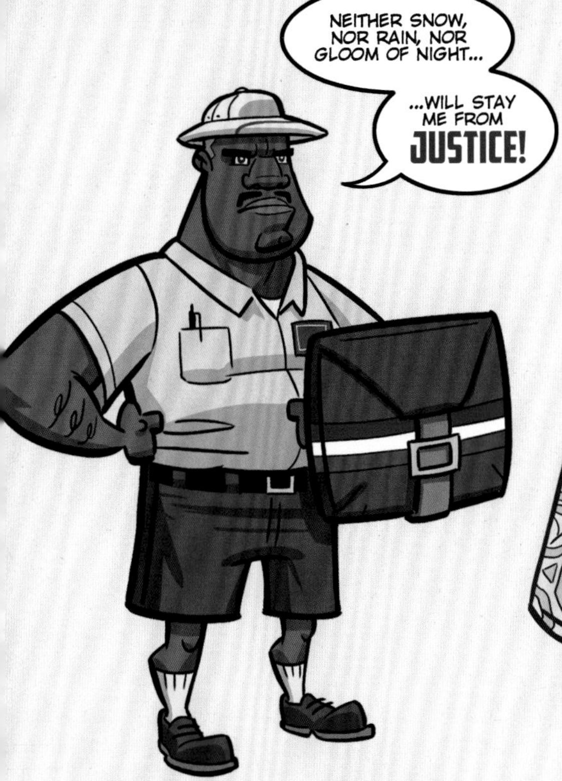
NEITHER SNOW, NOR RAIN, NOR GLOOM OF NIGHT...
...WILL STAY ME FROM JUSTICE!

THE MAILMAN

POWERS: *SUPER STRENGTH, SPEED, AND AGILITY*

WEAPONS: *INDESTRUCTIBLE MAILBAG*

WEAKNESS: *DOGS*

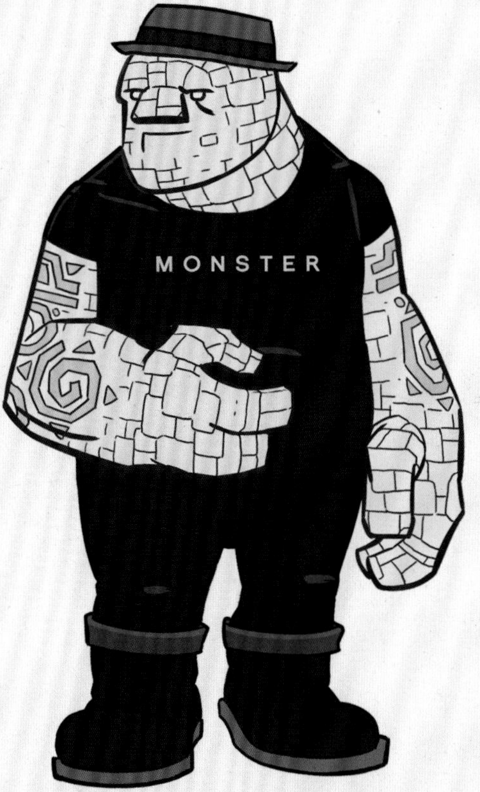
MONSTER

DAVE THE LIVING COLOSSUS

POWERS: *OFF-THE-CHARTS STRENGTH, IMPERVIOUS TO HARM OR INJURY, NEEDS NO FOOD, WATER, OR AIR TO SURVIVE*

WEAPONS: *HIS DISARMINGLY CALM DEMEANOR, HIS FISTS*

WEAKNESS: *ZENLIKE APPROACH TO LIFE, INABILITY TO RECOGNIZE DANGEROUS SITUATIONS*

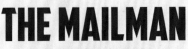

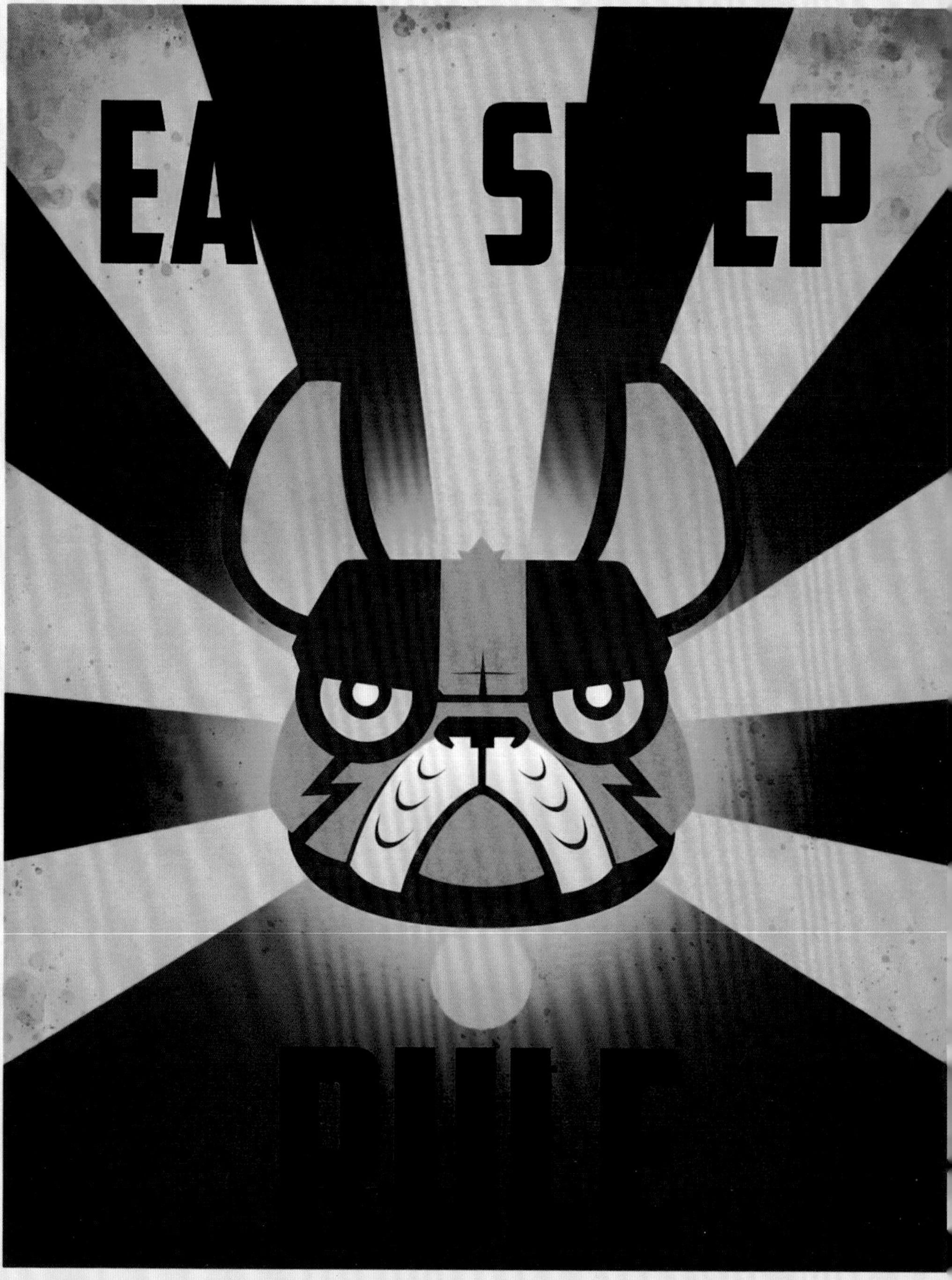
EA
S
EP

ACKNOWLEDGMENTS

A million thanks, as always, to my long suffering wife, LeeAnne. Kirby has a special place for you in his kingdom. Me, not so much.

Special thanks also to Christopher Golden for his enthusiasm on his project.

Thanks also to the crazies and all their fur-babies at Halloran Park, Michael Burke at Comicazie, Nicole Scopa, Ashlee Brienzo Lentini, Mom Sniegoski, Pat and Bob Dexter, Auntie Pam, Dr. Kris, and the crazies down at Cole's Comics in Lynn, MA.

And most especially to Tom McWeeney for making Kirby's story far better than I could have ever imagined.

—Thomas E. Sniegoski

A few special thanks:

First, to my brother Jim for cultivating my love of drawing and humor.

To my loving and supportive wife, Nanci, who spent countless weekends on her own while I was hunched over a computer screen and never once threw anything at me.

To my parents, James and Theresa, for never saying, "Art is not a viable career path."

And to Rich Hedden, who showed me how to turn funny ideas into comic pages.

—Tom McWeeney

CONTRIBUTING FRENCHIES

— Kirby Sniegoski

— Zelda Kubert

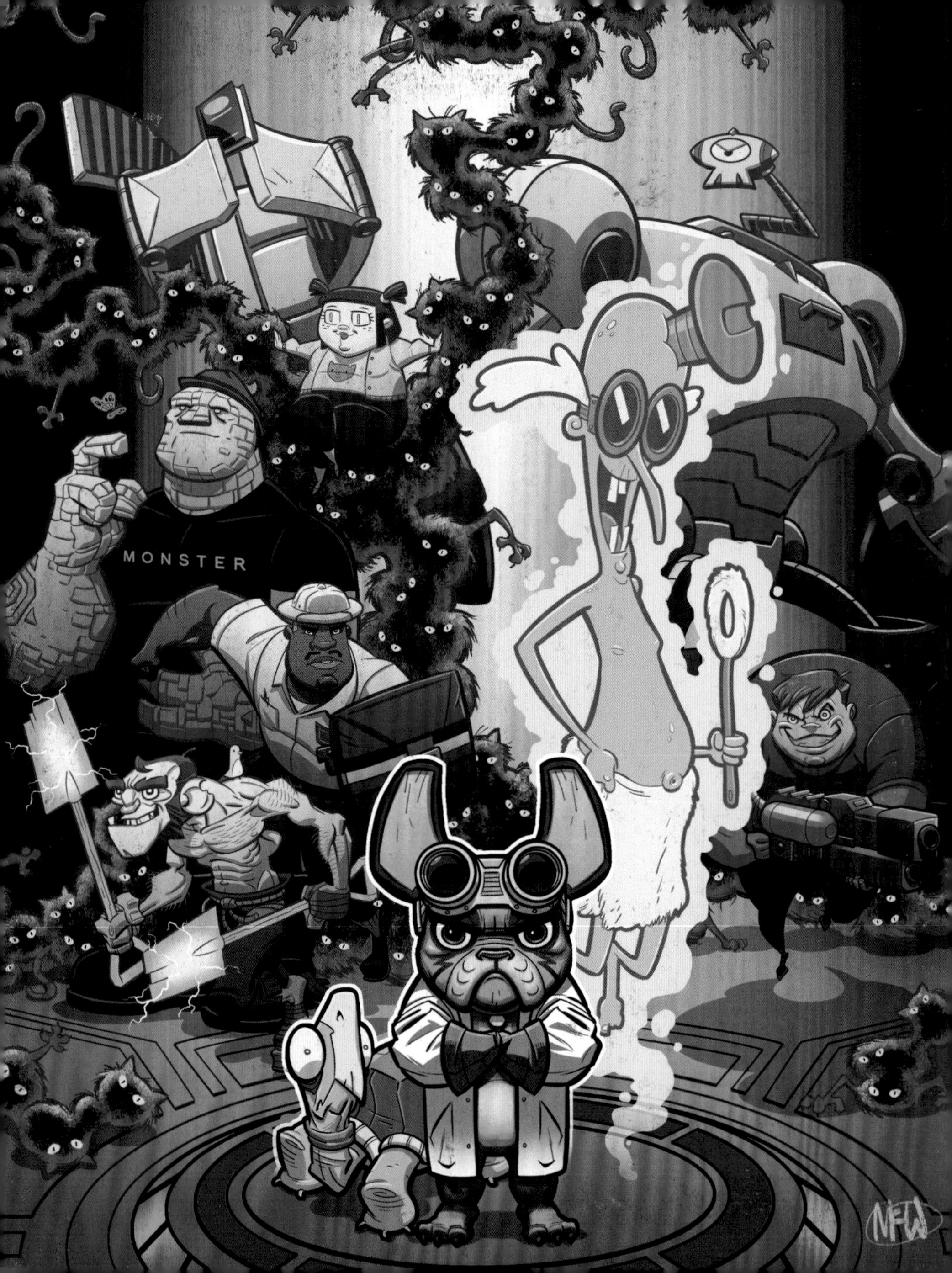
MONSTER
NFW

THE ADVENTURES OF ATOMIC FRENCHIE WILL CONTINUE...

PO Box 3088
San Rafael, CA 94912
www.insightcomics.com

Find us on Facebook: www.facebook.com/InsightEditions
Follow us on Twitter: @insighteditions

Copyright © 2018 Thomas E. Sniegoski and Tom McWeeney

Published by Insight Editions, San Rafael, California, in 2018. All rights reserved.
No part of this book may be reproduced in any form without written permission
from the publisher.

Library of Congress Cataloging-in-Publication Data available.

Publisher: Raoul Goff
Associate Publisher: Jon Goodspeed
Art Director: Chrissy Kwasnik
Designer: Evelyn Furuta
Senior Editor: Katie Kubert
Managing Editor: Alan Kaplan
Editorial Assistant: Holly Fisher
Senior Production Editor: Elaine Ou
Production Manager: Sam Taylor

ROOTS of PEACE · REPLANTED PAPER

Insight Editions, in association with Roots of Peace, will plant two trees for each
tree used in the manufacturing of this book. Roots of Peace is an internationally re-
nowned humanitarian organization dedicated to eradicating land mines worldwide
and converting war-torn lands into productive farms and wildlife habitats. Roots of
Peace will plant two million fruit and nut trees in Afghanistan and provide farmers
there with the skills and support necessary for sustainable land use.

Manufactured in China by Insight Editions

10 9 8 7 6 5 4 3 2

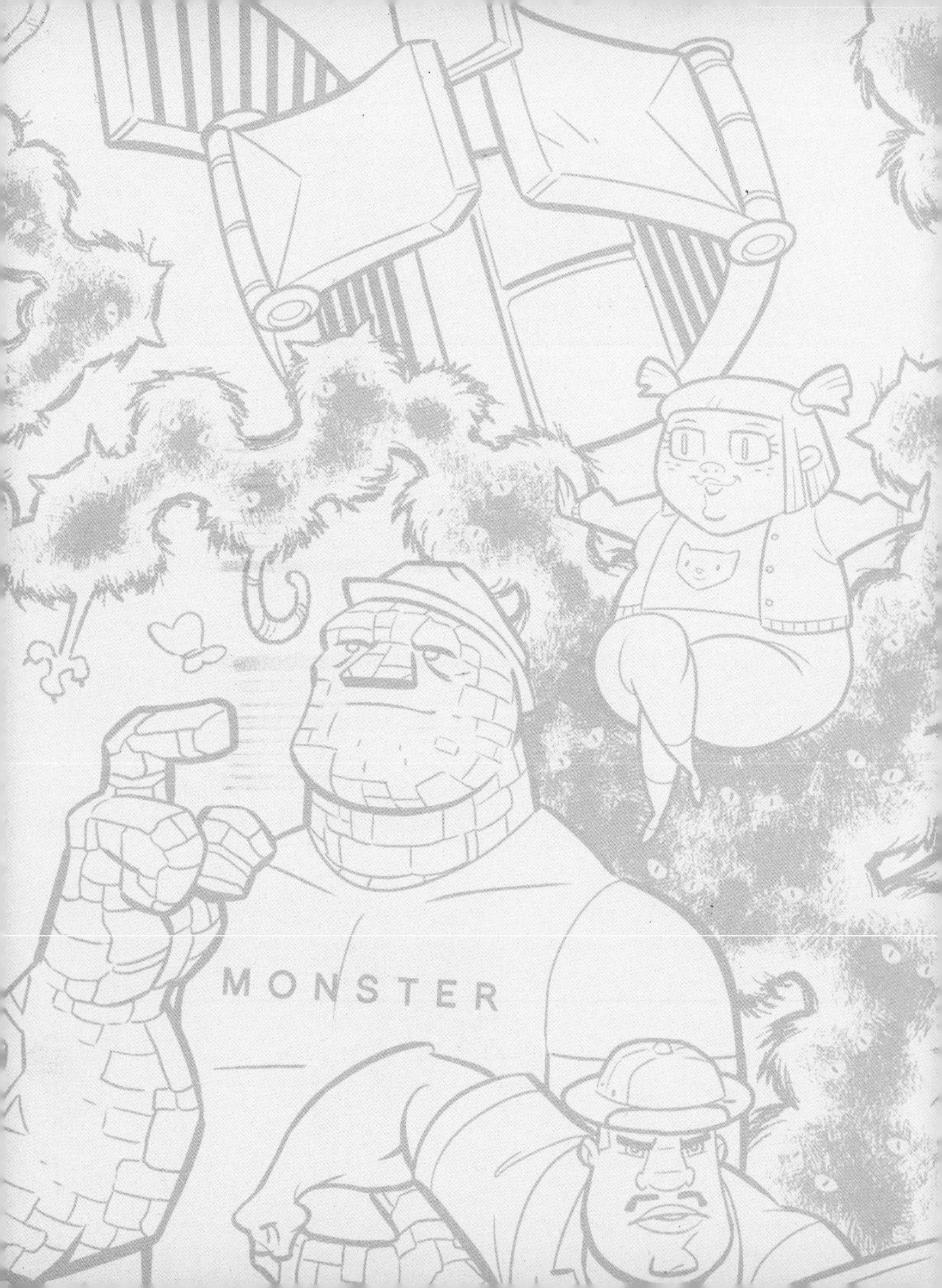
MONSTER